THE BIRD OF TIME

Books by George Alec Effinger

THE BIRD OF TIME

GEORGE ALEC EFFINGER

DOUBLEDAY & COMPANY, INC.

GARDEN CITY, NEW YORK

1986

All of the characters in this book
are fictitious, and any resemblance
to actual persons, living or dead,
is purely coincidental.

Library of Congress Cataloging in Publication Data
Effinger, George Alec.
    The bird of time.
    I. Title.
PS3555.F4B5   1986   813'.54   84-28776
ISBN 0-385-19232-0

For their advice and encouragement over the years, this book is for Robert Silverberg and Edward L. Ferman and Shawna McCarthy.

CONTENTS

The only way to predict the future is to have power
to shape the future. Those in possession of absolute power
can not only prophecy and make their prophecies come true,
but they can also lie and make their lies come true.

—Eric Hoffer

"Fiddle-dee-dee. War, war, war. This war talk's
spoiling all the fun at every party this spring. I get
so bored I could scream. Besides, there isn't going to
be any war!"

—Vivien Leigh as Scarlett O'Hara
Gone With the Wind

You can't sort jam and marbles.

—Walt Kelly

THE BIRD OF TIME

the Agency Building right in the middle of Agency Plaza downtown.
"Any luggage?" asked the uniformed man.

"Uh huh." Hartstein indicated a molded plastic suitcase he had
brought with him, with extra shirts and socks, camera and film, and whatever else he thought he'd need.

"They didn't have molded plastic suitcases in ancient times," said the
Agent.

"Oh," said Hartstein, "that's right." He looked confused.

"Don't worry. We'll provide you with everything you'll need, costume,
appropriate accessories, money, and so forth. We'll make sure your hairstyle and facial hair conforms to the local fashion. We'll give you a quick
ESB knowledge of language, customs, and background. You won't have to
worry about a thing."

"I'm not," said Hartstein in an uncertain voice. "Worried, I mean." He
looked at a framed quotation hanging on the wall behind the agent:

*When great causes are on the move in the world, we learn that we are
spirits, not animals, and that something is going on in space and time,
and beyond space and time, which, whether we like it or not, spells
duty.*

—*Sir Winston Churchill*

It made Hartstein feel better; that was what it was there for.

"Good," said the man in the uniform, "you're my kind of man." And
he smiled again, no more pleasantly than the first time. "Now don't tell
me, let me guess. You're either the Library at Alexandria or Catherine the
Great."

Hartstein was astonished. "The Library," he said. "How did you
know?"

"You college boys are all alike. Okay, take this receipt up to the ninth
floor, Room 972. They'll give you all the introductory material. You can
travel anytime you like, just give us twenty-four hours' notice. You come
in, take your ESB session, get outfitted, and we push you through the
screen for your day in the past. You don't—"

"Can I go today?"

"What?"

Hartstein swallowed. "Can I do it today?" he said.

The Agent shrugged. "Sure, of course. In a hurry? The Library isn't
going anywhere."

"It's going to burn to the ground, isn't it?"

The uniformed man gave Hartstein a long, disdainful look. "They
promised to hold off on that until after you leave," he said.

CHAPTER ONE

THE BIRD OF TIME BEARS
BITTER FRUIT

You know the shock of utter terror just as you're about to hand over a large sum of money for something you're no longer sure you really want. Hartstein felt it. He felt it in his stomach, and he felt his hand give a peculiar reluctant quiver as he gave his card to the man behind the counter.

The man smiled, not pleasantly. He was dressed in the uniform of the Agency, the silver and blue tunic with the leatherneck collar. There were five rows of ribbons on his breast, signifying one thing and another, all mysterious and unknown to Hartstein. The man was evidently a hardened veteran of the Agency; it seemed odd to Hartstein to see him behind the counter, like a travel agent or an airline ticket clerk. "Second thoughts?" said the Agency man.

"Well," said Hartstein, "no." He wasn't going to let this veteran see that the notion of a vacation in time made him just a little uneasy. It did, but not enough to make him change his mind. Really, it was the expense that staggered Hartstein more than the danger. But possibly, down underneath, buried successfully beneath rocky strata of more mundane worries, there was the tickling fear that he might be one of the 2 percent that never came back.

Hartstein was a young man, recently graduated from college in Mississippi, about to begin a new life as an employee in a doughnut shop, who had been given a large sum of money by his grandparents with the stipulation that he spend it broadening his horizons, by traveling either to Europe or into the past. "I'd love to go back in time," he explained to his father. "Europe will *always* be there."

Mr. Hartstein considered his son's urgency about the past, which, as far as he could see, would also always be there. "You're going to have a great future in doughnuts, son," he said.

And so Hartstein was standing at the Agency counter in the lobby of

"Oh, good."

The man handed the receipt across the counter. "Take that upstairs. Good luck. Next?"

Room 972 was a large room; there was a counter across the front of it, and many desks and cubicles dividing the vast space to the rear. It looked like the kind of place you went to when the Internal Revenue Service wants to ask you a few questions. Hartstein's stomach began to grumble again. He told himself that there was no reason for anxiety, but he couldn't shake the feeling of impending doom. Doom he had chosen and paid for himself, with his grandparents' money.

"May I help you?" asked a young woman. She seemed very bored. She was dressed in the same silver and blue uniform, but on hers there were no campaign ribbons. The cut of the tunic was less severe as well, permitting the general public to evaluate certain of her characteristics.

When Hartstein's eyes turned from the bustling activity around him to this attractive Agent, he lost some of his fear. "I'd like to go to the—"

"The Library, I know. Yellow slip, please." He gave the receipt to her. "When did you want to go?"

"I'd like to do it today, if I could."

She looked up at him and cracked her chewing gum. One eyebrow went up just a bit. "In a hurry?" she said.

Hartstein shrugged. There was a framed quotation at this counter, too:

> The Bird of Time has but a little way
> To fly—and Lo! the Bird is on the wing.
> —The Rubáiyát of Omar Khayyám

The lines didn't mean a damn thing to Hartstein.

"Today," said the Agent, "let's see." She consulted several clipboards and a large, black, vinyl-bound notebook. "Well, you're in luck. There's no real problem with that. It's, what? it's almost eleven o'clock. So we can have you ready by two o'clock. You realize that you will have exactly twenty-four hours in the past, no more and no less. So if you go through at two, then you'll be back tomorrow at two. Right?"

"I understand," said Hartstein.

"And you took care of everything downstairs? Uh huh, it's all here on the voucher. So, is there anything you'd like to change? This is your last chance."

Hartstein wasn't crazy about the way she phrased that remark. "My last chance?" he said.

She looked up at the ceiling impatiently. "You can't be yelling 'Wait a minute, I forgot something' when they're pushing you through the screen.

If you don't want to go to the Library, if you'd rather, say, go to see them assassinate Julius Caesar, you'd better do it now. We don't want to have to listen to your kvetching when you get back."

The idea of Julius Caesar and Brutus and Mark Antony's funeral oration and all that sounded very attractive to Hartstein, and he considered it for a moment.

"But if I were you," said the Agent, "I'd stick. You can spend all day in the Library. Caesar's down and dead in a minute, and then everybody goes to have lunch. The rest of the day you might as well be window-shopping in the Agency gift shop, for all the excitement there is."

"You're right. I'll just hang with my original plan."

"Good boy," said the young woman. "Take the voucher through the swinging gate, follow the yellow line on the floor, and see Sergeant Brannick. Have a good time in Alexandria." Like nightfall in the jungle, boredom reappeared with terrible suddenness on her ordinary face.

"Through the swinging gate," she said. She pushed a button and a buzzer sounded. Hartstein went through the gate and followed the yellow line. It went through a small village of polished desks until it came to an end abruptly, at the battered oak station of Sergeant Brannick.

"Voucher please," said the sergeant. He was a large man, as large as the Agent who had sold Hartstein the ticket. He wore the Agency uniform, decorated with as many ribbons as the man downstairs had had. It seemed just as odd to Hartstein that Brannick would be employed here, handling the routing of tourists. Didn't the Agency need its experienced personnel in the field, patrolling the freeways of time, fighting the unimaginable crimes that temporal terrorists would certainly be plotting against the sleeping citizens of the present? "Voucher, please," said Brannick more loudly.

"Sorry," said Hartstein. He gave the man the yellow slip, now bent into a tiny, neat square. "Will the Library be crowded full of other people from the present when I get there?"

Brannick's eyes narrowed. "You won't see anybody there except the locals," he said.

"Oh? Why is that? Why isn't the place crammed like sardines with us by now?"

"Because 'The Past' is an objective concept, and it doesn't exist like that. Just like that necklace you have on. Subjectively it's a chain, although objectively it's only a collection of links. The past doesn't work that way. It isn't really a long line of links extending from 'then' until 'now.' "

"Oh, I see," said Hartstein, even though he didn't have the slightest idea what Brannick was talking about. He didn't want to annoy the man. "I've done a lot of thinking about moving around in time and what it could mean and what terrible things could happen and all the awful accidents that might occur if you weren't careful and all that."

A visible change came over Sergeant Brannick. "You have? The time business interests you?" he asked, his voice suddenly hearty and full of hollow buddiness.

"Uh huh. What do you mean, no such thing as the past? Where am I going, then?"

"No *objective* past, I said. There's definitely a past, all right. You're going to Alexandria and you're going to see the Library. While you're in town, by the way, why don't you run up to Pharos and see the lighthouse? It was one of the Seven Wonders of the Ancient World, you know, and it was still standing where you're going. But tell me, you think that time travel is more exciting than, oh, spending a few days in Las Vegas?"

"I think so. I could have gone to Europe, but I decided to go back instead."

"No problem," said Brannick. "Like I said, we'll talk tomorrow. Give my regards to Cleopatra."

The doctor made Hartstein strip and stand with his toes on the yellow line. Then he told the young man to do all sorts of undignified things, some of which Hartstein couldn't believe had any diagnostic value. "Your injection," said the doctor in a tired voice.

"I've had all my shots and boosters," said Hartstein. "In school."

The doctor shook his head. "We have to inoculate you against things back there that don't even exist today. You'd have no protection at all against some of those diseases. You'd come back in such bad shape, in a week you'd look like Dorian Gray's painting."

"Like what?"

The doctor waved a hand. "Hold still," he said.

The yellow line took Hartstein to the ESB section. The procedure itself was quick, painless, and pleasant. He was given a mild sedative which had him drifting in a warm, secure dream in a few minutes. He wasn't sure exactly how the knowledge was put into his mind; all he knew was that the letters stood for Electrical Stimulation of the Brain. It sounded like a sinister process, but it had been used on Hartstein a dozen times since childhood, during his education. It was a routine procedure; he was no more afraid of it than he was of other forms of medical editing. He lay back on the molded couch and put the intangible contents of his mind in the care of the ESB trainee who took his voucher. An hour later Hartstein had been processed. He took back the yellow slip and set out along the line once more. He tried to draw on his new knowledge of Egyptian language and social behavior, but nothing came. He worried that perhaps the ESB treatment hadn't stuck, or that some kind of mistake had been made. He recalled, however, that he had had the same experience following his other ESB sessions. When he got to Alexandria, when he needed the knowledge, it would be there.

The last station was the costume department. A young man in a tight-fitting Agency uniform told Hartstein to have a seat. "It won't take long, God knows," said the costumer. "It isn't as if you're going to feudal France or someplace interesting." He gave a wistful sigh. "I've always wanted to work upstairs, you know. Fitting people for the Renaissance. Can you imagine the materials, the fashions? Maybe someday. Well, for now, here's yours." He handed Hartstein a large sealed plastic bag.

"This is it?" Hartstein asked dubiously. He tossed the bag in one hand. It weighed very little.

The young man shrugged. "It's hot there, I guess."

Hartstein opened the bag. "Do I have to try it on here?"

The Agent closed his eyes in exasperation. "One size fits all," he said in a dull voice. "Oh, Lord, why me?"

Inside the bag was a white cotton skirt and some jewelry. "No sandals?" asked Hartstein.

The young man massaged his forehead in supreme weariness. He shook his head.

"No robe? I go around bare-chested?"

The young man nodded. "You get a headdress, though. One of those bath-towel things."

"Wow," said Hartstein without enthusiasm. He examined the jewelry: there was a gold bracelet with a large golden scarab, which was inlaid with lapis lazuli; there was an elaborate golden necklace with a lapis moon riding in a golden boat; there were two beautiful earrings, made of gold with cloisonné falcons, their wings arching to form perfect circles, inlaid with quartz, faience, and colored glass; there was a heavy gold ring depicting some Egyptian god or other. The priceless jewelry contrasted with the simple, rough cotton skirt. "Is this real gold?" asked Hartstein.

"Certainly is. You can't get out of this building without giving it back. And we can always get more of that jewelry anytime we want, just by going to ancient Egypt and getting it. Let me help you with that skirt."

"That's all right," said Hartstein, "I can manage. But what am I supposed to be?"

The uniformed man scratched his wispy beard. "A scribe, I suppose, or a valuable slave in a wealthy household. I don't know. I've never been there myself."

"Well, in History 110 we had a couple of weeks about Egypt, and I've seen this before." Hartstein held up the lunar pectoral. "This is one of the King Tut treasures."

"They all are, honey."

Hartstein stared for a moment, not understanding. "But how am I going to get away with wearing all of this Pharaoh's stuff, walking around the streets pretending I'm just a middle-class country boy with a yen to read the classics? And anyway, I'm going to about 50 B.C., and King Tut lived almost fifteen hundred years before that. All of this stuff, the skirt and the jewelry, is an anachronism. And the headdress too. Where I'm going, they'll all be influenced by the Greek occupation and the Romans."

The costumer yawned. "No, they won't."

"They won't? Why not?"

"They just won't, that's all. Wait until you get back there and then take a look around. Just remember, sweetheart, that the past isn't always the way you expect it to be, from reading books. How dreary that would be."

Hartstein was having more misgivings. "You can help me with the earrings," he said. "Did they have screw bases during the reign of the Ptolemies?"

"No, of course not, but do you want me to pierce your ears instead?"

Hartstein shook his head.

"Then just shut up and hold still."

The transmission screen itself wasn't very impressive. Hartstein had heard about it since childhood, had even seen pictures of it, yet he had a mental image that included more adventure and excitement than did the real thing. He waited on a worn green-painted bench for twenty minutes while a couple of dozen other people ducked through on their way to various eras. Some of the destinations were easy to guess, because of the travelers' costumes: one fat, bald man in the October of his years wore the skins of some mottled animal and carried a crude stone hatchet; two teenage girls traveling together wore Agency-issue outfits that disguised them as flower children of the 1960s; a tall, thin man with a loud voice and a permanent sneer wore the toga of a Roman senator. It gave Hartstein a feeling of being backstage at the community theater as he glanced around the waiting room and catalogued the cultures and centuries represented by the panorama of styles. And, he reminded himself, they all came from plastic-wrapped packages in the Agency warehouse. The most complex courtier's costume must have seen constant use, worn and cleaned and stored away again like a rented dinner jacket after prom night.

"Mr. Hartstein?" called a woman. He got up and went to the screen. "Mr. Hartstein? Your voucher, please. Thank you. Okay, we're going to put you through to Alexandria now. You will arrive early in the morning of May 15, 48 B.C., a full year before the Library will burn during Julius Caesar's siege of the city. Are you ready?"

Hartstein swallowed. He felt very nervous. His stomach was sending him sterner messages than ever. "I feel like a fool, dressed like this," he said.

The Agent had probably heard that sentiment many times. She did not reply. She grasped him by the arm and led him to the flickering screen. Hartstein saw that here, too, there was a framed sentiment:

> *Lasciate ogni speranza, voi ch'entrate.*
> *—Dante Alighieri*

He couldn't read Italian, but his high school Latin enabled him to recognize one word; *speranza* meant either "hope" or "breath," but he couldn't remember which.

"You will pop back here tomorrow at this time," she said. "You won't be able to do anything about it. Wherever you are, whatever you're doing, you'll snap back to the present. Try to keep track of the time, just to avoid any kind of inconvenience or embarrassment."

"Right," said Hartstein absently, just as she shoved him into the purple glow.

Just like that, he was in Egypt. He could tell, because of the palm trees and the camels. His first thought was, "Gee, it's just the way I imagined it." He was standing on a long, broad street. He looked to his right and left, but the street went on in both directions, straight as a reed, farther than he could see. There were imposing buildings nearby, on both sides of the street, and he was startled to realize that he knew what they were: behind him was the great Hall of Justice and, beside it, the public gymnasium; before him to the left was the famous amphitheater; far away down the street in the other direction were the city's stadium and the hippodrome; directly in front of him was the immortal Library. He looked both ways again for traffic, out of habit, and crossed the street.

The Library's appearance surprised him. There was a huge flight of granite steps leading up to the main entrance; the stairs were like a tremendous cataract of stone, guarded on either side by placid-looking granite sphinxes. "It looks like the New York Public Library," he thought. The resemblance was reinforced by the scores of people sitting on the steps. There were young couples holding hands, people talking together in groups of two and three, individuals idly watching the commerce of the city pass by on the great avenue, solitary loiterers dozing in the warm sun. All the men were dressed exactly as he was—barefoot, cotton skirt, headdress, showy jewelry. The women were even more remarkable in their tight, straight linen dresses and pleated, thin shoulder capes, their wide golden collars and inlaid pectorals, golden bracelets on their arms and wrists, golden rings on their fingers. Hartstein noticed that there seemed to be a lot of gold distributed among the common citizens. Everyone wore black or green outlines around the eyes. All the men looked like pharaohs and all the women like empresses. They passed the time in the pleasant weather outside the Library.

Hartstein stood on the sidewalk, hesitating. Part of him wanted to rush up the steps and into the building, to get his hands on the great lost literary works of antiquity. Another part of him was still afraid. That part was momentarily stronger; it asked him first if he could account for the sidewalk. He could not. He accepted it as a fact of history that none of the present-day authorities had bothered to report. It wasn't important; it meant nothing to him. He forgot all about it before he had climbed ten steps.

"Do you know what time it is?" asked one of the sitting men, as Hartstein drew near. The Egyptian had his arm around an attractive dark-skinned young woman; when she turned her head sideways, she looked just like a hieroglyph.

Hartstein paused. Reflexively he glanced at his wrist, but he had no watch. He looked up into the sky and judged the time by the sun. "Nine o'clock, I'd guess," he said.

"Thanks." The man stood and offered a hand to the young woman. "Come on, baby, they'll be open now."

Hartstein passed them and continued up the steps. At the top were three great bronze doors. He went to the first. A little sign on a pole stood in front of it. The message was in two languages, like the English and Spanish signs in airports. Here, though, there were hieroglyphics on top and Latin on the bottom. "That's peculiar," thought Hartstein. "In History 110 they told me that demotic script replaced hieroglyphics long before now." Thanks to the ESB session, he could read the Egyptian symbols easily, while the only word of the Latin he knew was *ianuam*. The sign said PLEASE USE NEXT DOOR. Hartstein smiled. *"Plus ça change, plus c'est la même chose,"* he murmured. He went to the middle door and swung it open.

Inside, the Library was lit by sunlight streaming through huge windows on every wall set high above the bookshelves. Hartstein stood inside the door, paralyzed for the moment by the staggering value of this gigantic room, by the anticipation of browsing through the treasure of lost wisdom. He became aware of the silence, of the pervasive odor of old books decaying in their bindings, of the sense of great riches of the intellect not far away, on the shelves within his reach, on other shelves across the vast hall, in other chambers hidden beyond distant doorways, of uncounted volumes and forgotten authors . . .

And then, like a fish from the sky, a thought startled him. What was most unusual about the Library was its overwhelming familiarity. "It's the ESB treatment," he told himself. But it was more than that. There was too much that was just like the present. More than he would have guessed.

In the center of the immense open hall there was a large desk. Two women sat behind it and glanced through papers and books. They were evidently employees—Hartstein had some initial difficulty calling them librarians—and he decided to begin his tour of the Library with them. He went to the desk and waited for one of the women to look up. "Hello," he said.

"Hello," said the librarian, "can I help you?" Hartstein was stunned; she was the most beautiful woman he had ever met in his entire life. Her eyes were deep and bright and violet, lidded with Nile blue, made even larger by the black outlines that curved up toward her temples. She wore a braided wig as black as death. Her skin was tanned and smooth, the hairs on her forearms pale, bleached by the sun. Her features were striking and exotic in the way that those of some photographic models are, the type of woman one never meets in real life. She wore the same long, figure-hugging dress, the same short cape, and the same queen's ransom in jewelry. She smiled, and the stale, studious atmosphere in the chamber ignited.

"I'm . . ." Hartstein looked around in panic.

"Can I help you find something?" she asked.

He nodded, desperate for an idea. "Do you have anything on philosophy?" he said.

"Of course. Go to that cabinet and look up philosophy. When you find the book you want, make a note of the catalogue number. I'll help you locate it. It will be over in that section, against the wall." She pointed past his shoulder, off in the general direction of the Sinai Desert.

"Thanks." Hartstein knew immediately that he had made a bad mistake. He didn't want to do anything that would take him away from the desk and the librarian, but he went to the cabinet. It was made of blond wood and fashioned with wooden pins instead of iron nails. He put a hand on the solid door, but he did not open it. He didn't want to spend his time looking over copied manuscripts of things he hadn't enjoyed reading in college. He went back to the desk.

"Did you find anything?" asked the lovely librarian.

"No," said Hartstein, "I changed my mind. I was hoping I could find— by the way, what is your name?"

"I am Pamari," she said, looking down shyly at her work. Her long black lashes hid her eyes.

"My name is Stulectis, from the city of Mardenes." Both proper names had been inserted into his memory by the ESB process. They were both merely foreign-sounding nonsense words. There had never been any city called Mardenes, but it sounded as if there might. "I think I'd like something less difficult to read, something that would give me a good idea of how the citizens of this great city live."

"You can try over there," said Pamari, indicating a section of books opposite another desk near the rear exit.

"Thanks again. Oh, and would you forgive me if I ask you something personal?" Pamari glanced into his eyes and, embarrassed, looked back down at her papers. "Would you like to have lunch with me? I'm only going to be in Alexandria until tomorrow morning. I thought—"

"I don't really think so," she whispered. She was blushing furiously.

"I'm very sorry," said Hartstein, angry with his foolishness. "I shouldn't have—" He interrupted himself and went to look at the books. He tried to remind himself that he had come to examine them, and not to promote a twenty-four-hour romance with a woman who had been dead for more than two thousand years.

Another shock interrupted his internal scolding. The books on the shelves were just that—books. Not scrolls. Not whatever else the Egyptians might have done with papyrus pages (collected them in folders made of sheepskin, tied them together with cotton twine). They were modern-looking books, bound in leather, their titles and authors painted on the binding in neat hieroglyphics. Hartstein took one down and looked it over. It was called *Memnet's Shekel-Wise Guide to Parthia*. There was a neat cartouche of catalogue numbers at the base of the book's spine. Hartstein opened it up; instead of hand-copied hieroglyphics, as he expected, he was bewildered to see printed pages. He cried aloud in outrage, almost running back to Pamari's desk. He waved the book above his head. "What is this?" he said loudly.

"I'm sorry, sir," said the other librarian, "but you'll have to lower your voice. This is—"

"What *is* this? You can't have printing!"

"—this is a library."

Pamari took the book from him. "Mr. Stulectis, is there some problem?" She looked honestly upset by his attitude.

"Remember where you are, sir," said the other woman.

"Remember where I am," said Hartstein, more calmly. "Yes, I remember. I'm very sorry. No, there's nothing wrong. I made a mistake. I think I made a terrible, very expensive mistake."

Pamari didn't understand what he meant. She looked at him curiously; he felt the blood rushing to his face, and he went back to the books to hide his discomfort. He noticed that the sign above the section where he had found Memnet's magnum opus said SUMMER READING. He put the book back. Summer reading. "It figures," Hartstein muttered. He looked at other books nearby. There was one called *The Murder of a Simple Scribe*, by Adasirnat. There was *The Flax-Seed Diet*, by Architydes the Cytheran. There was *Self-Realization Through Hubris*, by Epimander. There were more: *Passion's Scarlet Scarab*, by Germanica Drusilla Tarquin; *The Hittite Conspiracy*, by Menotepset; a large volume of *Who's Who in the Lower Kingdom*; *Osiris Is Dead Again*, by Ekartis, formerly Associate High Priest of the Temple at Amarna; *War-Chariots of the Nineveh Conflict, Volume II; New Voices in Etruscan Fiction*, edited by Quintus Flavius Mummo; and many, many more. Hartstein's face was dark with rage as he continued to read the titles.

"If I can carry things back in time," he thought, "like this ridiculous jewelry, then I can probably take things with me to the present. I'll take one of these books with me. I want to see how Sergeant Brannick will explain this." Hartstein chose a book from the NEW & NOVEL section, *The Shriveling*, by Karheshut of Thosis, author of *The Yawning* and *The Theban Bronze-Implement Massacre*. "I can't wait for this." Hartstein's fury had settled into a deadly, cold anger. When he returned to his own time, he was going to expose the Agency and make such a disturbance that the time-travel swindle would be ended forever. He wandered around the Library for a while, making notes of everything he wanted to report.

BRITANNIA, ISLE OF BLUE MEN said a hand-glyphed poster above a small rack of books. Hartstein browsed among them for a few minutes, briefly amused by a volume entitled *Papyrus-Reed Boats of the Gods*, which attempted to prove that the monuments at Stonehenge and elsewhere in Britain were actually the docking sites used by Ra, Horus, Isis, and the rest for their celestial craft when they visited their summer homes in the north. The book gave Hartstein an idea; he decided that sometime he'd like to visit Stonehenge while it was being created, just to learn what its prehistoric architects thought they were making. But, he reminded himself, if this visit to Alexandria were typical of the Agency's command of history, he might well witness those ancient Britons building parking lots for the gods.

There was a bulletin board with plenty of community messages: scribes offering copying services, rummage sales, cats and mice mummified cheap, meetings of the Historic Obelisk Preservation Committee, lessons on traditional drum and improvisational cymbal, choice delta property shown by appointment only, a class in the cooking of transalpine Gaul, moonlight monument tours and tomb investigation, baby-sitting, pet-sitting, palace-sitting, the usual mix of come-ons and vital information. Hartstein was beginning to understand just how mundane the past could be.

There was a librarian telling a story to a group of children in the Young Adults division. The girls wore red-dyed shifts of light cotton; the youngest boys were naked except for the ubiquitous Tutankhamen-inspired golden ornaments. In the periodicals room were back issues of the Alexandria *News*, most of which was devoted to daily reports of fires in the suburbs and barge collisions on the Nile, with a few pages of personal ads ("SWM, 42, successful merchant, landowner, on intimate terms with Thoth, would like to meet SWF, 14–25, prefer broadminded enslaved foreign princess, for mutually enlightening cultural exchanges, etc. No phonies or Carthaginians"). There were public service messages posted on the walls (WHAT TO DO IN CASE OF PLAGUES. *Hail:* Go indoors at once. Hailstones can be lethal to human beings and animals. Do not try to protect exposed property. Do not venture outside until you are certain the plague has passed. *Boils:* Apply hot poultices and appropriate charms. If prayers and sacrifices are not effective, consult your physician. *Water turned to blood:* Do not mix with wine or fruit juices. Blood is not satisfactory for drinking, washing, laundering, or other purposes. Do not use the water until you are notified by the authorities that it is safe to do so. And so on). There was a huge section of mystery novels and a small section of books that tried to make sense of the mixture of Egyptian, Greek, Roman, and miscellaneous deities. There was a large selection of firsthand accounts of strange places beyond the known world (*Five Days on the Moon,* and *A Journey to Africa's Land of Living Fire,* by Philopeides the Lesser). There was everything, in short, that Hartstein would expect to find in his own neighborhood library, and nothing that he had hoped to see in Alexandria. Aristotle's lost books on comedy were missing, either checked out or stolen. The only thing by Aeschylus on the shelves was an early musical comedy called *Pythagoras Tonite!* which had been written in collaboration with friends while they were all still in school. There was very little in the Library that Hartstein found exciting or even interesting. There was nothing that he could carry breathlessly back to the present, nothing that shed light on the unanswered questions of the past, nothing that made Hart-stein's expense worthwhile. Except Pamari.

"I'd like to check this book out," he told her, giving her the copy of Karheshut's masterpiece of horror.

"Certainly." She seemed glad that his spell of madness and wrath had passed. She smiled at him; she almost made him forget his disappointment and frustration. "May I have your library card?"

"Card? I'm sorry, I don't have a card."

Pamari nodded. "That's right, you said you were from out of town. Well, if you're going to be here for any length of time—But you said you were leaving tomorrow! Why would you want to check out this book?"

Hartstein opened his mouth and, finding no answer, closed it. The silence stretched on.

"Something to read in your hotel room tonight?" she asked.

He was inexpressibly grateful. "Yes," he said. "I could return it in the morning."

"Well, then," said Pamari, "we could give you a temporary card for today. May I see your identification?"

His heart sank. "Never mind the book," he said lamely, "I probably wouldn't finish it anyway. And I'd much rather take you to dinner, and then maybe you could show me the city."

This time Pamari didn't crush him with her reply. "Yes," she said lightly, "we could do that."

Hartstein was ecstatic. "What time should I meet you?" he asked.

"Six-thirty," she said. "At the front door."

"I'll be there," said Hartstein. He left the Library thinking of her, forgetting entirely why he had come to Alexandria, forgetting the sham and farce the Agency had traded him for his grandparents' hard-earned savings.

While the Library had been one of the most unsatisfactory experiences of his entire life, that evening in Alexandria was perhaps the most memo-rable. Every minute he spent in Pamari's company made him regret his modern life and dull and ordinary friends so many centuries in the future. Hartstein had to remind himself again and again that very soon he would return to the present, leaving Pamari frozen like a rare and beautiful butterfly in the amber of time. It put a not unpleasant melancholy edge on his enjoyment of the ancient city.

Pamari suggested a small inn where they could have supper. Hartstein was curious about the kind of food he would get; he had no clear idea of what people in ancient times ate. As a matter of fact, he had no good idea of what people in modern Egypt ate. But yet it came as no surprise when the innkeeper brought large platters of roasted lamb and roasted camel, with bowls of dates and oranges. The innkeeper, a tall, burly man who looked as if he could handle any trouble that rowdy patrons might start in his establishment, carved the roasts himself. Hartstein was about to ask the man where he had obtained his golden necklace and golden bracelets and rings but, recalling what he had discovered in the Library earlier, he decided he didn't need to know any more answers.

There was a peculiar, sweet-tasting, light-colored wine with the meal, and as he drank more of it, Hartstein found the taste becoming more pleasant. "I thought there would be some Greek food," he said. "Because the Greeks ruled here for so long. The Ptolemies are a Greek family, and Cleopatra is more Greek than Egyptian."

"You do not like this food?" asked Pamari.

"I love it," said Hartstein, although he could have done without the roast camel. "But I expected more in the way of, oh, hummus and moussaka and baklava and that kind of stuff."

"I've never eaten those things," said Pamari. "You have traveled a great deal, haven't you? You've seen a lot of the world. I've never been outside the city of Alexandria."

Hartstein looked deeply into her sad eyes. "You would not believe the things I have seen," he said. He covered one of her small hands with his own.

"Tell me," she said excitedly. "Tell me what you've seen."

"I will. But I want you to tell me about Alexandria. I've seen nothing but the Library and this little inn. And you."

Pamari looked away, suddenly shy once again. "The Library is very famous," she murmured.

"But much less fascinating than you. Are you finished eating? Let me pay the man, and then we'll take a walk and you can show me the sights."

Pamari nodded. Hartstein drained the last of the wine in his golden goblet, left a few coins on the long table, and offered Pamari his hand. They left the inn and walked along the central avenue of the city, in the direction of the hippodrome. "What is back there?" asked Hartstein, pointing to the right, beyond the gymnasium, south toward what would have been the residential section of the city.

"Nothing of importance," she said. "I never go there."

"Why don't we? The stadium and hippodrome don't interest me. I'd rather walk with you toward nothing than spend my time looking at empty stone buildings." They turned away from the street and went along the eastern flank of the Hall of Justice. The way was dark and silent, and suddenly Hartstein was aware of how vulnerable the two of them were. He berated himself for leading Pamari toward who knew what kind of danger. There were surely thieves and robbers in ancient Alexandria, and there were no Agency uniforms around to persuade the criminals that Hartstein was to be treated as a guest of the past. "Let's go back," he said. But before he turned around, he saw something too strange to ignore. There were dark shapes ahead of him, houses and shops and other buildings, but none of them was distinct, even though a full moon shone down from the clear Mediterranean sky. The nearer they approached, the farther the shadows receded. After two hundred yards Hartstein knew that something was wrong. "Why aren't there any houses?" he asked. "Where are all the houses?"

Pamari was bewildered. "There they are," she said, pointing ahead of them. "Can't you see?"

Hartstein waved a hand impatiently. "They were just ahead of us ten minutes ago. We've been walking and walking, and I still can't make out any of them. I can't seem to focus on any single building. It's like everything away from the main street—away from the Library—is vague and formless and not really there. I'll bet we could walk from now until morning without ever coming on a real house. Or a real person either." He turned to her, wondering. He reached out and touched her face.

"I am real," she said, looking curiously at him.

"Are you?" he asked. He took her by the shoulders and pulled her nearer. She uttered a sigh; her languorous lashes hid the glistening eyes he would never see again. Hartstein bent to kiss her, cupping her delicate face in his rough hands. Just before his lips touched hers he fell forward, stumbling through a purple glow onto the Agency's temporal recovery stage.

"What the hell!" shouted Hartstein as he looked wildly around him.

"Welcome back, Mr. Hartstein," said Sergeant Brannick.

"What the hell is going on?" cried Hartstein. "What am I doing back here already?"

"It's two o'clock," said Brannick. "Twenty-four hours, just what you paid for. I suppose you're just a little disoriented. It takes some getting used to, flashing from one time to another like that."

"Twenty-four hours! It wasn't even twelve! I got there this morning and it wasn't even midnight yet. I had all night left. What kind of a cheat is this?"

Sergeant Brannick led Hartstein away from the recovery stage. Other travelers would be coming back soon, and it was important to keep the area clear. "I think someone neglected to tell you about the temporal Doppler effect," said the Agent.

"Somebody neglected to tell me about a whole lot of things," said Hartstein angrily. "And I'm going to get my answers, and then I'm going to make things pretty hot for your Agency, too."

"Why don't we talk about it?" said Brannick soothingly.

"Sure, I'd like that." Hartstein took out his page of notes, the ones he had made during his tour of the Library. He was dismayed to see that they were all written in hieroglyphics, which he could no longer decipher. "That's great," he muttered. "That's just typical." He crumpled the page into a ball and threw it on the floor.

"Sit down over here," said Brannick. "Some people are very upset when they come back. The past isn't always what they expected. Naturally we're anxious to make up for any unpleasantness. We don't want any unsatisfied customers, you know. Why don't you just tell me why you're so agitated?"

"Agitated!" shouted Hartstein.

"Shh." Brannick indicated a man dressed in the costume of a medieval Italian nobleman. "You'll spoil his fun."

"I'll tell you why I'm agitated," said Hartstein in a lower voice. "They had printed books! Bound, printed books!"

"Ah. You found ancient Alexandria very much like our world in some ways."

Hartstein looked disgusted. "Not just your crummy similarities. I mean out-and-out anachronisms. Historical impossibilities. It was like a low-budget film made by uneducated fools with no imagination. Where was I really, some back-lot construction in Arizona? All ESB-trained union labor? Costumes, props, and nine-to-five Egyptians?"

Brannick took a deep breath. "You were really back there, Hartstein. You were really in the past. In ancient Alexandria."

"But—"

The Agent silenced him with a curt gesture. "But the past isn't what you think it is. It isn't always what you expect. There is no such thing as the objective past."

"I know, I heard that before. What the hell does it mean?"

Brannick massaged his forehead with one hand. "It means that the past depends on our ideas. The past looks like what we *think* it looks like, our consensus. There is nothing in the past that the present hasn't put there. If the majority of people today think there were knights in shining armor in fifth-century England, when you go back to fifth-century England there will be knights in shining armor. It doesn't make any difference what historians and archaeologists know, what has come down to us preserved through the ages, what truly existed in those days. The past is a subjective museum of popular belief."

"What about the *real* past?"

"You were in the real past, the only past that actually exists. I know, I know. I understand what you mean: What about the objective past?" Sergeant Brannick seemed very tired; Hartstein wondered how many times a day he had to go through this explanation. "The objective past is closed to us. We can't find it, to be more precise, if in fact it really exists anywhere."

"So all time travel is a kind of legal con game," said Hartstein.

"Not really," said the Agent. "Almost everyone is thrilled and happy with their vacations. The past is exactly the way they expect it to be. After all, it's their ideas that make the past what it is. A few people are disappointed, those who know a little more, who know what they're looking for. We have to explain the situation and try to make them understand that we haven't cheated them." He indicated other returning travelers, all laughing and joking, dressed in costumes from many times and many lands. "If anyone is to blame, it's them. You visited their conception of ancient Alexandria, their idea of what the great Library was like."

"And that's why there wasn't much else to the city? Why I couldn't find the streets and the houses where the people lived? Why there was nothing but downtown history?"

"That's right. I'm glad you're catching on so quickly. People may know about the Library, but they give little thought to what Alexandria, the rest of Alexandria, was like. So it's all vague and half-formed and patched up with clichés and fog."

Hartstein nodded. He had lost some of the sharp force of his anger, but he still had questions. "Then why was I snapped back here so early? I didn't have a full day in the past. I met a girl—"

Brannick smiled. "You *always* meet a girl, Hartstein. That's part of the popular idea of the past. That's where all the romance in the universe is—yesterday. Everytime you go into the past, you'll meet a girl. Anyway, someone should have told you that time is subject to a kind of Doppler effect, the way light and sound are. The farther back in time you go, the shorter the minutes become. You were gone twenty-four hours by our clock. I don't know how many hours that would be in your Alexandria."

"You have an answer for everything, don't you?"

Sergeant Brannick looked down at his tunic, pulled it tight to eliminate some folds, and indicated his service ribbons. "Some of these I got for my distinguished career defending truth, justice, and the Agency way through all the eons of time. The rest I got for knowing all the answers. Listen, I know you're still unhappy about this Egyptian business. That's not good for you, it's not good for me, and it's not good for the Agency. We want to square things with you, Hartstein. We're ready to offer you another trip into the past, free of charge, all expenses paid, anywhere you want to go, stay as long as you like up to five days. How does that sound to you?"

Hartstein said nothing for a long time. He watched men and women returning through the glowing screen from their holidays, from dead ages they had not perceived as somehow very wrong. "Why can't I be like them?" he thought. "Why can't I just be satisfied with what I found?" Everyone else seemed to have had a great time; Hartstein felt a little envious. "No," he said at last, "you don't have anything I want. You can't give me the real past, and these adventures in Storyland of yours don't interest me." He got up and walked away.

"You don't realize what I'm offering you, Hartstein," said the Agency man. "I'm giving you access to the whole world. Think about it."

Hartstein turned and faced him. "Nothing you say will make me go back in time again."

Brannick laughed. "You're wrong, Hartstein," he said. "I see your type every single day. You'll come back, I can tell. Don't worry. That offer of ours will be waiting for you, whenever you decide to take it."

Later, after he had traded the Alexandrian costume for his own clothing, Hartstein left the Agency Building. A cloud passed in front of the sun, suddenly darkening the afternoon. Hartstein looked up, frightened, certain that he would see the Bird of Time overhead, blotting out the light and warmth. The great Bird had flown by, Hartstein knew, and dropped its little gift on him. Nevertheless, Brannick had been right. Sooner or later, Hartstein was sure that he'd have to try it again.

CHAPTER TWO

JUST THE FAMILY AND A FEW CLOSE FRIENDS

Then upon the passing of the season did Jesus go away from there and came into Shinabbeth, which lieth west of Tiberias the city of the Gentiles. And the rumor of him was great in all the nations of Galilee. And they brought unto him children wasted by sickness, and elders that bare the burden of grief, and though they did not receive him in their hearts yet did they call upon him, saying, If thou art truly the Teacher, then take away from us this bitter sorrow.

And Jesus saith unto them, Yea, if you would not suffer these afflictions, then it is upon the Son of Man that they must rest. Would you be made whole in this wise?

But the multitudes made no answer, yet even so was there sufficient reply in their silence.

And Jesus, perceiving all of this, preached unto them in the manner of a parable . . .

"My God," said Hartstein passionately, "you didn't tell me it was going to be so hot."

Sergeant Brannick mopped his face with the end of his linen headdress. "What did you expect?" he asked. "Even at Christmas, the three Wise Men came on camels, not reindeer. Hurry up or we'll be late."

They limped painfully through the narrow alleys of Shinabbeth, toward the home of a wealthy merchant who was giving a feast in honor of his son's bar mitzvah. Hartstein and Brannick were attending in order to hear Jesus, who had promised to drop by for a little while and say a few words. Brannick had managed to wangle an invitation from Judas Iscariot by donating a few silver coins to the apostles' treasury.

Sergeant Brannick, as a representative of the Agency on this trip into the distant past, was acting as Hartstein's personal tour guide. Generally the Agency didn't bother supplying guides; it preferred to fill up the traveler's brain with implanted memories of everything one needed to know—language, customs, geography, historical significance, points of interest—and then put the poor soul *in medias res*. But Hartstein had been so displeased by his adventure in ancient Egypt that to maintain his goodwill the Agency offered him an all-expense paid luxury trip anytime in the world.

The holiday in Egypt had been Hartstein's choice. His grandparents, who had footed the bill for that trip, suggested that now a firsthand experience of Jesus might improve his ambiguous moral posture. If Hartstein hadn't been so intimidated by his grandparents, he would have chosen to see something else instead, like the Jazz Age. He had discovered a native talent for licentiousness while in college.

But no; here he was in some sun-baked village between Nazareth and the Sea of Galilee itself. Shinabbeth called itself a city, but in his own time Hartstein knew of supermarkets whose parking lots were larger. It was hot, dusty, dry, and very dull. The only transportation was by foot *(pedibus* in Latin, Sergeant Brannick informed him; "Pedagogue," thought Hartstein, who already knew that), and despite all the claims the Romans made for the improvements they instituted in their colonies, the stone-paved ways were murder on blistered heels and twisted ankles.

Thanks to the Agency's extensive costume department, both men were impeccably dressed. They looked like two unemployed shepherds on an ill-conceived Christmas card. Sergeant Brannick even carried a long crook. "What do we tell people if they ask us who we are?" said Hartstein.

Brannick was a very patient man; that was one of the reasons he had been chosen for this job. "We tell them we're shepherds, of course."

"But shouldn't we be, you know, abiding in the fields and all that?"

Brannick shrugged. "I suppose shepherds get some time off, too. Or maybe we're looking for a stray. One of our sheep is lost and we think it headed straight for town."

Hartstein smiled dubiously. "We left the ninety and nine, and have come in search of the poor son of a bitch that ran off. Who's going to buy that, Brannick?"

"Don't worry about it, Hartstein, nobody's even going to ask. You got to remember that we fit into the scene. But if anybody *does* ask, you clam up. Let me do the talking. I'm the veteran around here, I'll handle everything."

Hartstein frowned. "I hate it when somebody says that," he muttered. It usually meant that he was being led blindly into some hopeless disaster.

Despite all his assurances, Sergeant Brannick was partially wrong: only *one* of them looked as if he belonged in the neighborhood. Brannick himself did not. Clad in a long cotton shirt bound with a leather girdle, the headdress, sandals, and a coarse cloak woven of goat's hair, he still looked like a hero. There was no way in the world that Brannick could have looked otherwise; every line was clean and sharp, every movement precise. Sergeant Brannick never stumbled, never stammered, never hesitated. He walked with an indefinable and immutable air of competence. His hair, black with gray highlights, was cropped short; his phony beard trimmed in a style more cinematic than shepherdic; his eyes were bright blue and piercing, a requirement for advancement in the Agency; his shoulders were as broad as a javelin thrower's, and his forty-year-old physique as trim as it had been the day he enlisted. Even draped in the shapeless Hebrew costume, the sergeant gave the impression that he was still in uniform, that he was still braced in his silver and blue Agency tunic with the sleeve full of hash marks. As much as Brannick knew about time travel, as much as he could tell Hartstein about the biblical era they were visiting, he did not belong. He looked as out of place as a straw in a beer bottle.

Hartstein, however, had found his milieu. If anyone could appreciate him, average joe that he was, it was the poor inhabitants of Shinabbeth. The town was the figment of the imagination of countless unexceptional people. There was no such place as Shinabbeth, there never had been; but Hartstein hadn't found that out yet, and Sergeant Brannick was in no hurry to tell him.

He was a nice guy, was Hartstein, but when these adventures began he was what one might call "ineffectual." Which is a nice way of saying he was a nebbish, which, let's face it, is what he was. But he didn't have to stay that way: the fortunate factor was that Hartstein's moment of trial and decision had not yet occurred; when it did, he could still leave nebbishness behind. And he did have Sergeant Brannick as an example of the kind of man he hoped to become. Hartstein was still potentially a lion among men.

It's just that he didn't look like one to the casual observer. But rather than get too far ahead of the story, let's content ourselves with watching him hobble painfully through the streets of this imaginary town in ancient Palestine, on his way to a catered meeting with Jesus Christ.

Shinabbeth lay in a low, flat place beneath a clutch of stony, barren hills. It was a small village, with but one main through road and several rutted cross-streets. Crowded together like sheep in the fold were a few dozen squat, white, flat-roofed houses. There was no order apparent in their placement; they clustered in the valley like dumplings dropped from a spoon onto the hard, dry earth. Just beyond the town proper, in a kind of

suburb notable only for its inconvenience, was a large estate belonging to
the wealthiest man in the area, a merchant called Jotham son of Nathan.
It was he whose son was being welcomed into manhood this day.

Jotham's residence was the only stone house in the neighborhood, but
even so it could not compare in magnificence to the homes in more
metropolitan centers of Palestine. It looked like a big gray box, three
stories high, made of dressed granite blocks with few windows looking out
upon the dreary vista. There was a heavy wooden gate closing the entrance, and an archway led from it into the central courtyard. An ancient,
slow-moving gentleman with the beard of a patriarch acted as porter and
unlocked the gate when Sergeant Brannick presented proof of their invitation.

"Are we early?" asked Brannick.

"Yes and no," said the old man. "Master Jotham has set out a great
feast and already several of his wife's relatives have descended on the meat
and wine. But the ceremony is going on now, and this Rabbi Jesus isn't
expected until later. Are you here for the bar mitzvah, the food, or the
rabbi's sermon?"

Sergeant Brannick gave Hartstein a quick look to remind him to say
nothing. "We've come to pay our respects and to congratulate your master
and his son."

The old man's eyes narrowed shrewdly. "You're here for the free meal,
then," he said. "But come in; Master Jotham would be upset if I turned
you away. There's no telling who may turn out to be of his wife's family.
They are as many as the fleas on a yellow dog's belly."

"Thank you," said Brannick. The two men touched the mezuzah nailed
to the gatepost and kissed their fingertips, and passed through. In the
courtyard there were several large trees, and benches had been placed in
the shade beneath them. The old man had been correct; already more
than a score of people were busily consuming the extravagant banquet
Jotham Ben-Nathan had provided.

A young woman dressed in a long blue cotton robe, with an apricot-
colored cloth covering her head and draping her shoulders, approached
them, carrying a platter of fruit. She regarded the two men curiously; all
the guests appeared to be of the upper strata of the local population, but
Brannick and Hartstein were clearly dressed as shepherds. "Welcome,"
said the young woman. "Please, refresh yourselves and receive the hospitality of the house of Jotham." She indicated a small wooden stand where
a pitcher of water and a basin had been set up to facilitate the washing of
hands before eating.

"Thank you," said Brannick. He started toward the washstand.

"Brannick!" said Hartstein urgently. "Do you know who that girl is?"

Brannick looked at him placidly. "I gather that she's one of our host's servants."

"She's Pamari! You remember, I told you about her when I came back from Alexandria. I met her in the Library. But that historical period was almost seventy years before this one. How can she be here?"

The sergeant shook his head sadly. "You'll get used to it, Hartstein," he said. "I tried to explain it to you after your trip to Egypt. Whenever you go into the past, you find your ideal mate there. When you were in Alexandria, it was Pamari. Here her name will be different, but she will look the same and she will sound the same and she will arouse the same feelings in you. If you go to Elizabethan England, she will be there. If you go to feudal Japan, she will be there. It can be painful until you've made a few trips and the shock wears off." He paused and looked around the courtyard. "Do you see that lady? Over by the fig tree? That woman with the maroon-and-white-striped robe? That is the love of my life. In Manchu China her name was Lai Lin. In Moscow, while we waited for Rasputin to die, her name was Lida. Her name here is Leah."

"But—"

Brannick interrupted him by raising a hand. "Go ahead," he said. "Meet your girl. Talk to her. At first you'll be amazed by how much she reminds you of the Egyptian girl. Then you'll beg me to take her back with us, and you won't believe that it's impossible. I've been through this a million times with other tourists."

Hartstein closed his gaping mouth. He knew Brannick was right. "It won't do any harm just to say a few words, though," he said. The sergeant only gave him a knowing smile.

Conceiving a great and sudden hunger for an orange or dates or whatever the young woman was serving, Hartstein followed her across the courtyard. "Say," he announced, "I'd sure like a piece of fruit."

She turned around, smiling, and held out the platter for his inspection. There was nothing on it that Hartstein felt like eating, but he took a fig just for appearance's sake. He had never eaten a fig before, except inside a Newton, and he wondered what he was supposed to do with it. "My name is Zaavan," he said. "It's sure a nice day for a party, isn't it?"

"Yes," she murmured shyly. She dropped her long dark lashes, hiding the gorgeous violet eyes he had fallen in love with in the great Library of Alexandria.

Hartstein wondered if there was any period in the entire history of the universe when he would have an easy time starting a conversation with a beautiful woman. Maybe if he were floating around in space watching the

Big Bang he could find something to talk about, but even then he suspected he'd sound like a moron. "Do you come here often?" he asked. Immediately he hated himself.

"I am the handmaiden of Abigail, wife of Jotham Ben-Nathan," she said. She looked at him curiously; he wasn't behaving like the simple shepherd he appeared to be.

"Maybe we've met before. Have you ever been to Bethsaida? I think we may have been invited to the same harvest celebration there."

"No," she said, "I've never been to Bethsaida."

"Oh." Hartstein's heart was breaking. He wished that she'd give him a little help.

"But you may be thinking of my sister; some people think we look alike. My name is Pamrah."

Hartstein smiled. "I would never in a million years confuse you with anyone else," he said. He waited a moment for her reaction, fearfully, and then realized that he had said the right thing.

Pamrah lowered her eyes and blushed—just the way she had in ancient Egypt. "I have to serve the other guests," she said.

Hartstein didn't want to let her go. "I know. But I'd like to speak to you later, if you get the chance."

"I'd like that, too." She fluttered her lashes once more, then turned away.

"Not bad, soldier." Hartstein spun around, startled. Sergeant Brannick had come up behind him silently.

"She's more beautiful here than she was before," said Hartstein.

"That's the way it works."

Hartstein looked at the fig in his hand and wondered what to do with it; there was nowhere to put it and he really didn't want to eat it. "I have to give you a lot of credit, Brannick," he said. "This is very accurate, very realistic. Alexandria was a fraud from the minute I got there. There wasn't a single thing about that place that I could believe. But this place is so real —the houses, the people, everything. Is that just because you're here with me? It makes me suspicious, as if you operate two separate pasts, one for the Agency and one for the tourists."

They walked across the yard, toward a long double row of tables set up in the shade. "Does this place seem more real to you than Alexandria?" asked the Agency man.

Hartstein nodded. "There's no comparison," he said. "I told you about all the anachronisms I saw. Look around here; this is what I expected, what I paid my money for."

"You said it yourself, Hartstein: it's what you expected. Never forget

that the past is what you make it. The past is a simulation of what you—
and everybody else—expect it to be. Now, in Alexandria you had a certain
familiarity with it through your studies. But the consensus of popular
belief sees that place just as you found it, glaring anachronisms and all.
There isn't any difference here, either. The mistakes are all around you,
but you don't have so great a knowledge of this locus in space and time. A
biblical scholar would spot the inaccuracies in a few seconds. On this trip,
your preconceptions match those of the rest of the people in our time.
That's all there is to it."

"Ah," said Hartstein. "Point out a couple of mistakes for me."

They sat down at one of the tables. "You'll see that though these people
are Jews living according to centuries-old traditions, there will be few of
the required observances. That's not because in the historical past they
were lax about these things, but because in our own time we are, as a
whole, unfamiliar with them. We kissed the mezuzah coming in; that's a
custom many people in our time might be expected to know about, and it
was included in the ESB-induced preparation you received before we left.
But as for specific prayers and such throughout the day, well, they ought
to be there but they won't be. If and when most people in our era learn of
these things, they will appear here, as a reflection."

"That's what I'm having trouble understanding," said Hartstein. He
scratched at the beard spirit-gummed to his chin. "I always thought that if
you went into the past and disturbed something, you'd create havoc back
in the present."

Brannick shook his head. "That's impossible," he said.

"Yet if you alter the present—or, at least, the common knowledge of
the present—you can change the past?"

"That's one of the principal duties of the Agency. We're trying to bring
the past into line. We're trying to make this shoddy past that we're able to
visit resemble the real past we know about through written records and
archaeology."

Hartstein thought that over while he sipped a cup of wine. "What
about the parts of the past that no one knows very much about? What
happens when you visit them?"

Brannick looked surprised, as if Hartstein had brought up a deeply
disturbing subject. "It's like a dream," he said, grimacing. "It's like waking
up from a nightmare and seeing the world while your eyes are still blurry
with sleep. Nothing is very distinct, but if you concentrate real hard, you
can find your way around all right. There's nothing to discover and nothing to learn in those places. Do yourself a favor, Hartstein, and forget
about that."

Brannick's description made Hartstein shudder. "Then the only clear, sharp spots are the exciting highlights. But what happens in between? What happens here, for example, between one documented event in Jesus' life and the next?"

"If you hung around long enough after the loaves and fishes, say, everybody would leave and it would get misty and hazy and you'd be all by yourself, even if you went into the middle of a big town. It can be very frightening. It's like that for all the great moments in history—a vivid day or week of events, just as you imagined them, followed by a gray and ominous nothing."

A bright burst of laughter behind them kept Hartstein from asking more about the mysteries of between-time. He turned around; there were three men, all wearing large, fringed prayer shawls over their shoulders. The shawls were bordered in black with black stripes, and seemed incongruous on the persons of their boisterous owners. One of the men pointed across the courtyard, where Pamrah was serving an elderly woman who sat in the meager shade of a stunted olive tree. The man said something in a voice too low for Hartstein to hear, and the others laughed again. A second man made a broad gesture in Pamrah's direction. This time they raised their eyebrows and shook their heads; the third man clapped a hand to his forehead in mock astonishment.

"Can you hear what they're saying?" asked Hartstein.

"Don't pay any attention," said Brannick. "Remember, we're guests here and we're more or less undercover. Don't get involved. Always tell yourself that you can't afford to mix with these people on a personal level. Remind yourself that they're not real and they don't matter."

Hartstein continued to watch the men; he grew angrier and more frustrated. "It's Pamrah they're discussing," he said.

"I know that."

"But I can't just—"

Brannick put a strong hand on Hartstein's arm. "Yes, you can, soldier. You're going to learn my way or you're going to learn the hard way, so you may as well get used to the idea. Forget about Pamrah and ignore those men. They mean nothing to you. We came here to listen to Jesus, and none of the rest of it is worth a tick's hatband."

Hartstein directed his fury at the Agency man. "What the hell are you talking about?" he demanded. "What do you mean, 'I'm going to learn the hard way?' I'm going to learn what? You're dragging me around with you as if this were some kind of training mission, like I signed up with the Agency myself. Well, here's the latest, buddy: *I haven't enlisted.* I'm no tenderfoot recruit for you to break into shape. This is my vacation. I think the weight of all those service stripes on your uniform sleeve has finally bent your brain. Maybe it's time for you to check into the Old Sergeants' Home."

Before Brannick could answer, a short, fat man ran through the courtyard, upsetting a bench and knocking over a plate of delicacies. He paid no attention to the indignant shouts behind him, but dodged through the crowd and disappeared into the archway leading to the road outside. Hartstein was mildly bemused; it was an incongruous thing to happen at such a pleasant and serene occasion. Brannick, however, responded as if the running man had committed some unimaginable outrage. "I've got to go," he said brusquely.

"Go?" cried Hartstein. "Where? What am I supposed to do here by myself?"

"You can handle it; you were on your own in Egypt. Just sit tight. Your show will get going here in a few minutes. I'll be back before it's over. In the meantime, have some more wine. Don't go anywhere. You'd better be right here when I get back. And try not to talk to anybody, too."

"But where—" Hartstein's fragment of a question went unanswered; Brannick tried to be inconspicuous, but it was perfectly obvious that he was chasing after the stranger. Then Hartstein was all alone, abandoned to his own devices in a land and a time that had no place for him.

Pamrah had come to his table, and now she stood beside him. "Did your friend go after that man?" she asked.

"I suppose so," said Hartstein, "but I don't know why. Who was that man? Is he a member of the household?"

Pamrah shook her head. "I've never seen him before today. He spoke to me earlier, before you and your friend arrived. He had an unusual accent —like yours. I thought you were all together. I thought you knew him."

There was a commotion in the archway. Hartstein expected to see Sergeant Brannick chasing the costumed stranger back through the courtyard. He wondered what it all meant: what possible reason could Brannick have had for his sudden disappearance? The way the Agency explained the nature of time travel, the past was subjective, a shifting balance of truth and myths, subtly different for each visitor. It was impossible for someone else from the present to appear in this version of the past unless, like Brannick, he had left the present at the same moment as Hartstein. Pamrah seemed to think that the stranger came from the same place as Brannick and Hartstein, but that was contrary to the laws of nature.

Yet, on the other hand, why would Brannick leap up and go after an unknown, unreal resident in this dream of yesterday?

There were only two choices: one was foolish, and the other impossible.

But there *could* be a third explanation—if Sergeant Brannick and the Agency were withholding certain important information. On second thought, that seemed to Hartstein likely to be the truth, much more likely than any other hypothesis. In that case, there was nothing to be done until Brannick decided to come across with the facts. Hartstein suspected that he might be in danger, after all, but he wouldn't panic until he got the high-sign from Brannick. At the moment, in any event, he had other things to occupy his imagination: the commotion at the gate turned out to be the arrival of Jesus Christ and the twelve disciples.

"Can you tell which one is the Rabbi?" asked Pamrah.

Hartstein looked at the group of men coming into the courtyard, but none of them resembled how he imagined Christ to look. Then he saw something that made his mouth fall open. "Oh no, I don't believe it," he murmured.

"What's wrong?" asked Pamrah. "Are they impostors? Master Jotham was afraid that thieves or Gentiles might take advantage of this celebration to despoil his house."

"Oh no," said Hartstein, suddenly disappointed and weary, "they're not impostors. I can vouch for them, all right. I can even tell you the names of most of them."

"Of the Rabbi's disciples? How do you know *their* names? Have you been following them around the countryside?"

Hartstein pointed to the first of the newcomers, a tall, determined-looking man with broad shoulders and great, strong hands. He wore a yellow mantle and carried, in one hand, a pair of crossed keys and, in the other, a fat, dead fish. A bantam cock followed him, making murmurous crowing sounds. "That's Simon called Peter," said Hartstein. "I didn't think he'd really be dragging all of his symbolic attributes around with him, but I should have been ready for it. I wonder what he thinks the rooster is all about. He's not going to find out about that until, well . . ." He didn't want to say anything more to Pamrah about his knowledge of what was to come. He was surprised by his reaction; he wasn't furious about the absurdity of it all, the way he had been in Alexandria. In a way, it was kind of amusing. He rather enjoyed sitting back and watching history being enacted before his eyes with all the charm and accuracy of an elementary school pageant.

"Is that the Rabbi?" asked Pamrah. She indicated another man coming into the courtyard; he carried a sword in one hand, but did not seem particularly fierce or threatening. He was speaking to a handsome young man with wings, and suddenly they both laughed out loud.

"That's Matthew, the one without the feathers. He's often shown with the winged man, just as Mark has a winged lion."

Pamrah didn't understand, but she was impressed. "He looks like an angel," she said softly.

Hartstein smiled. "Don't bother about that. The guy with the wings isn't anybody. He's just a prop for the real apostle."

The other disciples filed in: John, clad in red with an eagle on his shoulder, carrying a large cup with a snake coiling out of it; his brother James, carrying a scallop shell and looking around for a safe place to leave it; Thomas, skeptical as always, carrying a carpenter's rule and probably wondering why; and the remaining seven, whom Hartstein had difficulty identifying, although if he had to make a guess, it was a good bet that the man holding the purse and the hangman's noose was Judas Iscariot.

And behind them all, like a shepherd driving his flock, came Jesus, speaking in a quiet voice to a well-dressed, well-fed man, evidently Jotham Ben-Nathan, their benefactor on this afternoon.

"That must be the Rabbi," said Pamrah in hushed, awed tones.

Jesus was, well, just what Hartstein had expected. He wore a seamless white garment and a red cloak—the very one that Richard Burton, two thousand years later, would die to protect from the snotty Caligula in *The Robe*. Jesus moved with a magnificence and an unselfconscious grace that commanded the attention of everyone in the yard. Also the bright, radiating halo around his head was pretty eye-catching as well.

"A halo," muttered Hartstein. "I would have felt cheated if they hadn't included that." But even the special effects scintillating around Jesus' head did not diminish Hartstein's wonder.

Peter, the Rock, gave his keys to a less charismatic disciple to hold, put his rooster in the care of one of Jotham's servants, and tossed the fish onto a table with a flat smack. He directed his eleven fellows to take seats, and then went to Jesus and conferred for a moment in whispers. He nodded at last, shook hands with Jotham, and joined the other disciples.

Jotham Ben-Nathan raised his hands and smiled benevolently. "Hello, everybody. I'm glad you all could be with us as we celebrate this very special day in the life of my son, Asher. Crowning my joy on this occasion is the honor and privilege to welcome the Rabbi Jesus into my home. I hope that we will be able to prevail upon him to share with us his great wisdom, which has already won him such fame and renown throughout Galilee. But first, my friends, eat and drink your fill. I call upon Rabbi Eleazar to offer a prayer and a blessing."

"Okay," said Hartstein to himself, "but I didn't come two thousand years to listen to a lot of speeches by spear-carriers." He had the unpleasant feeling that the Agency had suckered him again.

"I cannot stay here, Zaavan," said Pamrah. "Master Jotham is giving me angry looks."

"I'm sorry, honey," Hartstein said. "I don't want to get you into trouble with him. After this party is over, maybe we'll have some time to ourselves."

Pamrah smiled sweetly and carried her tray to another table.

"Let us pray," cried Rabbi Eleazar in his best Old Testament God of Vengeance voice. He praised his Lord for bringing forth bread from the earth, and creating the fruit of the tree and the vine and the earth.

The rabbi paused, but Hartstein was too experienced to hope that he was finished. These were just preliminary benedictions, the general address preceding the specific one that was intended to knock the congregation back on their heels.

"We celebrate the maturity of this fine boy, O Lord, who even today becomes a member of the community of adults, and takes up the obligation of observing all the commandments which Thou, in Thy infinite wisdom, hast given unto us. Guide this young man, Asher Ben-Jotham, and if it be Thy will, let him not stray from the ways of his fathers and his people. Let him not listen foolishly to the teachings of *false prophets*, O Lord, as this is one example of the things today's young people take up in their misguided desire to rebel against the ways of their elders. Let him not follow after *errant shepherds*, who lose themselves and their flocks together in the Desert of Ignorance, in the Wastes of Desecration. Let young Asher listen instead to the wisdom of his father, to the loving words of his mother, and to the experience and judgment of his rabbi. Upon him and upon these Thy worshipful servants may Thy holy light shine, the light of love and truth, the light of peace and goodwill. Amen."

There was a long silence when the rabbi finished the invocation. Some of his remarks seemed unnecessarily pointed, and Hartstein looked at Jesus, who seemed quietly amused by the reference to lost shepherds. Hartstein smiled. Some of the disciples, however, were disturbed and angry, and Simon the Zealot looked as though he wanted to dump a jug of wine on Eleazar's head, but Jesus quieted them all with a small, silent gesture. The rabbi took a seat far down from them. The boy himself, Asher, stood and delivered a little memorized address, going on and on about how prepared he was now for manhood and responsibility and several other things about which he didn't have the faintest idea. It was a very touching, although tedious, display of adolescent confidence.

"I see the hand of the Agency in this," thought Hartstein. "This reminds me very much of those works of ancient wisdom I found in the Library. I'll bet I'm going to sit here all afternoon waiting to hear the words of Jesus Christ, but it will be one guest speaker after another. According to the Agency version of history, nothing important ever actually happened. It's all a long parade of banal events until the world, bored out of its goddamn mind, stumbled into the twenty-first century. I wish I had brought something to read."

The kid was still talking—now it had to do with how gravely he accepted the advice his elders offered him. "Like hell," thought Hartstein—and the sun was beating down into the courtyard, right onto Hartstein's cloth-covered head. The air was hot and sultry and still, and he felt as if he were suffocating. His cup of wine was empty and the jug had been passed far down the table, out of his reach. Hartstein was not enjoying himself. He stood up, paying no attention to the disdainful looks he drew from the family members sitting nearby, and crossed toward Pamrah, who had dispensed the last of her fruit and was now waiting patiently for Asher to shut his mouth at last.

"Where can I get something to drink?" asked Hartstein.

"Come with me," said Pamrah.

"I'll be glad to. I've had enough of these speeches. I came to hear Jesus."

Pamrah looked interested. "I suspected that you were no member of the family. I have heard a lot about Jesus, and I'm glad I'll be able to hear him, too. If he hadn't consented to come to this celebration, I would never have heard him; Master Jotham wouldn't have given me leave."

"Your master sounds like a hard man."

Pamrah raised an eyebrow. "No," she said, "not really. He's better than most, I guess."

Asher Ben-Jotham finished his little presentation, and there was strong applause from the relatives. The boy smiled bashfully, then hurried to his place beside his father. He had sailed through the difficult part; he had earned all the gifts and presents with his solemn recitation, and now he could relax a little.

Just then, as Jotham was preparing to speak, Brannick came back into the courtyard. Only Hartstein noticed him; the Agency man's face was streaked with dirt, his expression grim and forbidding. Hartstein was sure that something unpleasant was happening, something he didn't really want to know about, yet he felt obliged to find out whatever he could. Brannick sat down beside him. "How's the history lesson?" asked the sergeant.

"About as relevant as the last one. Listen, what are you up to? What's the big idea of playing secret agent on a hot day like today?"

Brannick tipped Hartstein's cup and looked disappointed that it was empty. "We may have a little problem," he said.

Hartstein felt suddenly cold all over. "What kind of problem?"

Brannick studied the young man's face before he answered. "We may not be able to go back to the present."

"Oh."

"We may be stranded here forever."

"Oh."

"But I think I know how to fix it."

Hartstein just nodded. "Then why don't you just do that, then. Say, tell me, Brannick, how the hell could we be stuck here? That's not supposed to happen."

Brannick made an airy, empty gesture. "You already knew that a small percentage of time travelers don't return."

It was a negligible factor. Hartstein nodded.

"This isn't related to that," said Brannick. "This is something else, something more sinister."

Hartstein was trying to keep himself under control. He wanted to scream; getting information from Brannick was like getting credit from the phone company. "I have a right to know," he said as forcefully as he could whisper. "I'm in the middle of it with you. Tell me what's going on!"

Brannick drummed his fingers on the table while he considered. "It's a long story," he said. "I'd have to explain about the Temporary Underground, and it would take too long. That guy I was chasing is from our era. This is their past we're in—not ours. It's a new weapon of theirs and it's got me scared. I don't know how they finagled us into the wrong past, but only he can return to the present. We can't, because we're not connected to our present any longer. Our only chance might be if that rebel dies somehow; then we can take his place in the pathway and we'll snap back to our proper time. I'm not even sure that will work, but it's our only chance. You stay here and don't worry. You're here to enjoy yourself. Leave it all to me."

Brannick got to his feet again. "Underground?" cried Hartstein. "Rebel? What the hell—" But it was no use; Brannick had already hurried out of the courtyard. "Enjoy myself," muttered Hartstein darkly.

"Thanks, everybody," said Jotham. His broad smile seemed to have gone a little crooked under the influence of a few cups of wine. "Rabbi Eleazar wanted me to make a few announcements before I introduced our guest. First of all, there will be a charity bazaar next Sunday, at the home of Adaiah, my dear neighbor. Everyone is invited, of course, and if you want to help out I'm sure you'll be welcome; see Rabbi Eleazar or Adaiah about that. Second, please don't leave your wagons in the road outside the temple. The Romans are kvetching about it, saying that we're denying them access or something like that. Just to avoid trouble from now on, park your vehicles off the road, even if you have to bump through a ditch. It will save us all trouble in the future. Finally, as you all know, Zechariah Ben-Shual has been quite sick, and could not join us today. Some members of the congregation are planning to travel into Capernaum to visit him. If you'd like to go along, see my wife later this afternoon. I think that's about it. If no one has anything else to announce, I'm going to have one of our guest's followers come up here and introduce him."

Jotham gestured toward the group of disciples, and Peter rose slowly to his feet and came forward. He towered over his host but did not seem the least bit ill at ease. Jotham returned to his seat and called to Pamrah for more wine. "I'll bring you some, too," she said to Hartstein, disappearing into the house.

"I'd like to thank Jotham Ben-Nathan for his kind invitation, and for his hospitality," said Peter. "Of course, we've been traveling around through Galilee, and we've had many pleasant experiences among the people of this part of the country. One of the countless things I've learned while following Jesus is that the less fortunate of our neighbors have just the same chance of obtaining the Lord's blessing in the world that is to come. I'm reminded of a funny story I heard while I was still a fisherman on the shores of Galilee. It seems there was this wealthy and powerful landowner who was very ill. All the people in the town were worried about his health, not because he was such a good neighbor, but because in one way or another all their occupations depended on him and the businesses he owned. So the village doctor was getting tired of all the calls he was getting morning and night, asking him how old Ebenezer was doing. The doctor decided he would have more peace and rest if he just put up progress reports down at the village market. The first day he put up a sign that said, 'Old Ebenezer is very sick. Condition serious.' Well, that worked pretty well, and the doctor was able to sleep a few hours without being disturbed. The next day the doctor put up a sign that said, 'Old Ebenezer is much worse. Condition critical.' Again, for the remainder of the day, the doctor was able to tend to his patient in peace. On the third morning, the doctor put up a sign, 'Old Ebenezer has gone to heaven.' Well, now that there was no way around it, some of the old man's neighbors realized that whether they liked it or not, Old Eb was gone for good along with their livelihoods, and they didn't have to pretend to like the old goat anymore. On the fourth morning, there was a new sign put up by one of the village comedians that said, 'Much distress in heaven. Old Ebenezer still hasn't arrived.' "

Hartstein watched Peter as the apostle waited for laughter, but they both waited in vain. "I'll bet that's the only story he knows," thought Hartstein. It had been the wrong occasion and certainly the wrong crowd to favor with that particular tale. It could be interpreted as an attack on wealthy landowners, and Jotham Ben-Nathan glowered at Peter and muttered to himself. It looked as if Peter were retaliating against the rabbi for the veiled references to Jesus as a false prophet. "This is going to be a tough act for Jesus to follow," thought Hartstein.

"Well," said Peter, dismayed by the reaction of his audience, "I guess I'd better just introduce my master and teacher, Jesus of Nazareth, who will enlighten all of us with more carefully chosen words than mine." He went over to where the other disciples were laughing behind their hands and sat down, embarrassed. Jesus put a gentle hand on Peter's shoulder and stood before the family of Jotham. His radiant halo didn't seem to bother anyone but Hartstein.

A man who sat at Jotham's table called out, "What do you have to say about the wealthy and powerful attaining eternal life?"

"Yes," said another man, "is the Kingdom of Heaven only for the poor?"

Hartstein settled back contentedly; this was, at last, what he had come to witness. Jesus smiled and spread his hands. "Now a priest was going down from Jerusalem to Jericho," he said. "And he came upon a Tar Baby left in the road; and when he saw the Tar Baby he passed by on the other side. So likewise a Levite, when he came to the place and saw the Tar Baby, passed by on the other side. But a Samaritan, as he journeyed, came to where it was; and when he saw it, he had compassion, for the Tar Baby appeared unto him as a man who had fallen among thieves, stripped and beaten and left half dead. And the Samaritan put his hand upon the shoulder of the Tar Baby, saying, 'Be of good cheer, for I will put you on my own beast and bring you to an inn.' But the Tar Baby replieth not, and the hand of the Samaritan was stuck fast. 'Release my hand,' said the Samaritan, 'or if you will not I must smite you,' but the Tar Baby replieth not, and the Samaritan smote it harshly with his other hand. That hand did also stick, and the Samaritan grew wroth, saying, 'Release my hands, or I shall kick you fiercely.' But the Tar Baby replieth not, and the man kicked it with his right foot, and his right foot did also stick. 'If you will not release my hands and my foot,' crieth the Samaritan, 'I shall kick you yet again,' but the Tar Baby replieth not. The Samaritan kicked with his left foot, and in like wise did his left foot also stick, and he said in anguish, 'Woe to you, if you do not release me, for I shall punish you severely with my head.' But the Tar Baby replieth not. The Samaritan did even as he said, and struck the Tar Baby with his head, and his head did stick fast. Now the Samaritan did cry out in alarm, and a centurion appeared from a place of concealment, laughing in his sinful pleasure at the other man's tribulation. 'What am I to do with this fool?' quoth the centurion. 'Shall I dispatch him here where he struggles, or bring him forth to the entertainment of the procurator?' 'Oh, noble Roman,' said the Samaritan, 'I beg thee, do not throw me to the lions. Slay me now or at thy leisure, but throw me not to the lions. Thy house and thy sons be an hundred times blest if thou wilt but refrain from throwing me to the lions.' And the centurion took counsel with himself, saying, 'What a great fear has this man for the lions. Yet it would be a seemly end for such an one as he. I will bring him to the procurator, who for his pleasure will have this Samaritan abandoned to the lions.' And so they came into the town and the Samaritan was parted from the Tar Baby and thrown into a circus of lions. 'They will rend him, for they are starved unto death,' said the centurion to his procurator. And yet there came glad cries from the Samaritan. 'Oh, thank you, thank you,' said he, for in truth he had grown to manhood among lions, and he had thus cleverly tricked his captors. And behold, the greatest lion among them came unto the Samaritan and licked the man's hand, in the manner of a faithful hound, for in elder days did the man pluck out a thorn from the foot of this same lion, and so did the beast gratefully spare the life of the Samaritan. And the procurator was sore astonished, and spake unto the Samaritan, saying, 'Go thou in freedom, and thy lion also, and live in peace.' And in such a way did the Samaritan win his liberty from the Tar Baby and the wicked sport of the Romans, and did the lion return to the forest, where it did feast upon the flesh of the wealthy and powerful."

Hartstein was simply appalled. The disciples sat in rapt amazement at this gem of wisdom from their master; the family of Jotham applauded politely, if in some bewilderment; but Hartstein was shocked that the Agency would present such an important figure as Jesus in what he thought was a foolish light. Is this how the people of Hartstein's time thought of Jesus? As a mixture of Will Rogers and Clark Kent? Hartstein didn't know where to look. He turned his attention to his hands, which for some reason were trembling on the table.

"Let me ask thee, is it not so that thou hast come a great way, and thou hast come but to hear me preach?"

Hartstein looked up, and his heart nearly exploded in his chest. Jesus stood before him, gazing down curiously, a pleasant smile on his handsome face. Hartstein didn't know how to answer. "Yes," he whispered.

"And what thinkest thou of my sayings?"

How could he reply? "I am unworthy to offer such judgments," he said.

"Yea, but whosoever maketh not judgments in his heart, even he shall curse the day when it shall happen that others inflict their judgments upon him."

"Yes, I know, but . . ." Hartstein felt too stupid to live. From the corner of his eye, he saw Matthew hurriedly scribbling down everything that was said. Hartstein hoped that when he returned home, he wouldn't find this pitiful interview recorded somewhere in the New Testament.

Jesus took the young man's hands in his own. Hartstein was astonished by how strong Jesus was; but of course, he had been a carpenter, he had never lived an easy or luxurious life. "Men will come unto thee," said Jesus, "and saying 'Join thy fortunes with us, for our destiny is great,' they shall demand that thou followeth their banner. And even other men will come, saying 'Go not down that way, for those men believeth only in death, therefore march with us, and we will shew unto you marvelous things.' And upon that terrible hour shalt thou know thy heart and thy judgment."

Hartstein had no idea what Jesus was saying. He was certain, gazing into the deep, sad, loving eyes, that this information was vital—but what did it mean? "What must I do?" he asked, sincerely tormented by his own ignorance.

Jesus released Hartstein's hands and looked beyond his audience, staring into the distance, or the future. "Thou suffereth and endureth all manner of things," he said. "Thou must cleave unto thy judgment even in the hour of peril itself, for behold, it is given unto they who bear such burdens great glory, even if that glory may not be seen until the passing of many days."

"Yes," said Hartstein, more miserable than ever. He had a cold feeling in the pit of his stomach. He thought he had a possible explanation of all this. He supposed that Brannick had made a bad mistake, and in a little while Hartstein would pay for it; he saw himself joining Jesus in the great moment of suffering, as the good thief on the cross right beside Jesus' own. That was how Hartstein interpreted Jesus' advice.

Jesus smiled once more. "Verily I say thee nay, that thou art mistaken about this, but go in peace and when the moment of need is come, then shalt thou ponder all these things thou hast heard me say."

"I will," said Hartstein.

Jesus nodded and turned away. Matthew was still taking notes frantically. The other disciples had stood and were milling about while Jesus offered young Asher his blessing. Hartstein sat stunned, dazed. His thoughts about the past and about the Agency had been turned upside down one more time: despite all the mistakes, the absurdities, the words that had been put into everyone's mouth, that *had* been Jesus who spoke to him. Hartstein had known it from the moment he looked into those gentle eyes (what color had they been?). The Tar Baby was a product of the mindlessness of the present; but he who had preached here this afternoon was no artifact of the Agency.

After a few minutes, when Jesus and his followers had said farewell and taken their leave, and the family of Jotham Ben-Nathan were standing in the courtyard, once more talking together in small groups, Sergeant Brannick returned with the short fat man he had pursued earlier. Both men were almost exhausted, although Brannick's expression seemed, for him, virtually exultant.

"Let's go," said the Agency man. He gave a little jerk with his head. He held one of his prisoner's arms twisted tightly behind the fat man's back.

"But—" Hartstein thought of Pamrah, then realized that the situation warranted no dallying. His heart breaking, he left her behind forever.

"I heard that you had an interview," said Brannick, smiling. "How did it make you feel?"

Hartstein wondered what the answer to that was. "First," he said, "I go back to Egypt and all my faith in the Agency is destroyed forever. Then you haul me back here, and it just makes things worse; I mean, the saints and the halo and that terrible story Jesus told. But then do you know what happened?"

Brannick urged the fat man toward the archway; Hartstein followed them. "No," said the sergeant, "what happened?"

"He spoke to me, and it seemed as if he knew me and was giving me some important message. Only I can't understand exactly what he meant."

Brannick laughed. "Didn't you more or less expect that, too?"

Hartstein frowned. "You mean, it was all part of the trip? Like finding Pamrah? Everybody who comes back here has a private conversation with Jesus?"

Brannick shook his head. "No, not at all. Jesus has never said a word to me. What I meant was, didn't you expect not to understand what he said to you, if he said anything to you?"

Hartstein thought that over and decided not to answer. They followed the main road away from the town of Shinabbeth, toward the hills.

"Where are we going?" asked Hartstein.

Brannick was quiet for a moment. "Do you remember what I said about our possible trouble here?"

"Of course I do."

"Well, look over there, where the sun is going down."

Hartstein turned and looked to the west. He saw nothing, just scrubby trees on the hillside, something that looked like a shepherd's hut on the summit. He heard a loud crack, as if someone's cervical vertebrae had been suddenly, powerfully snapped.

The short fat man, whose name Hartstein never knew, lay in the dust at the side of the road. There was no mistaking the awkward contortion of the body; the man was dead.

"You killed him," said Hartstein softly. "Ten minutes ago I was speaking with Jesus Christ. Then I walk out in the country with you, and you murder this total stranger." The circumstances were too bizarre for the young man to comprehend.

"Well," said Brannick, "there was no other way. I could tell you more if you were a recruit, if you were in the Agency. But I can't. You have to take my word, I guess."

"You *had* to do it?"

Brannick studied him for a long, silent moment. "War, all-out war." He indicated the fat man with his foot. "He knew what would happen if he was caught. Maybe *you* don't know about the war. Maybe most of the people in our time don't know about it. But it's real enough, and if we lose, we lose everything. The Underground doesn't want our power or our wealth or the kind of things rebel groups are usually after. The Temporary Underground wants to destroy the world—the whole universe as we know it. And only the Agency is standing in their way."

Hartstein wondered if this was what Jesus had been referring to; it sounded like a probable candidate. He closed one eye and looked sideways at Brannick. "Are you telling me the truth?" he asked.

The Agency man shrugged. "I'd tell you a lot more, but I can't. It's better that way. It's the Agency's fight."

Hartstein tried to keep himself from saying it; he held his breath as long as he could, and then, in a rush, he said, "All right, Brannick, all right, I'll enlist." He was thinking about Pamari and Pamrah and their countless sisters down all the ages. He was thinking about everyone and everything that was dear to him. "If you're really in this fight, then it's my fight, too."

Brannick didn't seem terribly overjoyed. He leaned on his shepherd's crook and rubbed one aching foot. "I knew you'd join up," he said.

"How did you know that? Did you peek into my future?"

"You don't have a future to look into. I told you about that before."

"I forgot," said Hartstein.

"You'll get used to it." Brannick looked at his watch and smiled—he wasn't really supposed to be wearing a watch in ancient Palestine, but he was an Agency noncom with many years of service, and he liked to bend the rules, and no one in the past had seemed to notice the watch anyway. "Congratulations, Hartstein. Any minute now we'll zap back to the present. *Our* present, where we belong. Then I can make my report, and you can take your oath. It will be a pleasure serving alongside you. Together we just might make the past safe for democracy."

Hartstein smiled weakly, but he recalled what Jesus had said to him. He wondered if the Agency was the group with the banner, and if the Temporary Underground would promise to show him great things; he still didn't really know what he was supposed to do about any of it. "I can't wait," he said.

CHAPTER THREE

CHE SARÀ SARÀ

It was a cinch for Hartstein to get into the Agency. He had Sergeant Brannick to sponsor him, and Brannick carried a lot of weight in the organization. And, of course, with the new threat from the Temporary Underground, the Agency was going to need all the cannon fodder it could recruit.

So just like that, Hartstein found himself wrapped in a silver and blue uniform and in the regulations and code of conduct that went with it. The Agency was one tough group of people. It began to be clear to Hartstein that whatever order there was in the world was due primarily to the efforts of the Agency. He was proud to be a part of it. Of course he was: his ESB training had insisted on that, just as the idea of enlisting had been implanted in his subbrain when he had been processed for his visit to ancient Palestine. Hartstein didn't realize that he'd been maneuvered ever since the first moment he had stepped into the Agency Building. Should he learn the truth, there was yet another suggestion planted that would make him feel that, whatever the ethics of the matter, the Agency had acted for his own good, and he should be grateful.

The ironic part was that it *had* been for his own good, and he was right to be grateful. The smart-looking tunic alone made him stand straighter, something Hartstein's mother had been unable to accomplish all through his adolescence. He was working now on getting his body into optimum condition; he was watching his diet carefully; he was getting plenty of rest and making a friend of soap and water; he was aware of his responsibility to his fellow man. Hartstein's grandparents nodded their heads wisely, positive that it had been the conversation with Jesus that had wrought this change. His parents couldn't understand it at all; it seemed to go against nature for a child to mature so quickly. Hartstein himself never gave it a thought.

His build was too narrow, his jaw too slight for Hartstein ever to be just like Sergeant Brannick. At least, he told himself, he might behave just like the veteran: he would perform his duty when he was called upon. He wondered if he could have killed the intruder in the peace of first-century Galilee. No, he decided, he couldn't have *then;* but he could *now.* That was the important distinction—he had been a tourist then, but now he was an Agency man.

And with the snappy uniform and the long, tedious oath, there came a bonus: just for signing up, he was entitled to take a three-day holiday in the future. In the future, which was completely closed to tourist travel. Most people believed that it was impossible to go into the future; it seemed that very little was impossible for the Agency.

"How can I go into the future in good conscience," objected Hartstein, "when I know what kind of desperate battles the Agency is preparing to fight? Isn't my place here, in case of emergency?"

Sergeant Brannick smiled a rough, manly, comradely smile. "A noble thought, Hartstein, a noble thought indeed. But no, the Agency knows what it's doing. In the first place, although you'll spend three days in the future, you'll be returned to the present only seconds after your departure. So you won't really be gone at all. In the second place, the Agency feels that the more trips you make into time, backward and forward, the more at ease you'll be anywhere and anywhen. Enjoy yourself. When you get back, you'll be scheduled for your training mission in the past. From then on, everything will get serious. You'll know you're in the Agency."

Hartstein nodded. He was ready for that. "Is the future like the past? Will there be a girl like Pamrah there?"

They were sitting in the transmission room, watching costumed tourists joyfully ducking through the screen into the quasi-past of their choice. Brannick laughed softly at the sight of a family of six, all dressed up like Halloween, frock-coated and hoop-skirted, off to visit the burning of Atlanta. "Some people in the Agency prefer the future," he said. "I don't. I don't like going ahead. I think it's boring, but many people disagree. The past, as you've discovered, is the home of romance. The future, in the same way, is the domain of hope. The future is different from the past, less predictable, but it springs from the same source; it's a reflection of what the people of the present think the future will be."

"Why don't you like it, then?"

The sergeant shrugged. "I like the past. Despite all that's wrong with it, I like it there. I don't like the future because it has no relevance to me. Each time I go, it's different. It changes from day to day, as our feelings and hopes change. At least the past is internally consistent. You can't say that about the future."

Hartstein was a little hesitant about leaving. "Is there any special advice?" he asked.

"None," said Brannick. "Don't get killed. Don't fall off a building or anything."

Hartstein chewed his lip for a few seconds. "What if I run into a rebel operative?"

"You won't," said Brannick. "They can't get into our future. And you don't know how to recognize them, in any event."

"Okay," said Hartstein. "Where are they aiming me?"

"One hundred years from today. Have fun. It's almost pointless to say goodbye, because in a minute or so you'll be right back here, and then we'll get you your basic training assignment."

"And then the fun begins."

"No," said Brannick, standing and leading Hartstein to the screen, "the fun begins now. It ends when you get back."

The purple glow of the transmission screen bathed them and made them look a little ghoulish. It was something else the sergeant said Hartstein would get used to. "Want me to bring something back for you?" asked Hartstein.

Brannick ignored him. He spoke to the woman operating the screen. "This joker's going up a hundred big ones, three-day interval, returned to this point." The woman nodded, reset her controls, and the screen's glow changed from purple to a pale jade green. They all looked even more undead.

"Brannick," said Hartstein dubiously, "I'm not sure about this."

The older man grabbed Hartstein's tunic by the shoulder. "You call me 'Sarge' now, kiddie," he growled. He shoved hard, and Hartstein stumbled through the green glowing screen, landing in the future on his face. It was a graceless way to meet his destiny, he thought.

They were all happy to see him. People cheered. People wept into hankies. People waved silver and blue Agency flags (Flags? mused Hartstein. Where he came from, the Agency didn't have a flag).

A short woman wearing a white lab coat stepped forward, one hand stretched out to greet him. "Mr. Hartstein," she said. "My name is Professor Smeth. I can't tell you what an honor it is to welcome you to our era."

Hartstein pushed himself up to a standing position and dusted off his tight-fitting tunic. He was glad to know that everyone liked him here, but he was curious. "How did you know I'd be arriving just now?" he asked. He didn't understand their adoration; he felt like Dorothy, greeted by the Munchkins.

Professor Smeth took his arm and led him by the delirious crowd that had turned out voluntarily, just the way in olden times crowds met victorious football teams at the airport. "Why," she said, "you were so impressed by your visit among us, that when you went back—that is, when you do go back—you gave—or will give—a series of lectures that will have a tremendous impact on world affairs, and you will be instrumental in turning your world into the wonderful, exciting, joyful world we have today. We all owe you so much. I personally owe you everything, because without your contribution I'm sure that I never could have led so fulfilling a life. And all these people agree with me." She indicated the hundreds of people, some of whom carried placards with Hartstein's picture on them.

Hartstein shook his head in bewilderment. "There's a paradox involved with this that I can't sort out."

"I know," said the professor.

"If your world was created in part through my efforts, then how can it exist now, before I give the lectures that will help to bring all this about?"

Professor Smeth led him down a long, curving ramp. The gray concrete walls were wet and glistening. There were glowing fixtures overhead that shed a peach-colored light on everything. Hartstein had no idea where they were or where they were going. "But this place isn't before you gave the lectures," said Smeth, with a smile that seemed to indicate that she had wrestled with paradoxes such as this many times, and that she usually emerged victorious. "This is a full hundred years later."

"But what happens if I don't give the lectures?"

Professor Smeth halted. She shrugged. "Then when you come to visit us, it won't be like this at all. It will be just like your world, or worse. But, as you can see, it isn't. And it won't be." Her gesture took in the concrete tunnel; Hartstein thought it would be ungenerous of him to point out that so far he hadn't seen anything to show that this future was wonderful, exciting, or joyful in the least. They walked farther down the ramp, until Hartstein lost all sense of how far they had come. Didn't they have elevators in the future?

At last they emerged from the tunnel, into a great round room walled with tinted windows. Hartstein almost threw up; they were on the top of an immensely tall building, so high that lacy white clouds obscured part of the landscape below. "What *is* this building?" he asked. No other structures speared into the heavens nearby.

"This is the Agency Building of our time," said Smeth proudly.

"The Agency always was big on impressing the citizens," said Hartstein. "And that ramp we walked down, why—"

Smeth anticipated his question. "Something to do with the drops. They can't operate above this level because it's harmful to delicate tissue. Crushes or explodes the capillaries. I'm not exactly sure; that isn't my field. But from here we can take a series of drops to the ground level."

"D—"

"Drops. They've replaced elevators."

"How do you always know what I'm going to ask?" said Hartstein warily.

"Easy," said Smeth. "I listened to your lectures again last night."

"The lectures," murmured Hartstein. He felt rebellious against the predetermined future Professor Smeth was offering him. He promised himself that he'd be damned if he was going to give any lectures when he got back.

Hartstein looked out the windows, over the patchy landscape of New York and New Jersey. The shape of Manhattan hadn't changed in a hundred years, but its population of buildings certainly had. There weren't very many; almost all of the island was the dark summer green that used to be visible only in Central Park.

"They all went underground," said Smeth. "During the war."

"The war with—"

"The war with the Temporary Underground. New York is now an underground city, as are most of the other large urban centers of the world."

"Then the Agency must have won that war," said Hartstein, feeling a great relief. He realized that what he'd like to do most was consult an encyclopedia or a few reference books, and learn what was going to happen to him and his compatriots.

"Of course the Agency won," said Smeth. "And it was very ironic, too. Our most irresistible weapon in that war was a chalked expression on a university blackboard. The rebels were manipulating reality through the use of something they called subjective differentials. One of the Agency's own mathematical philosophers discovered a weakness or a flaw in the Underground's reasoning, and developed a system that destroyed the theory of subjective differentials forever."

Hartstein felt his heart pounding. "Can you tell me that formula?" he asked.

Smeth shook her head sadly. "I don't know it. No one does. It was obliterated so that no one might make use of it to reconstruct and perfect the rebels' science. If we knew the equations, we could give them to you to take back, but we don't. In your time, things must take their course and many lives will be lost. It is unavoidable. But do not give up hope, because in the end the Agency will triumph."

So much for Hartstein's dream of returning as the savior of civilization as we know it.

"It's very hypnotic up here," Professor Smeth said. "Sometimes I stare out over the countryside and lose all sense of time. I find myself watching clouds chasing their shadows toward the ocean." She smiled, just a little embarrassed, and gently touched his arm, indicating that they were to move on.

The drops proved to be as sickening as the sudden view from the observation room. Hartstein followed Smeth, but balked when he saw her step into a clear plastic tube and plummet out of sight. "I'm a *hero* in this era," he muttered, trying to gather up his courage. "I'm a goddamn *hero*." He took a deep breath and stepped forward, falling through space at an absurd rate of speed. The drops, like the elevators of some hotels, were on the outside of the building; they gave an unobstructed though blurry view of the green checkered landscape hurtling ever nearer. "I hate this," growled Hartstein. He felt like a first-class letter abandoned to some immense mail chute. He wondered if his earthward plunge would end at the surface or if he'd just continue on down into the molten core of the planet.

He came to a sudden stop only a third of the way down the gigantic building. "What now?" he wondered. He wasn't standing on anything; he was sort of floating in the glass tube, unable to get himself going again. He thought he had broken something, or done something terribly wrong. He supposed that Professor Smeth had taken it for granted that Hartstein knew all about drops, and now he was stranded partway down, and sooner or later someone else would come screaming down from above and smash into him. "Hello?" he cried. There was no answer. He floated, suspended by some artifice of the future. He turned around with his back to the beautiful vista, and saw that there was an arched door. He went through it, and Professor Smeth was waiting for him. "Some fun," he said, covering his anxiety.

They walked across a concourse filled with potted trees and split-leafed plants, and before Hartstein could say anything else, Professor Smeth tossed herself down another drop. Hartstein did the same, and they fell earthward like eggshells in the disposal.

They made four drops in all, and when Hartstein emerged from the last one he was surprised to find that he was not, in fact, many miles beneath the earth's crust, but merely on the building's central plaza, which reached up from the ground floor to heights that vanished in mist and shadow above him. Smeth saw his expression and said, "Sometimes it rains in here." Hartstein saw no reason to doubt her.

There were more crowds of people, in vaster numbers, and they all cheered and wept and praised his name. He waved at them slowly, like a beauty queen in the Rose Parade.

Professor Smeth shouted in his ear, "I will leave you now. I have to get back to my duties. But I'll turn you over to your guide." She indicated a lovely young woman with violet—but it's not necessary to describe her: her name was Pamma'a.

"Hello, Mr. Hartstein," said Pamma'a. She smiled shyly. She was the first of her temporal duplicates who knew him by his correct name. He wondered what else she knew about him.

"Sergeant Brannick said that whenever I go into the past, I'll find you. He led me to think that you wouldn't be here in the future."

"Oh," said the young woman, "your Sergeant Brannick was too concerned with his own interests. The future is filled with hope, and if you hope for love, you will find it in the future just as you did in the past. Sergeant Brannick's ambitions and desires never included trivial matters like that. His futures must have been considerably different than yours."

Hartstein wished that he would be able to find happiness with her sometime. Pamari, Pamrah, Pamma'a: he had loved her, but time had denied her to him. Could he expect only scattered hours of bliss with her, when he visited one isolated moment or another, unrelated to the true present? He thought over what she had said. He realized that he could learn a great deal about himself by looking at what he found in this future he'd created. It would say a lot about his inner motives, those that were secret even from himself.

"What happens now?" he asked.

Pamma'a looked thoughtful. "Have you ever read *When the Sleeper Wakes*, by H. G. Wells?"

"Sure," said Hartstein, "hasn't everybody?"

"Or any of the various utopian novels that were popular a couple of hundred years ago?"

"We studied them in my sophomore year. Thomas More, Samuel Butler, Bellamy, Huxley, Skinner, Effinger, the rest of them. Why do you ask?"

"Because they all have one thing in common," she said. "They all stop the story dead in its tracks while one of the utopia's citizens gives the visitor a guided tour. That's what we're going to do now."

"Oh boy," said Hartstein.

But just then two men crashed through a door, weapons in their hands.

Hartstein reacted quickly; he grabbed Pamma'a around the waist and threw her to the side, then dived toward the gunmen, hitting the floor and rolling, intending to spring to his feet, chop the weapon out of the hand of the nearest thug, wing the other in the shoulder, and stand there, panting but victorious, to the plaudits of the crowd.

He was deprived of his plaudits. There was a surprised and not too pleased cry from Pamma'a as she landed heavily on the floor. Hartstein made his dive and roll, but as he came up (more slowly than he had planned) he saw that ten other men had followed the gunmen through the door. He stood very still, staring blankly. The gunmen were also a little astonished. They looked over their shoulders at the Agency uniforms behind them, and dropped their weapons. Hartstein scooped them up and covered the hapless villains from the front. He felt grotesquely foolish.

"Good work, Mr. Hartstein," said the leader of the Agency squad.

"It was nothing," said Hartstein. He wanted to go back home.

Pamma'a joined him, brushing off her silver and blue uniform. She tried to seem as if it had been exciting, that in fact she rather enjoyed being flung around like a sack of onions. "Thank you," she said breathlessly, "you saved my life."

"It was nothing," said Hartstein. He shrugged.

"We'll take care of these guys now," said the squad leader. He indicated that they were to march through the door, off to some futuristic jailhouse. The armed men followed the prisoners, trooping out in absolute precision.

"All right," said Hartstein, alone again with Pamma'a and the cheering throngs, "what was that all about?"

Pamma'a led him out of the towering lobby of the Agency Building, through some kind of invisible barrier, into the fresh air of Hartstein's future. "We still get stray elements of the Temporary Underground now and then," she said. "They pop up sometimes. If they left their own time before the end of the war, then we have to take care of them here before they do any damage. But we never know when they're going to appear. We have a complete roster of all their forces; those two will be taken care of and crossed off the list. Eventually we'll have accounted for every man, woman, child, and creature of the rebel army, and we can stop worrying."

They walked toward the entrance to another building. As he had learned before, most of the other buildings were subterranean, and their entrances were similar to the drops he had used in the Agency Building. If these structures were any larger than the one he had just left, it was possible that he might, after all, emerge perilously close to the center of the earth.

"How did those Agency guards know the two rebels would materialize here and now?" he asked.

Pamma'a was surprised that he had to ask. "You mentioned it in the first of your great lectures," she said. "Would you like to watch yourself? We have all of them available in the Agency Library."

Hartstein decided that he didn't really want to watch himself. But he thought that if he could get a transcription of the lectures themselves, it might save him a lot of work in the event that he decided to give them after all.

Pamma'a went down the drop like Alice down the rabbit hole. Hartstein, blithely now, followed her. He came to rest some moments later upon a broad, sunlit plaza some quarter mile below the surface. Handsome people were walking about, looking into shop windows, resting beside babbling fountains, and arguing obscure points of philosophy or scientific theory. Everyone seemed happy, healthy, and extremely polite. It was too good to be true.

"Where are we?" asked Hartstein.

"This is the, ah, Hartstein Building," said Pamma'a, smiling. "This is Hartstein Place, that's the Hartstein Memorial Fountain, beyond that is the Hartstein Eternal Flame, the Hartstein Obelisk, Hartstein Park, and the Hartstein Arena."

Hartstein was impressed. "Wow," he said, "I must sure have been somebody."

Pamma'a laughed at his modesty. "Somebody is right," she said. "Do you realize that in order to be your guide today, I was selected from over three hundred million applicants? The selection process began over ten years ago."

He was astonished. "And you were chosen—"

"For my physical characteristics, as well as personality, neatness, and my ability to get along well with my peers."

"And no doubt I mentioned you in my lectures. Why did it take ten years for them to find you?"

Pamma'a's face darkened. "For some reason, sir, you made no mention of me in any of your recorded lectures."

Hartstein laughed. "Well, I can take care of that. I'll make sure to mention your name, and then I'll save the future some ten years of costly decision-making."

"Do you mean it? Will you really mention my name?"

"Yes, sure," said Hartstein. Something nagged at him. He didn't understand what would happen if he went back and did mention her name; how would that alter the present moment (that is, the present-in-the-future moment)? Another leering paradox hovered just outside the field of vision of his mind's eye. Hartstein shuddered and looked away.

Pamma'a led him to another drop. "I want you to see the new New York," she said.

He gazed at the drop in wonder. "Do you mean there are more levels below this?"

She laughed; it was a musical sound. "This is the leisure level," she said. "The very tip of the city, like the revolving restaurants atop skyscrapers in your time."

Hartstein shook his head. "Not in my time," he said. "We've become much too sophisticated for that. Those things belong to the century before mine. But how far down is the, uh, ground level of the city?"

"Maybe I shouldn't tell you. It may make you claustrophobic."

"You're right, don't tell me. But does the sun shine down there, like it does here? How is that possible?"

Pamma'a looked up into the warm, bright sunlight. "It's all done with mirrors," she said. "A lot of things here in your future are done with mirrors."

"That's something I want to remember," said Hartstein. "The World of Tomorrow. Wow."

Down they went, falling until Hartstein grew first uncomfortable, then bored, then drowsy. He almost fell asleep, but was jolted wide awake on his arrival at the lowest level.

The city, from this perspective, was just how he always imagined futuristic cities to look. There were gigantic buildings that dwarfed anything in the twenty-first century. Slender aerial walkways like cobwebs of steel linked the skyscrapers (well, they couldn't correctly be called skyscrapers, but Hartstein was not interested in developing a new name for them); transportation was provided by an intricate system of monorails, carrying the laughing, happy, productive men and women to their destinations; broad, clean expanses of parkland provided wholesome places to relax and meditate; carefully planned fourteen-lane highways efficiently directed the pollution-free automobiles on their way from city to city; beside them ran sparkling, man-made waterways that were used more for recreation than transportation; all of this brought tears to Hartstein's eyes, because he realized that this exciting, happy future was due in large part to his own contributions. He was proud, and he couldn't wait to get back to his own time. His grandparents would be proud, and his father would know at last that Hartstein was cut out for more than merely selling doughnuts.

"Wow," murmured Hartstein.

"Impressed?" asked Pamma'a.

"You bet."

"Superscience in action," she said. "Look over there." She led him to the entrance of a building faced with polished black stone. There was a plaque bolted to the front, with two quotations:

Time is but the stream I go a-fishing in.
—Thoreau

Ladies and gentlemen, it gives me great pleasure to announce that we are all poised on the verge of the Conquest of Time. Please extinguish all smoking materials.

—Hartstein

"Wow," said Hartstein. Seeing his name in bronze relief gave him a little shiver. "Can I jot that down somewhere? I've got to remember it."
"You will, don't worry," said Pamma'a. "Let's go inside."
"What is this place?"
She indicated the impressive bronze doors, which reminded Hartstein of the doors to the Library of Alexandria. "This is the Mihalik Building," she said. "It houses the Time Museum."
"Oh boy," said Hartstein.
Just inside the bronze doors, in a high vaulted hall that echoed like a train station, there was a massive statue of Frank Mihalik, the first person to travel backward through time. Mihalik, like many pioneers, had experienced danger and adventure and tedium, and finally became a hero in the truest sense. There was an inscription carved into the base of the statue:

The past is really something. And the future is really something, too.
But I'll tell you one thing: don't nothing hold a candle to being home
where I belong, right here in the present. There should be some kind of
agency or something to protect it, because it's the only now we've got.
—Frank Mihalik
"The Odysseus of Time"

"He sure was something," said Hartstein in awe.
"Yes," said Pamma'a, "but come with me. I have something else to show you." He went with her across the tessellated floor; they passed through another vaulted chamber, where there was a statue of Mihalik's girlfriend, Cheryl, who accompanied him on some of his adventures. Beyond that hall was one devoted to Hartstein himself. He was uncomfortably surprised by his own statue. There were exhibits all around the perimeter of the room; he debated with himself about the propriety of looking at them, because he felt that it wasn't wise to know too much about his future. He didn't want to spoil the nice surprises, and he didn't want to know about the bad parts. But he ended up looking anyway.

"What year did I die?" he asked.

Pamma'a showed him the recording of his state funeral. "You died in 2096, precisely one hundred years to the day after Mihalik made his first journey through time. The whole world made much of that coincidence."

"Who are these people?" He pointed to the weeping men and women sitting in the front row during his eulogy.

"That's your wife," said Pamma'a, "and these are some of your eight children, with their families."

Hartstein felt his pulse quicken. "What was my wife's name?"

Pamma'a looked down at the floor shyly. "Pamela," she said. "I don't recall her unmarried name."

"Ah," said Hartstein. It seemed that he would find one of Pamma'a's temporal cousins in his own time. That fact made the record of his death bearable. "What did I do to warrant a state funeral? Surely it took more than a few lectures."

"Behold: Your accomplishments are writ large upon the walls of this chamber in letters of gold."

Hartstein looked up and saw the most astonishing list of victories, achievements, exploits, brave deeds, noble acts, feats of valor and virtue, and just plain gallantry that he had ever seen. There was no way that he could copy down all those attainments. He would have to perform them the hard way, as they were required, one by one in his lifetime.

"Pamma'a," he said in a quiet voice, "let's go on. I don't want to study my own life very closely. For some reason it makes me queasy. Let's go look at somebody else."

"How well modesty suits you," she said. "You're just the way I've always imagined you to be." Her expression was frankly adoring. It pleased Hartstein. It gave him renewed hope for the future, for the time when he would meet the woman who would, at last, be his own version of Pamma'a, the one destined to share his life of triumph.

There was a special display tank in a corner of the Hartstein Gallery. It had been dark and vacant, but now it came to life. A hologram appeared of a saturnine man with vital, magnetic eyes. "Mr. Hartstein," said the man, "my name is Dr. Bertram Waters. Perhaps you are familiar with my name, although we have never met. It was my work, along with that of many of my colleagues, that led to the development of the selenium pulse projector which makes time travel possible. I was on hand when Frank Mihalik departed on his epoch-making journey. Then later, when such travel had been perfected to the degree which you enjoy, I myself made many trips into the past and into the future. In this way I have seen the story of your adventures, and I wish to join the people of our descendants' era in expressing my honest admiration and gratitude to you. You represent the best of what my twentieth-century world attempted to preserve. Now—that is to say, in the year in which you momentarily find yourself— you are learning just how great your achievements will be. This is a gift that is given to few people, but it is given to you so that you may return to your time equipped to encourage others more hesitant than yourself, to rally them to join you in the essential fight for their very existence. Go then, and do your work cheerfully, and know that your name rings down the passages of time, never to be forgotten, forever to be blessed." The hologram of the great man faded, but his rich voice still lingered in the vaulted chamber.

"Gee," said Hartstein, "what a good man. Dr. Waters himself. I can't wait to tell Sergeant Brannick all about this."

"A wonderful thing," said Pamma'a. "A glorious tribute."

They wandered from Hartstein's memorial to other parts of the Time Museum. "What is the world like today?" he asked. "Have other troubles come along to take the place of the defeated rebels? Are there cells of the Temporary Underground still plotting away in secret? Can it be that the world at last is united under one flag, with one common goal of prosperity and happiness for all? What message of hope do you give me to take back to my fellows?"

"Listen, then," said Pamma'a. "We suffer no divisive factions, because the world and its colonies among the stars are governed in the most benign sense by the Agency. Yes, following the time war the governments of nations realized how petty was their jurisdiction, fixed as it was to the present moment. They abdicated in favor of the Agency, which was the only body capable of policing not only the present, but also the past and future. Our only problems today concern ourselves as individuals, in choosing the best way of expressing our inborn talents and abilities. And in this area also the Agency is our counselor, offering a vast array of subtle tests which evaluate and suggest likely careers to anyone who asks. We are happy, fulfilled, and unworried. We have arrived at last at the ultimate consummation of civilization. We owe that to the Agency, and the Agency owes its gratitude to you."

Hartstein was at a loss for words, overcome with emotion.

There was a small noise—*thitt.* Hartstein ignored it. It was like the buzz of an insect's wings zipping by his ear. *Thitt.* He heard it again. He walked on with Pamma'a, into a room devoted to re-creations of dreadful carnage during the war against the Underground.

Thitt.

"Say," said Hartstein, a puzzled frown on his face, "do you keep hearing a kind of little sound, like air escaping from a beach ball?"

"No," said Pamma'a.

Thitt. Thitt. Thitt.

"There," said Hartstein. "Didn't you hear that?"

"No."

One of the *thitts* hit Pamma'a in the leg. She screamed and fell to the cold terrazzo floor. Blood flowed freely from the wound, and Hartstein was momentarily confused. He didn't know what to do; it seemed that they were under attack, but from where? And by whom? Where were the Agency guards now?

"Mr. Hartstein!" cried Pamma'a. She had pulled herself across the floor to a place against the wall, trying to make herself invisible in the dim light of the gallery.

"Pamma'a, don't speak," said Hartstein. He tried to think of a plan, but he seemed entirely in the power of the unseen ambushers. Whoever they were, they held all the trumps: Hartstein was afraid, unarmed, and ignorant of the number, identity, and location of his enemy.

First he had to see how badly Pamma'a was wounded. He crawled to her; she huddled shivering against the wall. Above her were holograms depicting great battles in the war against the Temporary Underground. It was possible that, for Hartstein, the greatest battle of that war was being fought right now, in this very room. There was a nice irony in the notion, and Hartstein intended to appreciate it at a later time. He was aware of a sudden silence; there were no more shots—with a shudder, Hartstein realized that he wasn't even certain of the type of weapon he was facing. It might be some unimaginable futuristic death ray, acquired by the assassins anywhen at all. He was certain that he was marked for death by the Temporary Underground.

It made sense. If he was prevented from leaving the future, he could not return to his present and begin the great life of notable achievements he had seen celebrated only minutes before. Those deeds included playing no small role in the destruction of the Underground itself. He should have anticipated another attack, when the two armed men had been so easily overcome by the Agency guards. But then, each and every attack ought to have been anticipated in just the same way. Hartstein was having trouble sorting out his time-lines. He had not yet learned to think chronically, something Sergeant Brannick did so easily. He wished Brannick were with him now; Hartstein was perfectly willing to forgo all of his impending fame and glory just for the assurance that he would live to go home again.

Pamma'a's condition was not serious. Hartstein used a handkerchief to press against the wound. There seemed at first to be a lot of blood, but it looked like it might be controlled by direct pressure.

"I'll hold it," she whispered. She had regained her spirit, and Hartstein was proud of her courage. He fell in love with her all over again. She took the handkerchief from him and pressed it tightly against the wound. "You'll have to search for a way out of this trap," she said.

There were two exits from the room. The gunman might be in any of the adjacent galleries, firing at them whenever they silhouetted themselves in the doorways. But in which direction, and how near, Hartstein had no clue. It seemed useless to cry for help; if the enemy hadn't ambushed the guards first, then there was some other reason for their puzzling absence, and yelling bloody murder was not the answer. Besides, that wasn't something that the Hartstein this future loved so well would do. How odd, he thought, that he could think of his pride at a time like this.

"Pamma'a," he whispered, "we need a weapon."

She nodded. "Remember where we are. There is an entire arsenal in this building. In the displays. Most of them are nonfunctional, but in the next room"—she pointed to the doorway on her left, leading farther into the maze of galleries—"there is a collection of captured Underground weaponry. Those that fire projectiles are not loaded, of course, but the static guns will still be useful."

Hartstein said nothing. He maneuvered his way slowly along the wall toward the doorway. When he was beside it he paused, breathing in and out, slowly and deeply. He got down on the floor and pressed himself as flat as he could; then he crawled into the doorway, raised his head, and took a look.

There was no one there. He looked beyond the next room, through the doorway on the far side, and he saw no one. The gunman—it seemed to him that there was probably only one, but he had no evidence to support that belief—must be behind, between this room and the entrance to the museum. Hartstein lifted himself slowly, just a little way off the floor, trying to stay as small a target as possible. He was in a sort of push-up position, and was bringing one leg forward, ready to dive over the threshold, when two quick *thitts* splintered the wall beside him.

Hartstein found himself in the next room. He didn't recall moving, but he had definitely arrived—and in one piece; he congratulated himself. He realized that he had left Pamma'a, a marvelous candidate for hostagery, alone in the other room. If the gunman ran up and captured her, Hartstein was as good as lost. He gave the exhibit a hurried examination. In one display case there were five weapons, all unfamiliar to him. Three were evidently pistols that fired bullets; he ignored those. The other two, according to their labels, were static guns. Hartstein took off one of his boots and tried to smash the case. It was, of course, impervious to that sort of attack. He tried again and again with no more success, while a sick feeling of helplessness almost overcame him. He muttered prayers, trying to bargain with God or Nature or the Lords of Karma or Dr. Bertram Waters or anybody who'd listen. He hadn't even smudged the case.

"Stand aside," said a familiar voice.

Hartstein whirled around. In the doorway stood Sergeant Brannick, holding a static gun in his hand. At first Hartstein felt an incredible relief wash through him. And then, in utter terror, he realized that it had been Brannick who had ambushed him. Hartstein tried to speak, but his throat was too dry. "Why?" he managed to croak.

"Stand aside," repeated Brannick sternly. Hartstein obeyed; Brannick fired once at the display case, and it shattered into fine, sparkling dust, filling the air with a misty cloud of stinging particles. Hartstein turned away quickly, shielding his eyes. When he looked again, Brannick was standing in the doorway, waiting. The Agency man pointed to the display. Hartstein went hesitantly to the ruined case, put his trembling hand down through the ragged hole, and grasped a static gun.

With his back turned to Brannick, Hartstein spoke up. "I don't know how to use this thing," he said.

"You pull the trigger," said Brannick coldly. "A thin red laser beam will show you where you're aiming. There's no recoil to worry about. You just point and shoot."

"I don't want to do this," said Hartstein. He looked at the weapon in his hand. He was in no great hurry to turn around.

"I know," said Brannick. "But you're going to face me, or I'll shoot you in the back. This isn't some kind of entertainment, Hartstein. There's no code of honor here. Making you dead is the only concern. Nobody's going to censure me if I get you between the shoulder blades."

"Will you tell me why you're doing this?"

"Shut up, Hartstein. And turn around."

There was a moment for one more quick prayer, and a thought of Pamma'a. The only thing he felt as he turned was regret, more regret than he had ever known. He was able to fire his weapon once, and then he was hit. He fell to the floor; the strange thing was that he had never felt so marvelous in his life. He remarked to himself that dying just wasn't what he had expected. In the few seconds of consciousness left to him, he wished that he could tell someone about it. There really wasn't anything to be afraid of.

Yet he woke up in pain so intense that he thought at first he was being punished for his sins, and that this was eternity and that if he had known it was going to be like this, he would have made other arrangements while he was still alive. But then he began to make sense of where he was: a hospital bed in a private room crowded with flowers and greeting cards. Pamma'a was asleep in a chair beside his bed. Her leg was bandaged, and Hartstein wondered why she wasn't in a room of her own.

"Pamma'a?" he murmured. He couldn't seem to make his voice any louder.

She awoke and smiled. "Welcome back," she said.

"What happened?"

"You saved my life, and you saved our world. That man wounded you, but you got him. Right through the heart, cleanly. If you hadn't, if you'd been . . . killed, you wouldn't have been able to do all the things you're going to do, and the Temporary Underground might have won the war, and . . ." The paradoxes involved were too taxing for either of them to think about. If Brannick's shot had killed Hartstein, the whole world of the future might have changed instantly, with no one living in it aware of the drastic alteration.

"He recruited me," said Hartstein. "In my own time. We were becoming friends."

The door opened and Professor Smeth entered, followed by doctors, nurses, orderlies, and men and women wearing Agency uniforms. "You're a big hero," said Professor Smeth, putting a box of candy on Hartstein's nightstand. He glanced at it; even one hundred years in the future, some of the candies still had soft cream centers. On some fronts, civilization progresses all too slowly.

"All your recorded accomplishments are insignificant compared to what you did two days ago," said one of the Agency men.

"Two days ago?" said Hartstein. "That means I'll be going back soon."

"Yes," said Pamma'a sadly.

"Tell me one thing," said Hartstein. "Why weren't there any Agency guards waiting for Brannick to show up?"

Professor Smeth sat on the edge of his bed. "There is only one explanation," she said. "In your own era—" But that was all she was able to say; she disappeared in a green glow, and Hartstein, lying in bed, was dumped heavily to the floor of the Agency's recovery stage. He was home.

Sergeant Brannick was waiting to meet him. "How did it go?" he asked jovially.

Hartstein's eyes opened wider. He started to cry out, but then he realized that Brannick might not have followed directly after him; Brannick might have gone to meet Hartstein from any moment in the future.

Perhaps Brannick was not yet a double agent for the Temporary Underground. Hartstein would have to play this very carefully. "Nice," he said. "Not bad at all."

Brannick indicated Hartstein's hospital gown. "An accident?"

"Uh huh," said Hartstein. "Nothing serious."

"I have to debrief you about everything you did and saw. We have to make sure you understand that none of it was real. Some people have a hard time letting go of things they've seen in the future."

Was this a trick of Brannick's to throw Hartstein off the track? Was the sergeant desperate to protect himself, knowing what was going to happen in the future? "I was a hero, Brannick. They all loved me. There were buildings and parks named after me. And then you showed up and tried to kill me, to prevent all the things I'm going to do. You wanted to ensure a victory for the Underground. But I killed you instead."

Brannick laughed long and hard. "I warned you all about that, Hartstein," he said. "You went into the future, into your own daydreams. All of it was wish fulfillment, every tiny bit. The future is even more subjective than the past. Now, why would you daydream about killing me?"

Hartstein considered. It made some sense; he didn't really think he was capable of doing all the things Pamma'a said he would. But before he made any decisions one way or the other, he wanted to talk about the nature of the future with someone else. A higher authority.

He described his adventures in detail, and Brannick explained that if Hartstein returned there, it would all be different. The next time, the city might not be underground but built up into the stratosphere. Or any of an infinite variety of alternate future possibilities. As for why the Agency guards hadn't anticipated Brannick's attack, Hartstein knew the answer to that. He had always known, but hadn't acknowledged it to himself: he never intended to mention the incident to anyone, least of all in his "lectures," so that when he came to the future he would be a hero all over again. That truth made him feel just a bit unclean; he had been willing to let Pamma'a suffer pain and injury—she might even have been killed— just so that he would be a hero.

But then, if he didn't mention the incident, how could Brannick have known when and where Hartstein would be vulnerable? And if he did mention the incident, Brannick would know that the attempt was hopeless, that the sergeant would only be killed for his treachery. So that seemed to corroborate what Brannick had told him. Everything that happened to him in the future had been a wish, a fantasy . . .

He would have no statues dedicated to him, no tributes, no cheering crowds. The equation that defeated the Underground might never be discovered. In fact, there was no guarantee now that the Agency would win the war. And Pamela, his promised bride of the future, was she also only a phantom of his desires? All the security and peace he had found in the future slipped away from him, dissolving like a dream in the cold light of morning.

And yet he was no worse off than he had been before the trip. Now, at last, Hartstein would never again be seduced by the false charms of the past or future. He understood the nature of time travel, and it was a disheartening knowledge. It had shown him shabby truths about himself: he had probably daydreamed about defeating Brannick because the sergeant represented Hartstein's ideal of the competent individual. A dream world was possibly the only place Hartstein might hope to best him in such a deadly contest.

But there was one other consolation. It struck Hartstein suddenly, and it almost compensated for the disappointments. "This means, I guess, that I won't need to worry about the lecture series."

Brannick smiled patiently. "You don't have anything to say to anybody," he said.

"Thank God," said Hartstein. That took a great load from his shoulders.

CHAPTER FOUR

NO BUNNIES, THANK GOD

In order to review the unusual circumstances Hartstein had endured in the future, and to recognize his exemplary courage in a moment of great danger, a formal board of inquiry met to decide how best to reward the brave recruit. Five men wearing blue and gold uniforms of Agency Chronic Marshals gazed at him impassively, as Hartstein told the tale of his adventure as a hunted man in an unreal world. Sergeant Brannick sat beside Hartstein, trying not to look like a proud parent.

"Tell me," said Marshal Hsien, Overlord of Benevolent Futures, "what did you think while you were under attack?"

Hartstein tried to make light of the whole affair. "It wasn't so bad, sir," he said, a modest smile upon his lips. The smile was the same that he had seen Brannick use from time to time. "I got a chance to do a lot of thinking, about what the security of our time frame means to me and to those I love. I am sure that I was placed in peril only because it would further the greater good of the Agency's cause."

"Yet it was clear to you that the false Sergeant Brannick was prepared to kill you," said Marshal Farias, Overlord of Unhappy Pasts. He was a huge man, with a thick head of silver hair and cold black eyes that glared out beneath a craggy brow.

"That was his duty, sir, by the logic of that future."

Marshal Kourjadian, Overlord of Dire Futures, nodded. "You represent more than a soldier of the Agency," he said in his deep, rumbling voice. "You are a well-trained instrument, a weapon of the forces of order, and damned expensive to replace. It is a truism of war that infantrymen are expendable, but that is not so in this conflict. You have been tested and you have proved your mettle."

Hartstein bowed his head, but did not reply. His opinion counted for little against the unanimity of the marshals.

"But this is not a theoretical discussion," said Marshal Hsien. "This board has met to review the actions of Private Hartstein, and after adequate consideration it has determined that Private Hartstein represents the best qualities of the Agency's tradition. Sergeant Brannick is to be commended for the work he has done in preparing so worthy a young man. And, Private Hartstein, while it is not the policy of the Agency to bestow honors, awards, or medals for the pursuance of one's duty, we five marshals concur in the opinion that a token of our gratitude and respect is in order. Therefore, from this moment you are elevated to the rank of corporal, with all the privileges, duties, and perquisites that attach to that rank. You will be given your own remote temporal tap, with which you will be able to travel through time at will, unaccompanied by senior Agents. And you will be given your first solo mission. We wish you the best of luck, and want you to know that the Agency will be watching your future career with special interest. This inquiry is adjourned."

Hartstein was a little startled by the magnanimity of the board's decision. Of course, he realized that the wartime conditions made promotion easier, but he never expected to be trusted with his own temporal tap so soon. Now all the eras of the past were open to him, endlessly, as well as the bizarre, dreamlike futures. He could visit Pamari and remain in Alexandria for months or years, and then return to this moment when he felt ready to take up his responsibility to the Agency. Or he might decide never to return . . .

A familiar iron clamp on his shoulder brought him back to reality. "You did fine, soldier," said Sergeant Brannick. He nodded his head a little to indicate the depth of his approval.

"Oh, it was nothing, Sarge," said Hartstein.

Brannick laid a finger beside his nose and murmured, "You know that and I know that, but don't let *them* find out about it. Now, I guess you think you've been given a rich widow's freedom to go playing around through time while we grizzled veterans fight this battle. I got to knock that out of your head and give you some more information."

A coldness Hartstein had experienced before crept through him. Here came more bad news, and more things that he ought to have been told before but Brannick had decided it wasn't time yet.

"This war isn't being fought in the costume departments of the Agency and the Underground," said Brannick. "It isn't being fought in ancient Turkey or with Balboa in Panama. It is being won or lost on the blackboards and computer screens of our mathematical armaments boys. They're mostly kids just like you. Oh, maybe they have a little more between the ears, but they're good boys, too. But I tell you, I'd rather have one of you than a dozen of them behind me when I charge up some blind alley God-knows-when. Still, their little variables and decimal points are going to save this or lose it for us, and our bloody skirmishes are just buying them time."

"Just like they told me in the future, about the—"

"Shut up, son," said Brannick coldly. "Now, they're going to send you out on your own. You've never been on your own in a wartime situation. And the situation, timewise, travelwise, time-travelwise, is a little different."

"Different, Sarge?"

"Uh huh. They—or we—have introduced a kind of local stability factor. If you understood more math I could explain it to you. What it means is that you can go back somewhere and run into other people from our side or their side, all in the same quasi-past that used to be in existence just for the travelers on that particular jump."

"Sure, Sarge, I've seen that already. First there was that guy in Galilee, remember, and then—"

"Shut up, son. Now the problem is that they're learning to build time-bridges from one era to another, a sneaky kind of thing, going through times and places no one would ever bother about, and we figure they're trying to come up behind us somehow. But don't let none of that worry you. Our math boys are just as good as theirs, and we'll have it shut off real soon now. You just go back to whatever godawful place they're shipping you, and make me proud of you all over again."

"It means a lot to me to hear you say that, Sergeant Brannick." Hartstein put out his hand and the older man grasped it. "Everything I am, I owe to you."

"Don't you forget it, neither," laughed Brannick in the hearty, manly, well-rehearsed way of his.

"Do I have to leave soon?"

Brannick handed him a sealed envelope. "In six hours. Sorry, Corporal, that's all the notice you get. Wartime, you know. So you'll have to rush through outfitting and ESB prep, and then I'll meet you by the Big O." That's what the old-timers called the transmission screen. They called it nine or ten other things, too, every single one of which had an obscene connotation. It made Hartstein feel good to have Brannick use all kinds of insiders' jargon with him. He kept forgetting that he was becoming a veteran insider himself. "There's something important I want to say to you," said Brannick.

That last bit bothered Hartstein just a little, but he hustled off to get his brain basted with all the essential knowledge; and he picked up a thin plastic package from the costuming department that was the most unpromising disguise he had ever seen. There were only a few broad brownish leaves and a kind of rough belt made of bark. "This is it?" he asked.

"This is *it*, Hartstein," said the young man in the costuming department. "This is absolutely the worst. They must really love you. I thought you had a kind of dash in that scruffy shepherd rig, you know. Although," and here the young man paused thoughtfully, critically, giving Hartstein the fullest of his professional attention, "this might suit you, too. One banana leaf, maybe two, what do you think? Possibly too devastating." He glanced at the package. "It *was* a thirty-two waist, wasn't it? I have a positive genius for remembering things like that."

Hartstein held the plastic bag in one hand, feeling nothing but revulsion. There was no golden jewelry, not so much as a stone ear plug. "Where the hell am I going?" he asked.

"Sealed orders?" asked the young man.

Hartstein nodded.

The young man reached forward, making an elegant gesture of it, languidly turning the palm of his right hand over like a heliotrope seeking the sun. Hartstein hesitated, then put the sealed envelope in the man's hand. The young man smiled, tore open an end in careful little rips, blew gently into the envelope, and took out the Most Secret, Burn Before Reading dictates of the highest of the High Command. "Easter Island," said the young man. "Sixteen-oh-two. More than a hundred years before the first European ship discovered the place." He tapped the sheet of paper on his fingertips. "You may decide to leave your tennis whites at home," he said mockingly.

Hartstein stared silently. He waited for the punch line. He knew there must be one coming.

"The white-god routine," said the young man, yawning. He gave Hartstein yet another complete evaluation, then shook his head decidedly "no." "But of course," he sighed, "there are white gods *and* white gods, if you know what I mean. You're no Thor, that's for certain, but to those ape-men, who knows? They may have an opening for a savage clam god or something. What do the people on Easter Island do?"

"Easter Island is the place with all the big stone heads," said Hartstein. "That's as much as I know about it."

"I'm sure I've never heard anything more about the place. But once you've gone through the ESB—"

"I already did that."

"And you still don't have any idea?" The young man shrugged. "Think of it this way: in a place like that, centuries ago, with nothing but sun and fish and lotus blossoms, what's there to worry about?"

Hartstein leaned forward on the man's counter, on the little territorial limit of the costume department. He felt an odd fierceness rising in him, and he wanted somehow to spend it on someone. "You know what could go wrong?" he asked in a cold voice. "From what I've seen in other places, in other pasts, when I get to Easter Island all the big stone heads may be big stone Easter bunnies. Or they'll be giant heads of men, but made of hollow chocolate. I'm in no hurry to find out."

"Yes, well, you *have* to go now. They're waiting for you, I'm sure. Take your little leafy G-string and run. I'll bet you're going off with your Sergeant Brannick again, aren't you?"

Hartstein's eyes flashed. "I'm no shavetail anymore, buddy," he snarled. "This is *my* mission, and I don't need any sergeant looking over my shoulder. And I don't need any props-department gunsel giving me advice, either."

The young man turned away, unconcerned. "My," he said, "the gods are restless tonight." He laughed.

At the transmission stage, as promised, Sergeant Brannick stood waiting impatiently, slamming one huge fist into the palm of his other hand. Hartstein, dressed in the absurd costume of an Easter Islander—little more than foliage and goosebumps—watched as several wide-eyed tourists, all dressed as Viet Cong, disappeared through the purple glow into their vacation. A man dressed the same as Hartstein, down to the same yellow patches on his frondy knickers, went through the screen; Hartstein's eyebrows raised. More people stood in line for their turn. Brannick saw him, and walked across the vast hall. Hartstein felt naked, which, in point of fact, was virtually true.

"I got to tell you something," said Brannick.

"You said that before. Hurry up, I'm starting to catch a cold."

"Don't worry about that. I want to be sure you don't believe everything you hear back there."

Hartstein's eyes narrowed. "Back where?"

Brannick looked away, into nowhere. "Back where they're sending you."

"Do you know where they're sending me?"

Brannick coughed softly into one gnarled hand. "Uh, yes, I do. I took a peek. Don't believe everything they say to you."

"Everything *who* says to me?"

"The Underground."

Hartstein's shoulders sagged. "I'm going to run into the Underground again. Well, I should have expected that. Another battle. Another fine mess, and you took a look at it already. You know what's going to happen.

And you're not going to tell me anything about it except I'm not supposed to believe what they're going to tell me."

Brannick smiled. "That's right," he said. Hartstein didn't buy it for a moment.

"So if you saw how it turns out, why are you standing around here chewing your nails? Why am I bothering to go back there now in the first place?"

Brannick looked around impatiently, but there would never be any help coming for him. "Because it doesn't *have* to turn out the way I saw it," he said.

"Ah," said Hartstein.

"Why do you always have to have all of this explained to you every time?"

Hartstein looked Brannick directly in the eyes. Brannick didn't flinch. "Because," said Hartstein slowly, "the rules keep changing. All the time."

"Well," said Brannick lamely.

"And if it doesn't *have* to turn out the way you saw it," said Hartstein, "why did you bother taking a peek?"

Brannick looked hurt. "Because I care about you, son," he said. Hartstein didn't buy that one, either.

"Got to go," said Hartstein. He didn't wait for Brannick's shove; he stepped through the transmission screen's purple glow and found himself on a broad patch of slippery stones beside a low mountain. Behind him was the ocean, cold and restless as a cat in the rain. Above him were some of the famous stone idols, huge, forbidding, frightening. Great sea birds wheeled in numberless flocks above the cliff, crying a shrill, endless complaint. Four men stood in a silent huddle not far from Hartstein, staring at him, pointing. The great white god of something-or-other had arrived.

One of the men stepped forward, raising his right hand. Hartstein, new at the white-god business, did the same. The other man, he recognized immediately, was the tourist or Agent who had gone through the screen while Hartstein talked with Brannick. "Welcome," said the man.

"Thank you," said Hartstein. The man had a beard now; he hadn't a few minutes ago. He was also sunburnt to a dark brown, indistinguishable from the leathery skin of the natives.

"Let us go to my lodge and we will eat. My name is Tipchak. You're probably wondering what I'm doing here."

They proceeded up a narrow, rocky path. From higher up the view was astonishing. The air was clear and sharp and fresh, and the sights and sounds so commanded Hartstein's attention that he did not answer. All around him people were at work, feverishly laboring at countless tasks involving the great stone heads. The statues themselves, of some ceremonial importance, Hartstein believed, were being prepared by crews of men, women, and children. It seemed to be an isolated stone-age culture. This was A.D. 1600; why were the people here still living the life that had been left behind by the inhabitants of even the most remote regions of the world centuries ago? The black natives of the Congo had been more sophisticated when they first met European adventurers; the same thing was true of the peoples of the frozen North and equatorial South America. In all the world, there have been only a few pockets of truly Mesolithic culture left for civilized men to stumble upon. The mystery of Easter Island—or, to be accurate, one of its principal mysteries—was that the place itself was new, a volcanic island which did not support human habitation much before A.D. 900. When the islanders' ancestors first arrived, they must even then have been more advanced than the stone carvers Hartstein saw toiling upon the side of the ancient volcano called Rano Raraku.

There were about ninety great stone faces set in a huge circle on the slope, in the midst of a broad, grassy area that overlooked the sea. The faces were all turned in the same direction, to the south, toward nothing. Mexico lay three thousand miles to the north, Chile two thousand miles to the east, Tahiti, Pitcairn, and the Tuamotu Archipelago two thousand miles to the west. The great long-faced statues, called *moai* by the islanders, gazed thoughtfully across the creeping white waves.

The moai, hacked from a brownish volcanic tuff within the crater of Rano Raraku, were set up on pedestals in a great ring that enclosed another formation of them in the shape of a horseshoe. A worn path leading down the hillside was guarded by two faces at the upper end, two more in line, and, at the lower end, the largest statue of all. On the flat crowns of some of the heads there were balanced huge stone topknots made separately of some red stone, brought from some other place and somehow raised to their precarious positions. Men worked with stone axes, chipping bits away from the great heads, finishing the carving, hurrying to complete the monoliths in a frenzy of some sort. Women and children helped, directed by some unspoken plan or ritual. It was a marvelous and breathtaking scene, but it was all wrong.

"You're probably wondering what I'm doing here," said the man again. Hartstein had forgotten all about him.

"Well, yes. Who are you?" Hartstein shaded his eyes with one hand and stared up at the immense guardian moai that blocked the lower end of the path.

"My name is Tipchak. I told you that. I arrived here forty-five years ago, the first white man these islanders had ever seen. I played the conventional divinity routine, Plan Six in the book, and it's gone very well. I foretold these people of your coming, and here you are, and that makes me look very good. Or it will, when I present you to the villagers tonight."

"You went through the screen just before I did," said Hartstein. "And you say you've been here for forty-five years? You only look a few years older, at the very most." Hartstein saw a definite resemblance between the moai of Rano Raraku and this short, nervous man. Tipchak had the same narrow forehead, prominent nose, long-lobed ears, and compressed lips. All these phenomenal stone giants were tributes to this weaselly little man.

"I haven't stayed here the whole time," said Tipchak. "I didn't think that was necessary. I told the people that I had to go back to heaven on occasion, and I left them and skipped ahead a year and a half or so. I stay with them about a month at a time, to make sure the work gets done right. I've been here, oh, maybe three years in all. Getting ready."

Hartstein nodded. That made good sense. "Getting ready for me," he said.

Tipchak shook his head. "Getting ready for the attack of the Temporary Underground that's coming tomorrow morning."

Hartstein closed his eyes and waited for his anger to subside. "No one spoke to me about an immediate attack," he said.

"Well, I jumped ahead to tomorrow several times during the last three years, and I've seen it."

"Good thinking. What's going to happen?"

Tipchak took him by the arm; for some reason, Hartstein resented the man's touch. They walked toward the center of the activity, to the center of the inner horseshoe of statues. There was a small dwelling there, about twenty feet long, five feet wide, and five feet tall, made of lashed stakes and walled with matted reeds. This was the great god Tipchak's official residence. Tipchak indicated that Hartstein should enter; they stooped to get through the low doorway. Inside, the place smelled like the wet part of the stable Hercules hadn't cleaned out yet. Hartstein fought down a touch of nausea. He was offered refreshments, bits of hard yams and a gourd of cloudy water. He declined both.

"Local stability, that's the point," said Tipchak, munching some yam. "Just a matter of months ago, the quasi-past in general existed only near the historically significant points. The rest was the realm of chaos, really, if you'll allow a poetic way of putting it. Swirling fog and a feeling that there was more metaphysics around than solid ground."

Hartstein was taking shallow breaths through his mouth. He was trying to keep as little of the fetid air as possible from entering his lungs. "Sergeant Brannick tried to describe that to me once. I've never seen it, though."

Tipchak nodded, chewing. He finished the piece of yam and pushed the chunks around in the bowl with a filthy forefinger, as if one piece of dry tuber could be more attractive than another. He chose one. "There's less of the fog. More order, less chaos. And the odd thing is, you got the Underground to thank for it. Isn't that just the opposite of what's supposed to be going on? The Underground is fighting *against* order, but for the time being they're creating more of it because right now it's useful to them."

Hartstein shrugged. "I suppose they figure that if they win, the new order will disappear along with all the old order anyway."

The little man pointed at Hartstein and smiled. "Exactly! See, you're not as slow as they said. You just got to understand the sigma effect. That's the Underground's new stability factor."

"Who said I was slow?" asked Hartstein grumpily.

Tipchak ignored him. "How are you at visualizing things in a Cartesian system?"

"A what?"

"A graph. What was your major in school?"

Hartstein looked down at the basalt floor. "I was going into doughnuts," he said.

"Not a lot of abstract thinking in doughnuts," said Tipchak.

"I specialized in jelly intrusion," said Hartstein. "Filling 'em. I was at the top of my class in jelly doughnut resuscitation. Sometimes one of them will start bleeding, and you have to know where to put pressure and how much. And if you drop a pan of them, you got to learn not to panic. You take the critical ones first—"

Tipchak waved an impatient hand. "In a matter of hours the Underground will be blasting this hillside with stuff you've never even imagined. Leave me do the talking. Where was I? Graphs, right." He patted the muck on the stone flooring into a smooth layer. With a finger he drew a long, straight line. "This is space," he said. "Distance."

"Distance," murmured Hartstein, as if it were a brand-new concept to him.

"Say, from here to there. What we do, we divide it up into units. Any kind of units. Feet, meters, light-years, whatever. Now look at this." He drew a second line that crossed the first at right angles. "This is distance, but instead of from here to there, it measures from my left to my right, got it?"

"And you can divide that up into units too, I'll just bet. I know all this."

Tipchak sneered. "You must have slept through your doughnut lecture and woke up in the middle of something where people was actually thinking. Now, pretend there was another line sticking straight up from the place where the first two lines cross. What's that?"

Hartstein thought. "You mean, if it were really there?"

"Yeah."

"It would be a stick."

Tipchak accepted that. "Maybe," he said. "Maybe a stick. But what would it measure?"

"It wouldn't measure anything until you looked at it and saw it was made up into units, too."

Tipchak spat out the yam he was chewing. He seemed very easily frustrated. "And so?" he asked.

"Distance," Hartstein said. "Up and down."

"All right. Three lines measuring distance in three dimensions. The lines run from behind me, past you into infinity; from right to left to the far ends of the universe; up and down until there isn't any such things any more. Now we come to the fourth dimension."

Hartstein smiled. "I know about the fourth dimension," he said. "Impossible."

"The fourth dimension is heat. You put a measuring stick in the deep fryer, and you see about the temperature of the oil."

There was an ominous rumble from beyond the small shack. It could have been thunder, or the displeasure of God, or the arrival of the Underground's armada, or all of the moai toppling each other like dominoes, but Tipchak paid no attention. "The fourth dimension," he said, "is time. There *is* a fourth line, marked off into units, that measures distance back and forth from the past into the future. We can locate our positions in the universe using these four lines. We find our location along each line, and together they give us a single point, a unique point, a point that belongs only to right here and right now."

There was silence. Seconds, minutes passed. Tipchak waited for Hartstein to absorb all this. More rumbling came from outside; it was, after all, only a distant storm over the heedless ocean. In the dark, damp hut Hartstein struggled until, like a miracle, the idea of a mappable universe came alive in his mind. He had been prepared for this by his ESB-training since his first day in the Agency, but abstract thought had so little value in his world that Hartstein rebelled against it unconsciously.

"I understand by your expression," said Tipchak, "that you are prepared to listen to more."

"This is exciting," said Hartstein in an awed murmur. "It's like finding out all about yeast dough for the first time, all over again."

"Marvelous. So now that I've explained the nature of the universe to you, kid, I got to do this. I got to kick out the legs it stands on. Remember the units I was talking about? Well, it seems that these days they don't stay the same, even though by definition they're supposed to. It turns out that a unit on one line doesn't have to equal the same unit on another line, and that now the Underground has figured out ways to stretch or shrink units on the same line."

Hartstein grew disgusted. "Then why bother having measuring lines to begin with?" he asked.

"Right!" shouted Tipchak, jumping to his feet, banging his head on the low ceiling. "That's the whole philosophy that gave birth to the Temporary Underground. They claim that order and life and a neat universe are contrary to the laws of nature. They say that man should do everything possible to restore things to the way they're evidently supposed to be: in utter chaos."

Hartstein shook his head. "Nature or God or whatever you want to call it wouldn't create the universe just to let it fall into chaos. Nature doesn't work that way. Nature makes order out of chaos, not the other way around."

Tipchak shook his head. "When you get home," he said, "you better have somebody explain entropy to you. If you can understand it, you may live through this yet." He thought that over and shrugged. "Never mind. Forget what I just said. Now, the Underground has been using the stretched and squeezed-together points on the measuring lines, thanks to some mathematical magic they found inside a set of parentheses. In some places—like here—they've taken the mixed-up units and sorted them out and made them all equal again. They've introduced order, more order than there should be: the sigma effect. They've made a quasi-past here on Easter Island that is continuous for decades, rather than days or weeks. And they're coming tomorrow to establish a base of operations here."

"How did you know about that? How did the Agency know to meet them here ahead of time?"

Tipchak shrugged again. "We have spies, they have spies . . ."

"Uh huh," said Hartstein.

"Let's go outside again," said Tipchak. Hartstein scooted out through the door opening before Tipchak could finish the sentence. In the fresh air, Hartstein's mind began to function clearly again. The squalor of the hut and the opacity of the conversation disappeared together from his memory.

One of the loinclothed island men came up to Tipchak and spoke deferentially, addressing him as Me-Ki, or "Little God." There was some problem about the stone topknots, which Hartstein now saw were modeled after the artificially colored, bound-up hairstyle of the islanders themselves, and not Tipchak's own thinning dark locks. It was obvious that not all of the stone caps could be put in place before morning, some sort of deadline that Tipchak had given them.

"Speak not to me of this," said Tipchak. He gestured to Hartstein. "Let the judgment be Me-Ah's." He had called Hartstein "Big God."

As much as Hartstein enjoyed the novelty of the situation, he didn't have a clue as to the correct response. He looked at Tipchak, who gave a little shrug. Hartstein raised both hands. "It does not matter, for I am generous. I am pleased," he cried. The islander looked relieved. He ran back to the other workers to spread the news; in a few minutes, almost all work had stopped.

"The hell with it," said Tipchak. "They've just spent forty-five years getting it all ready for you, but now that you're here, the rest of it can sit around and wait for the next big god."

"Okay by me." They walked up to the rim of the crater, from which Hartstein could survey much of the island. "What preparations have been made for the battle tomorrow?" he asked.

"None, really," said Tipchak.

Hartstein didn't know how to respond to that, either. "And why not?" he asked.

Tipchak's expression grew shrewd. "Forty-five quasi-years ago, I predicted your coming. Along with the little bits of magic I did for them along the way, your arrival here today makes me a big shot. Now the other thing that I did was have them move all their big stone heads into that arrangement. If you stand by the biggest one, the Guardian Face, on midsummer's morning the sun ought to rise straight over the arch of the horseshoe. They just put the Guardian up last month, so this year will be the first time we get to see it happen. Tomorrow's the day."

"The heads aren't arranged like this on Easter Island," Hartstein pointed out. "There isn't anything about the sun rising over them. They were just burial markers or something for their big chiefs."

"No, no, no. I've spent forty-five years working up to this. First I—"

"It's Stonehenge that's arranged like that, not Easter Island."

Tipchak's mouth opened, then closed, then opened again. He said nothing.

Hartstein sighed. "You have the wrong place, the wrong time, the wrong people, the wrong objects. I'll bet you used the Stonehenge layout for it, didn't you?" Tipchak nodded slowly. "But Easter Island is in the other hemisphere, on the opposite side of the equator, and two thousand years away from the plan that made Stonehenge work. For all you know, the sun might rise out over the water." He pointed to a bay not far away from the volcano's foot.

"I kind of wondered a little about that when the sun came up there this morning," said Tipchak in a small voice.

Hartstein shook his head wonderingly. "It looks like it's time to go home and bring in Sergeant Brannick and the reinforcements."

"No," said Tipchak quickly, "you can't do that."

"Why not?"

The little weasel looked around for a good reason. "Because the Underground might change units on you while you were gone, and you'd never be able to find this locus in four dimensions again."

That sounded reasonable. Hartstein chewed his lip. "So what are we going to do?"

Tipchak smiled. "Leave that to me. I've played the white god thing longer than you have. I see a way out."

The way out, it appeared, was to have the islanders revise the very notions Tipchak had fostered for forty-five quasi-years. He presented Hartstein as a newer, bigger, more powerful god, with a *"Please disregard previous divine revelation"* message. There was a new revelation.

"And here he is to tell us all about it," cried Tipchak. There was a smattering of Easter Island applause, and then Hartstein was supposed to stand up and cobble together a battle plan. He had taken a few hints from Tipchak during the rest of the afternoon. It had developed that the man was a weasel, but he was a *very good* weasel.

The women served a feast. It was night; a full moon hung fat and yellow over the Pacific. The breeze from the bay was sharp with salt, but after the heat of the afternoon, a little coolness made Hartstein feel better about everything. He wished that he had been given a banana-leaf shirt or something; the night promised to be even cooler.

"Tomorrow, my enemy, Nu-Ru, the god of yams, will come here," said Hartstein. He paused; everyone in the village made appropriate sounds of concern. "He will attack me. He will try to destroy me." There were cries of alarm. "But he will not succeed. He will not destroy me, Me-Ah, Great God, because you will be beside me to drive Nu-Ru away."

There were shouts and fierce cries from the men. There were wails of fear and dread from the women. The children were already asleep, all tucked into their banana-leaf beds with woven dolls in the shape of Easter Island stone heads.

One of the men leaped to his feet and gave a boastful account of how he would slay the minions of Nu-Ru and win a place for himself in heaven. Another man jumped up and tried to top that story; as Tipchak had predicted, the affair went on for hours. Neither man from the future was required to say another word, or perform a single act of magic. As far as Hartstein was concerned, the only unpleasant aspect of the evening was that he was served by a young woman who was, of course, Pamari's duplicate here in this quasi-past. Her name was Pā-Eh-Ah-Me-Ah, or Lovely Woman of Big God. It was disconcerting because Brannick had been proved right: Hartstein had indeed become used to seeing her again and again, in one quasi-past after another, and this time, to his dismay, he found his thoughts centered on the impending battle rather than on her. She tried to distract him all evening long, but he paid her little attention. Deep inside, Hartstein was hurt by this knowledge. He would not have believed it possible for him to become so much an Agency man.

During the feast of fish and yams there was the drinking of much native beer, which had been brewed from fish and yams. One taste was sufficient for Hartstein; he passed on his bowl to a young man sitting near him, who seemed to have a bottomless reservoir for the stuff. "Is this wise?" asked Hartstein. "If they all get bombed tonight, are they going to be in any shape to fight tomorrow?"

"It makes little difference," said Tipchak. He was letting himself float along on the tide of good cheer.

"You've seen what happens in the morning, you said so. Let me know what to expect."

Tipchak drained his bowl and waited for one of the women to refill it. He waved a hand in the air. "You're going to make a speech before dawn," he said. "You're going to tell the warriors that one of two things is going to happen. You and this Nu-Ru person are brother gods, see, and your daddy is Me-So-Tā, the Sun God. The Sun God couldn't care less about who wins your battle tomorrow, so whichever side impresses Me-So-Tā the most before the battle gets his blessing, and victory. All these warriors will want a sign or something. They'll want to know ahead of time that you and they are going to win. So here's what you tell them. You say that we all have to go to the horseshoe of stone faces and wait for the 'sun canoe' of your enemy. About eight o'clock, the Underground's ship is going to come flaming across the sky. Every damn one of these brave idiots is going to fall down on his flat-nosed face in the mud, bawling in terror. You tell 'em ahead of time, you say that your daddy's sign is like this: if the sun canoe comes down behind us, behind the crater of Rano Raraku, then all will be well and we can charge down to glory and all like that. But if the sun canoe climbs down the sky in front of us, so that it disappears behind the Guardian Face, then we are doomed. It's that easy."

Hartstein didn't understand any of Tipchak's reasoning. "Why won't the Underground come down there? Behind the Guardian Face?"

Tipchak looked at Hartstein unsteadily. "Because if they do that, kid, they're going to put their ship down in the middle of the ocean. But these sons of bitches won't think about that. All they'll know is that the Sun God is on your side, and they'll go whooping and hollering down the other side of the volcano, right into the static guns of the Temporary Underground."

A chill went through Hartstein that had nothing to do with the offshore breeze. "Static guns?" he asked. He thought static guns were part of the unreal future only he had ever seen.

"I told you they were bringing all kinds of new stuff with them. Even the warship itself. It's all from the future. They're going to fight us with a whole destroyer full of stuff they dragged back from one of the worst possible futures. We don't stand a chance."

"But that isn't possible. The futures don't really exist, and you can't import nonexistent technology from a nonexistent future. That's one of the most basic laws of time travel."

Tipchak shook his head. "Sigma effect," he said, as if that explained everything. Maybe it did.

"And all these native men."

Tipchak's hands turned over, thumbs down, spilling all his beer into his lap.

"And us?" asked Hartstein.

Tipchak shrugged. "We do all right. After the battle, we get invited aboard the ship and interviewed."

Hartstein's stomach started to hurt. "You mean they're going to torture us."

"No," said Tipchak, "interviewed. Asked questions, get our pictures taken. You know. For the Underground press. It won't be bad; you're going to be offered a job with the Underground. The Commander is a nice guy, I've worked with him before. If you're smart, you'll take him up on his offer. If you turn him down, you're dead. If you try to run out of here, we'll jam your temporal tap in one or more dimensions, and you'll never be able to control it again. You'll dash helplessly around in both time and space. You might end up circling Barnard's Star in time for New Year's, who knows?"

Hartstein thought about his father, who never had a tremendous amount of confidence in him. He thought about Sergeant Brannick, who was, down deep, not such a bad guy. And he thought about Pamari and all the others of her. It seemed doubtful that he would ever resolve his situation concerning them, not in any satisfactory way. Not now.

But what Tipchak said made some sense. It cleared up one little element that had been troubling Hartstein all day. A good Agent—even a *bad* Agent—wouldn't have made the mistake Tipchak had: confusing Stonehenge and Easter Island. That would have been impossible, because the Agency's ESB-training would have laid in specific information, and would never have included such an error. That meant that Tipchak had jumped back to Easter Island inadequately prepared. Therefore he wasn't an Agent, after all.

He had to be working for the other side. He was a member of the Temporary Underground who had bought a tourist ticket back to Easter Island forty-five quasi-years before Hartstein's appearance, and then used his Underground temporal tap to jump back and forth. "You're a rebel, aren't you?" asked Hartstein.

"Yep," said Tipchak drunkenly. He giggled.

"Just checking." Hartstein signaled for some more baked fish. "I want to talk to you in the morning. When you're sober, I want to break your face."

Tipchak grinned and almost fell over. "Make sure I'm awake for your great-god act; don't want to miss that. 'Night." And he fell face forward into a bowl of beer.

And as the others, one by one, joined Tipchak in drunken slumber, Hartstein's fear grew stronger. He remembered that someone had warned him about this, somewhere, sometime. But he couldn't remember who, or when, or what he was supposed to do about it. He rubbed his head wearily, wondering why he wasn't more concerned about all the islanders who would be massacred in the morning. He wondered where all his human feelings had gone. He felt like a hollow shell operating for the Agency, and that his true emotions had been left behind in the present, in a locker with his uniform and valuables. Pā-Eh-Ah-Me-Ah led him away from the ruin of the banquet, to a fresh and clean bower she had built overlooking the crashing surf. He was glad for her presence and solicitous tenderness, but nothing she could say or do all night long was able to comfort him. He did not sleep.

CHAPTER FIVE

HARTSTEIN'S ADVENTURES UNDERGROUND

During the long dark hours of the night, Hartstein wondered if there were things he could do to change the course of events, to save the lives of the islanders. Merely to demonstrate its strength, the Temporary Underground appeared ready to slaughter every one of them, to make a demonstration that would impress Hartstein. It wasn't necessary; Hartstein was already impressed with its ruthlessness and cynical power. But try as he might, he failed to come up with anything that would be able to defy the Underground and its weapons out of some nightmarish quasi-future.

If there were enough time and the right materials on the island, Hartstein might have shown the warriors how to build war-chariots, if there had been horses to pull them. All they had were bows and arrows and hand weapons of the sharp or blunt varieties. They wouldn't get within five hundred meters of the static guns—and that was assuming that the rebels would be using hand-held pistols similar to the ones Hartstein had seen in the nonexistent Mihalik Building's Time Museum. There was no guarantee of that. Who could say what the Underground would use in its attack: static rifles, cannon, missiles? Tipchak could say, but he wouldn't. He just snickered and said that he wanted to leave it as a surprise. Maybe the Underground would arrive with more sinister weapons, based on ideas and science that Hartstein's era hadn't even begun to imagine. The empty hours until eight o'clock would bring no solace.

As the first pale signs of dawn glimmered over the eastern horizon, Hartstein stood and stretched his aching body. Pā-Eh-Ah-Me-Ah clung to him and whispered in his ear, but he did not listen to her. He looked out across the narrow bay where the sea still slept, the color of iron. He waited for some strong emotion to take possession of him, but none came. He waited for fear or hate or anger, but he felt only tiredness and hunger. The young woman took his hand and led him from the bower to the Guardian

Face, the great moai that stood at the foot of the path to Tipchak's absurd Polynesian Stonehenge.

"You are worried," said Pā-Eh-Ah-Me-Ah.

"Yes," said Hartstein. In the dawn's early light, the Guardian Face reminded him of his father, disapproving and silent.

"But you are Me-Ah, the Big God. Do you think your father, Me-So-Tā, will favor your enemy?"

Hartstein turned to her, bewildered. What difference did it make? Whatever happened, he would not have to live out his own life on the devastated island. If there were native survivors, they would cease to exist whenever the Underground abandoned its base on the island. This was, after all, only a quasi-past. It was longer-lived than most, of course, but if he visited Easter Island again in the year 1620 or 1630, everything would be whole, healthy, untouched by the conflict that would destroy this culture in this particular quasi-past. The moai would be standing where they belonged. And Pā-Eh-Ah-Me-Ah would be there to greet him. So what difference did it make? What was the value of life in a quasi-past? If there was an infinitude of Easter Islanders living in an infinitude of similar quasi-pasts, why grieve over the loss of a few here and there?

"I have seen a day when these great moai did not stand in this horseshoe and ring," he said, brooding. "They were scattered about the island, standing upon basalt platforms, dreaming upon the hillsides and beaches."

"Yes," said Pā-Eh-Ah-Me-Ah, "as they were before Me-Ki told our fathers to move them."

"And tomorrow, when I must return to heaven, will you build more faces?"

"No," said the young woman.

Her answer surprised Hartstein. "No? Why not?"

"We have enough," she said simply. She smiled as the carmine limb of the sun flung itself over the edge of the world. "I greet your heavenly father."

"Oh, sure." Although he didn't know what the moai were built for in the first place, Hartstein had to agree that the islanders probably had plenty of them. And so was solved one of the great mysteries of Easter Island: why did the islanders suddenly stop making the immense statues, sometime just before the first Europeans landed on their shores? "They had enough," murmured Hartstein. He marveled at the innocence of that reason; anthropologists always expected more.

Hartstein's speech to the assembled tribesmen was short and direct. Everyone was gathered within the central horseshoe of moai, shivering in the damp coolness of early morning. Hartstein pointed at the Guardian

Face which stood a few hundred yards down the narrow path, its back turned on them as it meditated on the sea. The young Agent recited the story of Nu-Ru and the sun canoe and the omen from the Sun God, and the warriors seemed cheered by it. They were happy with the idea of magic. They preferred advance knowledge, even if, as in this case, it turned out to be false. Signs and portents had a comforting effect on these people.

"Very good, very nice presentation," said Tipchak. "Now there's nothing to do but wait."

Hartstein watched the islanders working themselves up to a fighting frenzy, chanting and dancing. "What's the point of killing all these people?" he asked.

Tipchak shrugged. "It will be easier to operate here without them. And besides—"

Hartstein stopped him. "I know, I know: they don't really exist. Well, stick that one in your ear. I don't want to hear it anymore."

"We're going to watch the battle from up there," said Tipchak, pointing to the rim of the volcanic crater. "Out of harm's way."

"That figures. Some god I am. I ought to be leading them into battle."

"Did you expect that this was going to turn into your own little myth?" asked Tipchak, sneering. "Sorry. Maybe next time."

Hartstein remembered what he had promised the weasel the night before. He turned, letting his shoulder drop, and swung his right fist in a long, beautiful arc that ended with shattering impact on the point of Tipchak's chin. The rebel staggered backward, grunting, and sat down heavily. He wobbled for a moment, dazed, his hands covering his face. When his head cleared, he looked slowly up at Hartstein. There was no anger or surprise in Tipchak's expression; he was probably used to getting slugged. "Some lousy temper you got," he murmured resentfully. Both men were suddenly aware that the islanders had stopped their war chant and were watching. "Goddamn dangerous thing, too."

"It was just something I needed to do," said Hartstein. He walked over beside Tipchak.

"So, did you get it out of your system?"

"I don't think so." Hartstein turned and addressed the warriors: "Do not be astonished," he said in a loud, commanding voice. "Gods, too, have battle rituals we must perform." The islanders swallowed that easily enough and went back to their own hopping around.

One man separated from the group and approached Hartstein timidly. "Me-Ah," he murmured, nervously bowing his head again and again as a gesture of respect.

"Speak," said Hartstein.

"Nu-Ru is your enemy," said the islander. "He is coming here to fight with you. That is as it should be; there is always war among the gods. But Nu-Ru is the god of yams, who provides such of our food that we do not harvest from the sea. Will he not be angry with us, too, for fighting against him, as your allies?"

Hartstein wanted to tell this poor guy that next year's yam crop was absolutely the least of everyone's worries. "Concern yourself not with the policies of heaven," Hartstein said. "We must wait for the omen. If the Sun God is against us, then this day you will depart this world, fish and yams and everything. If we march together to victory, then Nu-Ru will be your servant forever, and the yams will grow as plentifully as pebbles upon the beach."

"That sounds just fine," said the islander. He went back to his crowd and repeated what Hartstein had told him.

The weasel, Tipchak, looked at Hartstein with a kind of grudging respect. "You got a natural talent for this, kid," he said, still holding his dented jaw. "I'm going to let the Commander know about it. We might have a place for somebody like you."

Hartstein paid no attention. "Why don't I just tell them all to run?" he said. "They could scatter all over the island."

Tipchak shook his head. "You'd pay for it," he said. "You'd really regret it."

Before Hartstein could say anything more, things began to happen very quickly. He didn't see the Underground ship explode into existence, but he heard the shuddering boom, and the shock wave almost threw him on his face. There were shrieks from the islanders. Hartstein turned to look and saw a huge needle-nosed silver ship screaming across the island, low enough for him to count the black tips of the baryon masts on the edge of each stabilizing plane. The ship was unlike any he'd ever seen, although there were certain similarities to the Agency craft of Hartstein's era. But he saw sinister weapons and unknown devices that meant that Tipchak had spoken the truth: this ship could have come only from some hopeless future.

Shrieking blasts of energy cushioned the craft's descent. The islanders had their sign, even though none of them was watching; they were prostrate with fear. For a moment the ship hovered, flame licking out from its steering jets, and then all was suddenly silent. The Underground's destroyer settled down out of sight on the grassy plain on the far side of Rano Raraku. Slowly the men of Easter Island raised their heads and

looked around; it was obvious that the sign had been favorable, that the
Sun God had chosen them for glory. A cheer went up among them.

"Come on," whispered Tipchak urgently, "we got to get out of here,
and fast."

"Hey," said Hartstein, "what's the—"

The dry grass between Hartstein and the warriors, the thin layer of soil,
and the volcanic rock beneath it erupted into the air. There was a sharp
crack of thunder as air rushed into a deep crater that only an instant
before had been solid basalt. Hartstein was thrown across the landscape
and landed about twenty feet away. He stared at the new hole, wondering
where it had come from. His thoughts were slow and unclear. A hand
tried to pull him up. His shoulder hurt. He got slowly to his feet, and he
felt dizzy. He put a hand to his forehead and it came away bloody. Someone pulled him, and he followed; it seemed like a good idea at the time.

"Come on, Hartstein, come on, I'm not going to carry you."

Hartstein smiled crazily. "You don't have to carry me. I'm fine. I'm—"

A second blast from the Underground's ship struck the stone pedestal
of one of the moai in the outer ring. The pedestal fractured into a fine
grayish-red powder that showered away on the tropical breeze. The great
stone statue trembled as if it had come alive and then toppled forward,
burying its insensible face in the soft mud. One of the screaming, terrified
islanders was crushed beneath it.

Then there was a volley of beams from the warship. The air was filled
with the cries of the natives, the splintering of the rock that made up the
mountainside, the thudding crash of falling statues, the concussions of air
masses colliding. Tipchak dragged and pulled and hauled Hartstein away
from the scene, up toward the summit of Rano Raraku. Hartstein's head
cleared after a few moments. He sat down helplessly, sickened, and
watched the destruction below. It did not take long. The Underground
shot the arrangement of moai apart like bottles off a fence. The south face
of the volcano became a blackened, pitted no-man's-land. Each shot killed
and destroyed with an economy that seemed almost miserly. If the warship had appeared at eight o'clock, then the carnage was over by eight
fifteen.

Hartstein was hypnotized by the sight. When the explosions ended, the
sudden stillness hit him like a physical blow. He found the morbid silence
more terrible than the attack itself. "How," he said in a croaking voice.

"What was that?" asked Tipchak, who sat on the edge of the crater, his
chin propped by one hand, as if he were watching a bunch of kids playing
kickball in the street.

"How can they do that? They're on the plain on the north side of the mountain. How can they hit targets on the south face?"

"In the future, the weapons don't necessarily work the way you expect them to," said Tipchak. "They're not shooting those beams through the volcano. They're projecting them to specific co-ordinates, materializing them where their targets are. The first shots were just calibrating range-finders, or else we might have been killed. Of course, I'd seen it before and I knew where to stand. You owe me your life, you realize."

Hartstein glared at him. "You want another clip on the jaw like I gave you before?" Tipchak flinched. Hartstein's face changed. "Oh my God," he whispered. "Oh, God. Pā-Eh-Ah-Me-Ah."

Tipchak relaxed when he saw that he wasn't going to be hit again. "She's down there, of course."

Hartstein jumped up and ran a few steps down the path, but then he stopped. He didn't want to go down there. He didn't want to look around.

"We got business, Hartstein," the little weasel was shouting. "We're expected."

Hartstein's expression was grim. "That's fine with me. Let's go."

The bottom of slumbering Rano Raraku's crater had filled with rainwater over the centuries, and now it reflected the pure blue of the fresh, empty sky. Unfinished moai lay like stunned giants on the rocky shores. Hartstein and Tipchak picked their way halfway around the volcano, and then climbed down the steep slope of the north side. The Underground's destroyer waited silently at the edge of a stand of tall, supple palm trees.

"When we get there," said Tipchak, "you better let me do the talking."

"Sure," said Hartstein bitterly, "you know these people better than I do."

"You bet your sweet ass."

Hartstein promised himself that Tipchak would pay for what had happened that morning. He didn't know how or when; but Hartstein was glad that he had the means to look through all of eternity for something horribly appropriate.

The smooth silver fuselage of the warship was unmarked. The Underground didn't go in much for flags or symbols. They were more interested in action, more effective than most revolutionaries because they neglected rhetoric in favor of unabashed demolition. They let great, smoking craters and slaughtered people do their speechmaking for them.

There was a low buzzing sound and a portion of the destroyer's hull slid back, revealing a dark interior. "Please come in, Brother Tipchak," said a familiar voice, "and bring our guest with you."

"That's the Commander," said Tipchak nervously. "I think we ought to hurry. He sounds impatient."

"Why is he impatient?" asked Hartstein. "Time running out or something?"

" 'Time running out,' " muttered Tipchak, "very funny." He shook his head disgustedly. The weasel grabbed Hartstein's arm and dragged him into the Underground's craft. The sliding panel closed behind them and for a moment they were swallowed up in the darkness. Hartstein wished that he had taken a last look at the sky, the sea, the sun: there was a moderately good chance he'd never see these things again.

Tipchak led the way. If this really was a ship from the future, Hartstein asked himself, how could Tipchak know his way around it? They passed by great boards of flashing lights, red, green, yellow. Digital meters measured one thing or another. Animated readouts spoke in low, sweet voices, advising the human crew members who ought to have been paying attention. The ship seemed deserted. No one minded the dials and controls.

"Where is everybody?" asked Hartstein.

"I don't know," said Tipchak. "They've just fought a hard battle; maybe they're celebrating. Or taking showers. Maybe they're watching tapes of the fighting and improving their skills."

"You're a big help," said Hartstein.

They passed along the corridor until they met one that crossed it and led deeper into the heart of the destroyer. They climbed up a level, then turned into another gangway, then down again, then to the left—after a while Hartstein was lost. He didn't think he'd ever be able to find his way to the outside again.

"This is the Commander's wardroom," said Tipchak. There was a solid steel bulkhead in front of them, with no hatchway evident. Hartstein waited for some futuristic miracle.

The solid bulkhead vanished. Beyond it was a spacious, comfortable room paneled in dark oak. The Commander sat at a long table of richly stained wood. He sipped from a glass of sherry and waited.

"Was that steel wall an illusion?" asked Hartstein.

"No," said Tipchak.

"Then where did it go?"

Tipchak shrugged. "I don't know how they did that."

"Secrets of the future," said the Commander. He indicated that Hartstein should take a seat at the table. He also indicated that Tipchak should get lost.

"So this is the Underground," said Hartstein. He looked around at the paneled study. "Nice."

"Thank you," said the Commander. "It's an illusion. The reality is gray-painted titanium-alloy walls with corrugations and rivets. But because this is a ship from the future, it has a few civilized features. I think these surroundings are much more pleasant, don't you? More conducive to, shall we say, plain speaking."

"Is that sherry an illusion, too?"

The Commander looked sad. "Yes, unfortunately, or I'd offer you some."

"You brought up plain speaking," said Hartstein. "How will I know when you're telling the truth?"

The Commander jerked, startled by the question. "You think I'd lie to you?" he said in a low, tightly controlled voice.

"I saw what you're capable of. I saw what you did to those—"

The Commander cut him off. "You saw an efficient and essential war-time operation," he said. "You saw the unavoidable human tragedy. You saw a cleanly executed military maneuver, planned by tactical computers, made necessary by the exigencies of this conflict. I do not need to debate the Underground's position with you; you know it already. But do not think that because my loyalties are not in harmony with yours, I am therefore a dishonorable man. I do not kill for the love of killing, but for the establishment of something you cannot even comprehend. Just because we are on opposite sides, do not do me the insult of assuming I am a criminal and a monster, a murderer, a liar and thief, a mad despoiler of women and children. You must believe my word, or else taste the sherry yourself. But then be prepared to accept the consequences."

Hartstein looked into the hard, stern eyes of the Commander and knew that he would never find out what was in the decanter.

The Commander waved a hand. "Let's talk about reality, shall we? You are aware that there's no such thing as an objective past."

"Yes, I've had that drummed into me again and again."

"Good." The Commander smiled pleasantly. "And the future?"

"I've been there."

"So you know. Can you make any statements then about the present?"

Hartstein didn't know what the Underground officer was driving at. "The present seems to be the only sane place in the universe. Where the four space-time lines come together. The only place where I really know what's going on and what's what."

"Ha ha," laughed the Commander, "how lovely if it were only so. But the present is another illusion you cherish, my son, as fragile and vulnerable as a soap bubble. The present exists with no more solidity than the oak paneling or the lush carpeting you can see but not touch."

"You must be trying to trick me," said Hartstein. He remembered what Brannick had told him: don't believe everything they tell you.

"Ha ha," said the Commander. "Why for all I hold dear would I want to trick you? Listen, what I want—and this is 'putting my cards on the table' time, you understand—what I want is for you to come to work for us. To work for the Temporary Underground against the evil forces of the Agency. There. Now that I've told you my ultimate goal, what point is there in fooling you?"

"Why me? What have I ever done? You want Sergeant Brannick or somebody like him."

"Sergeant Brannick!" said the Commander, smiling some more.

"You've met him?"

The Commander's brows narrowed. "Yes, son," he said softly, "we've met. But I want to talk about you. Why won't you switch sides and join the Underground?"

Hartstein shrugged. "Because I joined the Agency first. I gave them my word."

The Commander stared into space, evidently annoyed. "That's no reason," he said. "Do you even know what the Underground is trying to accomplish? Do you know what you're fighting?"

Hartstein's face flushed warmly. "Of course I do. You're trying to destroy the entire universe. What kind of sane organization wants to do that?"

When the Commander looked back at him, the man's eyes didn't seem to be those of a lunatic. "If the universe craves to return to its original state," he said evenly, "then we in the Underground are fighting the most holy of wars."

"I'll grant you that," said Hartstein with a tight smile. "But how can you make an assumption about what the universe wants? What did you get, a special little note from God or something?"

The Commander stood and indicated that Hartstein should follow him. "In a way, young man," he said, putting his arm around Hartstein's dirty, crumpled Agency tunic, "that's exactly what we've got. In God's own code, mathematics. One day, one of our people solved a series of very difficult equations that unlocked the meaning of life, death, energy, time, and all that kind of thing."

Hartstein was skeptical. They walked through the phantom study, through a narrow gangway dotted with tiny blinking lights. The Commander opened a round hatch, and Hartstein stepped into a bright room. This was the destroyer's Ops Center, but there were no conventional weapons in sight. There were blackboards and small computer consoles and several men and women with nervous expressions and lots of papers and reference material and source books. All the young men wore clip-on bow ties and all the young women wore white blouses with Peter Pan collars and circle pins.

"This is where it all happens," said the Commander proudly.

"Where what happens?" asked Hartstein.

The Commander suggested that they sit at one of the long tables. "Sister Spence, put up the Prime Sequence for this young man."

One of the Peter Pan collars nodded and began scribbling on the blackboard. It was a long, complex set of equations, but Spence never consulted her notes. Evidently they all worked with these expressions enough so that they were burned forever into their memories. When she finished, Spence had filled one whole board and half of another.

"It all equals zero," said Hartstein, thinking that the right side of the equations looked thin.

"Just mathematical fiddling," said the Commander in a friendly way. "We call them 'identities.' But bits and chunks of that huge group of equations can be pulled together into smaller units, factored out, rearranged. That makes it easier to deal with. For instance, when we realized that the exponent of θ^k"—he pointed vaguely into the morass of math— "had to be an even positive integer, it gave us the opportunity to establish temporary stability loci. Like here on Easter Island. Isn't that marvelous?"

"Terrific. But what about that quantity there in the ninth expression down? Didn't you divide through by $(3-f/3+f)$?"

"Of course," said the young woman. "That's the term for local conservation of random chronons."

"Then," said Hartstein, frowning, "the seventh term ought to be $5px^{n-3}-\mu$ all over $D_m V_c$. You've got the sign wrong."

The Commander looked at the blackboard for a moment. "Is he right?" he snapped.

Hartstein looked around, just a little stunned. How had he known that?

"He's right, sir," said Spence, doing some figuring with her slide rule. Some of the Underground's people were whizzes with the slipstick, taking less time to make computations than other people needed to punch the data into a computer terminal. All Hartstein could do with a slide rule was multiply and find square roots.

"How did you know that?" said the Commander in a dangerous voice. "Oh, it's obvious: the Agency outfitted you. When they prepped you for Easter Island, they peeked in here and gave you a little calling card. Quite amusing; how typical of Sergeant Brannick. I must do the same for him some time. How bad is the damage, Sister?"

The young woman shook her head slowly. "Very bad, sir," said Spence. "What it means . . ." She paused, afraid to go on.

The Commander put his kind hand on the young woman's shoulder. "Tell it to me straight," he said. Hartstein realized that the Commander was a wonderful man, just as full of compassion as Sergeant Brannick. Too bad they fought on opposite sides.

"It means that the sigma effect is . . . no effect at all. Not yet. We don't really have control over local stability the way we thought we had."

The Commander was silent. All the other young men and women in the Ops Center regarded him tensely. They were in a tough spot.

"Listen," said Hartstein. "You want to get rid of the $D_m V_c$ term or else the points along the various axes will stay equal no matter what you do. You can't do anything about V_c—that's a constant. So why don't you try to find values for D_m that will make the value of the denominator approach infinity? That will make the whole fraction negligibly small and that's where you can manipulate reality. You'll never be able to make $D_m V_c$ actually equal infinity, but you can come pretty damn close."

"Why, I think that'll work!" cried the Underground math star.

Hartstein just gazed at his feet shyly.

"Where did you learn that, boy?" asked the Commander.

"I was wondering that myself. Just the other day I couldn't add four doughnuts and six doughnuts. Today I'm solving high-order equations in my head. It's like my grandparents always say, that travel is educational."

The Commander sighed. "It's the Agency, youngster. You don't think that every time they give you the ESB preparation to go someplace, they don't take the opportunity to fill your head with all kinds of propaganda and who-knows-what as well? That's probably why you joined them so suddenly. They planted the hint on your first trip and reinforced it on your second."

Hartstein thought about it. "Why, those dirty—"

"Hold it a minute, son," said the Commander evenly. "They're fighting for their existence. They may be dead wrong, but they're struggling for their very way of life. They deserve a little respect for showing guts in the face of the inevitable."

"The inevitable, sir?" Somehow, this gruff, manly, likable Commander was just the kind of person Hartstein *wanted* to call sir, even though he was a leader of the enemy. Hartstein had trouble remembering that part.

"That equation," said the Commander, pointing to the blackboards filled with symbols. "You spotted the inconsistency in it, and we're awfully grateful to you. If you hadn't seen that, we might have begun our operations here in false security, and the Agency could have come roaring up our tails one fine morning. Now take a look at it again. Look deep. Do you see anything else? Take your time and look . . ." The Commander's voice was murmurous, confident, friendly. It was warm in the Ops Center, and Hartstein felt an overpowering desire to . . .

"Sir?" he cried.

"It's all right, lad," said the Commander, chuckling. "You just drifted off for a little while. You had a long day yesterday and a tough night. And this morning hasn't been at all restful. I was just asking you about the equation."

"Well . . ." Hartstein looked at the long strings of terms and bit by bit, like magic, they began to make sense to him. He began to see an interplay of forces, a cosmic balancing, that before had been only a cold scribbling of letters and numbers. "Why, what you told me before, it's true!" said Hartstein, astonished. "That is, if your mathematical reasoning can be trusted. It means that the universe is desperately trying to reform in its original condition, dispersed and quiet, and mankind is its greatest enemy, seeking to create filthy order where there should be peace."

"It seems so simple, doesn't it?" whispered the Commander. "Yet your Sergeant Brannick and the rest of the Agency forces have arguments, too, and I'm sure they sound just as good. But you can see for yourself: our story is told in unemotional algebra, the language of science. Their reasons are mere appeals to fear and selfishness."

"But . . . but . . ."

The Commander stood up and stretched. "It will take you some time to sort out all this in your mind. When you do, come see me and we'll have another talk. Until then, you'll have the freedom of my ship. Talk to anyone. Ask anything. You'll see what a marvelous and heroic task the Temporary Underground has assumed!"

Hartstein stared after him as the Commander left the room. Only Sergeant Brannick himself had ever inspired such devotion in him. "He's some man," said Hartstein. "And some leader."

There was a question he wanted to ask Spence. The young woman was coding material at her desk console. She looked up pleasantly as Hartstein sat down beside her. "Yes?" she said. "Can I help you?" She sounded just like a saleswoman at a perfume counter.

"The Commander said I could kind of wander around and ask questions. There's something I'd like to explain, if I'm not bothering you."

Her pleasant smile showed no sign of going away. Hartstein waited in vain for some word of encouragement. "Well," he said at last, "if the Agency can peek in here and copy down your whole Prime Sequence and arm me with some error you've made, then why couldn't they shut you down altogether a long time ago? I mean, all this peeking ahead in time and stuff."

"Oh," said Spence, dismissing the notion, "we peek ahead, too. We stay a step ahead of them, then they jump ahead of us, and it all evens out. By tomorrow we'll have the Prime Sequence fixed up and our math weapons back in order. We'll introduce some squiggle that will foul up their computations, and then *we'll* be back on top. You'll see."

"But isn't there an end to how much back and forth wrestling you can do?"

"Sure," said Spence. "It's not that difficult to establish the limits. You sum the series of the Agency's peeking, and you sum the series of the Underground's peeking, and whoever comes out ahead wins the war."

Hartstein was losing his patience again. "Then why the hell doesn't somebody do that already and let us all go home?" he cried.

Spence shook her head. This young man was evidently an idiot savant; maybe not even a savant. "Because a great deal depends on where you begin the two series. It's a matter of opinion who had the first advantage." She shrugged her shoulders; everything was supposed to be perfectly obvious from that point on, but it wasn't. Hartstein wished, not for the first time or the last, that he was back home pumping jelly.

"You're supposed to help me make up my mind about joining the Underground, aren't you?"

"Yes," she said. "That's why I'm here. You're supposed to like me, and I'm supposed to persuade you."

"And you knew all about me—"

"—because we peeked ahead and saw it all."

Hartstein closed his eyes wearily. "I can't stand it," he murmured.

"That's why I'm not bothering to try very hard. Nothing personal. Because we already know what your decision is going to be."

"Oh?" said Hartstein, interested despite himself. *He* didn't know what his decision was going to be.

"Sure," said Spence, "you're going to join us."

"So you're not going to try to talk me into it."

Her puzzlement didn't show in her expression. Her smile looked as though it had been applied carefully, in layers, with a fine brush. "Why should I?" she asked.

"Right. Never mind. How do you know—now, you realize this is just me talking out of my ignorance—but how do you know that this, right here, this Underground ship, isn't a quasi-past or a quasi-future I'm visiting? That you aren't any more real than those Easter Islanders were?

Maybe I'm real and you and all your buddies are just window dressing in the vast pawnshop of time?"

She thought over her reply for a moment. "You aren't married or anything, are you?" she asked.

Hartstein was startled. "No," he said.

"Didn't think so. Would you like to fool around a little? With me, I mean."

"Is that the Underground sales pitch? It's not very original."

Spence looked around furtively. "No," she whispered, "it's an idea of my own. I was thinking that if both the Agency and the Underground are working so hard to get you to cooperate, you must be very important. They must know that you're destined to do or discover something really big, something they wouldn't explain to us non-coms. And if that's true, well, I want to be with you when this whole thing is over."

Hartstein laughed derisively. "Me?"

Spence looked hurt. "Well, how do you know you won't? And why shouldn't I make a good deal for myself if I can?"

"No reason," said Hartstein. "But why should I want to fool around with you, if I'm such an important person?"

Spence glanced around again. "Because," she said. "Because I know how to make the past and the future responsive. To the present, I mean. So that the past will be the real past and the future will be the real future. So when you go there, you can trust what you see and hear and learn. I haven't told anyone else about it yet, and I need you to get there."

Hartstein felt a familiar, hollow coldness inside. "Get where?" he asked.

She snuggled closer to him. "You name it," she said.

And right then he recalled the words of Jesus in the courtyard of Jotham son of Nathan. Hartstein had been promised marvelous things and banners and great destinies. All he seemed to be getting was a girl with an Underground-issue smile and a quick hand on the slide rule. He felt somehow that he deserved more. Jesus had promised him too that Hartstein would know now what he must do. Jesus had been right about that; Hartstein did know. He wanted more and he knew how to get it: on the snow-white wings of the great soaring Bird of Time.

CHAPTER SIX

IN THE MEANTIME, IN BETWEEN TIME

Sister Spence was trying to explain a concept to Hartstein. "It's probably the most important idea in mathematics since the apple fell on Newton."

"Uh huh," said Hartstein. "It sounds like old-fashioned doubletalk to me. The kind of stuff that gets published in journals but never has any practical use."

"No practical use!" Spence was astonished by Hartstein's obtuseness. They were walking through the Underground destroyer's main galley. She led him into a small pantry. He turned on the lights, but she turned them off again. "If anyone comes in," she said in a low voice, "it will look like we're having physical intimacy. They're expecting that, anyway. How can you say something as stupid as that? This has more practical value than you can imagine. More than I can imagine, really. Let me undo a couple of buttons."

Hartstein was still dubious. "I still don't even understand what you're talking about."

"I can see that. Listen, it's simple. A long time ago, people believed that atomic particles were simple little charged things. Little bits of positively charged stuff, little bits of negatively charged stuff."

"Sure. I studied that in Outmoded Ideas 101."

"Then they found out that things could be partially charged."

"I learned that too," said Hartstein, "but I don't know what it means. It always sounded like being partially pregnant to me. Something either *is* charged or it *isn't.*"

"You're missing the point." Spence put a hand around Hartstein's neck and drew him nearer, just in case anyone came in and found them not being close. "A proton is supposed to have a certain unit charge for its mass. An electron is supposed to have a certain unit charge of the opposite kind for *its* mass. All of nuclear physics was built on a few basic ideas like that; but with the development of more refined measuring apparatus, some experimenters found out that their test results weren't exactly matching their predictions."

Hartstein kissed her just below the ear. "What does that have to do with your idea?" he murmured.

"Well, one of the founding principles of the Underground is that everything in the universe is tied together. You wouldn't know about that, being a dog of an unbeliever. But we think mathematics and physics and biology and everything are inseparable in the practical world. These aren't independent fields of study. They all operate under one single set of unified laws." She lifted his chin and kissed his lips, and he shifted his position so that his arm wouldn't dig into her back, and they learned that they could get very comfortable indeed in very little space. If they were discovered, they would look just like two young people not exercising self-restraint. It was a great plan.

"So?" said Hartstein.

"Here, let me help you with that. No, listen to me. If all that's true, numbers ought to reflect the real world, and not just the other way around. So I came up with the notion of partially signed numbers. Numbers that are maybe two-thirds positive and one-third negative. Or any combination at all. And that's how we're going to get out of this war."

"You came up with that idea? All by yourself?"

She shrugged. "I think I must have dreamed it. I woke up one morning and there were these notes on a pad beside my bunk, in my handwriting and everything. I just don't remember waking up and writing it all down. But the ship's computer hasn't been able to find any logical or operational flaw in what I want to do."

"Sister—"

"Call me Melissa."

"All right. Maybe you could move just a— That's better. What *do* you want to do?"

"You mean with my idea? I want to get out of here. At first glance the implications seemed to support the Underground's position. But then I realized that what it all really means is that life is more important in the universe than an eternity of emptiness."

They didn't say anything more for a few minutes while they attended to their camouflage. "Melissa," said Hartstein at last, "why did you tell me all that? When you know that I'm going to join the Underground?"

Her eyes opened wider. "You're not really, are you?"

"No, I'm not. But just a little while ago you said you knew that I was."

"Oh, *that.* Never mind about that. They told me you would, but after a while I could tell they were wrong. And that gave me a clue that my idea

is right, after all. That we can influence the past or the future, and escape
there if we're careful."

"Oh. What do you want from me?"

She raised her eyebrows. He kissed her lightly on the lips. "I can manipulate the reality," she said softly, "but I don't have a temporal tap. You do.
Help me to escape, and I'll help you. You must have found somewhere
you'd rather live than our present."

"Yes," he whispered.

There was a cool breeze from the hills, blowing the heavy afternoon air
away toward the jungle, and the voracious insects with it. Hartstein and
Melissa Spence stood on the banks of the river and watched the coffee-
brown water roll by. Behind them, in the African village, the native
women were chanting timeless rhythms as they prepared the evening
meal. It was 1914, German Central Africa, and this was where she had
decided to spend the rest of her life. Waiting for Charlie Allnutt to steam
by in *The African Queen*.

"Well," said Hartstein uncomfortably. He wiped the sweat out of his
eyes and wondered what else to say. He was still dressed in the Easter
Island outfit. His banana leaves were fraying badly.

"Yes, well," said Spence. If she had chosen, she could have given her
notion of partially signed numbers to the Underground, and they could
have used it to win the war. But she didn't want to do that.

If Hartstein had chosen, he could have given the idea to the Agency,
and *they* could have won the war. But he didn't want to do that, either.
"Oops," he said.

"What do you mean, 'oops'?"

"I just thought of something. It's not going to do me much good to hop
back to Alexandria. I don't have all the stuff the Agency gave me when I
went there the first time. I don't know if the ESB training lasts this long. I
might not know the language or anything. And I'm going to look awful
silly wandering around ancient Egypt dressed like this."

"I took care of that for you. It was just a matter of changing a couple of
digits 'way out around the fifteenth decimal place. I could make the past
any way you wanted it, so I just included a Hartstein appropriate to the
time. Good luck."

He hesitated to go. "You're sure you want to be here?" he asked. "I
mean, once I leave, you're stuck. You won't be able to jump out of this
past without a temporal tap."

She smiled. "It's all right. This is my fantasy past. Just as Alexandria is
yours."

"Okay, then. I guess I'll go." He gave her a kiss goodbye. "I wish you happiness, Melissa," he said. Then he took a deep breath and touched his temporal tap.

Dusk turned into afternoon. Central Africa turned into northern Africa. Hartstein winced in the sudden brightness, and noticed that he was dressed in the skirt and headdress costume, standing in the street in front of the Great Library of Alexandria.

Hartstein had crossed the street and started up the steps before a vague fear stopped him. There was something very wrong, but he didn't know what it was. He looked around: the Library, the people, the city looked just as they had the first time he had seen them. There was no obvious threat; none of the citizens looked like disguised Agents or rebels. What was he afraid of? Was it just the tension of seeing Pamari again? He suspected that she would have no memory of having seen him before, but he had the knowledge that she would soon be attracted to him. After all, they had done all that once before.

That thought identified the source of his uneasiness. Alexandria and the Library *shouldn't* look the same as they had. This was supposed to be the real past, the historical Egypt. "I don't understand," Hartstein thought as he climbed the stairs, "this is just a quasi-past." Melissa Spence's new mathematics didn't affect the real world, after all.

Following the initial shock, Hartstein accepted the idea. In some ways, living with Pamari in this mock Alexandria wasn't so terrible a fate. It beat all hell out of living in the present in the midst of an all-out time war.

As he swung open the great door, he thought that he had become some kind of guy, a real Agency rogue, romancing women in the enemy camp and women who never existed. The Don Juan of Time, that was Hartstein. He wore a crooked little smile as he entered the Library.

It was just as he remembered it: shafts of warm sunlight spearing down from the high windows, washing the stone floor; shelves of old books in black or brown or dull blue bindings; a scattered handful of people, some of them vagrants, some of them kids doing schoolwork, maybe one or two people looking for something interesting to read. And there, in the middle of the vast reading room, was the librarians' desk. And Pamari.

His heart started to pound so fast and so loud that it frightened Hartstein for a moment. His mouth was dry, but his hands were damp with perspiration. He approached the desk and waited. She was still the most beautiful woman he had ever seen.

"Hello," said Pamari, "can I help you?" Her violet eyes regarded him blankly for a few seconds. Then a rosy flush colored her cheeks. She dropped her eyes shyly.

"Hello," he said, "my name is Hartstein."

Things just got better from there. In a few minutes he had invited her to dinner and she had accepted. He browsed in the stacks until the Library closed; then he led her to the same inn where she had taken him on his first visit. "How nice," she said delightedly. "This is one of my favorite little places."

"I'm glad," he said. He poured her some wine. After a while they both relaxed a little.

For some reason that he couldn't explain, she was more interesting and more exciting than any of her twins throughout the mansions of time. He had cared for them all, as lovely reflections of Pamari, but only she was able to make him feel so joyful and so anxious at the same time. He was glad that he had his own temporal tap. It meant that he didn't have to worry about being recalled to the present abruptly, the way his previous meeting with her had ended.

After dinner they walked through the city, as they had once before; it made no difference to Hartstein that she had no memories of that other night. They had begun again. It seemed like so long ago, yet it had been only a few months. Hartstein's former life, the time before he joined the Agency, was impossible to retrieve, almost impossible to remember. But then, there had been very little about it worth remembering.

The full moon lit their way through the quiet streets of the city he had chosen as his new home. He hadn't even hesitated; he hadn't even thought to return to the present to say goodbye to his family. But that was because he believed Melissa Spence when she said she could transport him to the real past, where he could have the best of both worlds: Pamari and the true Alexandria.

The nearer they approached the houses and shops, the farther the shadows receded before them. It did not disturb Hartstein; he had grown used to that effect. He stopped and pulled Pamari into his arms. She pressed herself to him as he kissed her, and the strength of emotion he felt made him tremble. How odd that he had Sergeant Brannick and the Agency to thank for this happiness. Certainly he owed them for nothing else.

Fog billowed along the deserted street. The night was cool and sweet and clean, and the fragrance of unknown tropical blossoms filled the air. They walked on, speaking little, enjoying each other's presence, happy just to hold hands and be together. The fog swirled around their feet. Soon it had become so dense that they seemed to be wading knee-deep through it.

"That's strange," thought Hartstein. "Fog usually comes in off the water like a cloud. The only time you see fog like this—" he stopped again.

Pamari looked at him curiously. Hartstein turned to look behind him; everything was all right back there.

"What's wrong?" asked Pamari.

"Oh, nothing," he said. "It's just that I've only seen fog like this in horror films, rising from the ground in graveyards and like that. This doesn't look like real fog. It looks like vapors rising from dry ice spread around a sound stage." He laughed. "But you don't even know what I mean. I guess I'll just have to get used to living in a world that looks like an amateur theater stage set. But it's all worth it to me, sweetheart, because—"

He turned to Pamari. She wasn't there.

Hartstein looked around wildly. The street was just as deserted as it had been before. More deserted, because now he couldn't even see the ghostly backdrop of buildings. "Pamari!" he called. There wasn't even an echo. It seemed to him that he was in the middle of a vast, empty plain that stretched out forever in all directions. He looked up; the moon had disappeared, yet there was a mild suffusion of light. It didn't seem to be coming from anywhere. The fog lifted tendrils and wreathed him as he began to run through it. He ran in blind panic toward where he thought the Library should be. He called Pamari's name again and again. There was no answer, no sound at all. There was no sign of Pamari or of anywhere she might have gone.

At last, exhausted, he stopped. He didn't know where he was, but wherever it was it was nowhere. There was nothing to see, no buildings, no features to the landscape. Just the dim light and the creeping fog.

"Where the hell am I?" cried Hartstein, gasping air into his aching lungs. A terrible pain in his side doubled him over, and he closed his eyes for a moment. He calmed down a bit. When he straightened up and opened his eyes again, nothing had improved. There was still—nothing.

It was deadly quiet. The fog shrouded all sound, even the noise of his feet hitting the hard, unbroken ground. It felt like metal plate, an immense single sheet of it that now formed the floor of the entire universe. He lost track of the passage of time quickly, unable to say how long he ran in one direction and then another, searching for something, anything. It was as if he had fallen off the earth, into limbo. This was no real place and he was in no real time. That was all he knew.

With fumbling fingers he adjusted his temporal tap to return him to the present. He thought that if he found his way home, perhaps he could learn how to return to Pamari and remain with her. "It's Melissa's fault," he said, not hearing how near to hysteria his voice was. When he touched the tap, nothing happened. He went nowhere. Nothing changed. The fog rolled around him and the ghastly thin glow showed him only that he was trapped somewhere he could not even imagine.

Sergeant Brannick had warned him about this, about the world that existed when the bright moments of history had passed and all that remained was the eerie nonworld of between time. Sergeant Brannick had not even wanted to describe this place. Even he had seemed afraid.

After a while Hartstein wondered if this was what death was like. Perhaps that was an explanation: perhaps he was merely dead. If it was death, it was a disappointment. If it was some aspect of the real universe, it was terrifying; but if it was death, it wasn't so bad. Hartstein had not thought of death very often. To him, the immediate crises of daily life were more fearful than the vague threat of death. Of course, he was learning better.

Hartstein had had a nightmare once, about being lost or abandoned in the dark. He remembered it from childhood. It had ended with a hideous noise, like the rasping of a machined screw pulled from a hole in a sheet of galvanized iron, but infinitely louder. It had been the sound of the sky tearing. Hartstein looked up dazedly. He could not actually see the sky. There was just darkness above—not the blackness of the night sky, but the darkness of shadows in far, unlit corners. He crouched down and buried his head in his arms. "Get me *out of here!*" he screamed.

The end of the world was overdue, and he screamed again in the suspense. Any second now . . . Now . . . He felt the terror building, and he begged for deliverance. When the sky lit up like fire and the universe disappeared, God would find him all alone in this place, naked and lonely and worthless. He listened to the sound of the blood rushing in his ears.

When nothing happened after a long time, Hartstein looked up again. He saw fearful things. He saw time laid out like cards along a magician's sleeve. With one quick movement of the wrist the magician flipped all the cards over, but Hartstein knew he could not learn that trick. He knew that he could not even hope to grasp a single card, and that immense deck was too much for any man or any army of men to manipulate. He saw moments of his life etched into a strip of time. He saw himself now, in this instant, trapped on a frame of time. He saw everything that had ever happened in the world, each event caught irrevocably on a slide of time. He saw rows and ranks and files and strips and spools of time, unreeling and twisting off toward infinity.

He was not alone. There were evil things here, too. They ate at the edges of time. They browsed recklessly among the years, feeding greedily on hours of glory and days of shame. They left corruption and foulness on some of the frames. There were moments of unbearable filth and stench and absolute degradation, and Hartstein passed through them, pleading for an end to it. He had seen now what exists along with time, along with space, and they were loathsome, these things that chewed away at the borders of the real world.

A voice spoke to him. "Now, you see?" it said. "You didn't listen to me. You went and believed everything they told you."

"Sergeant Brannick?"

"Yeah. Come on, soldier, let's get out of here."

Hartstein looked around and spotted Brannick standing not far away, extending a hand toward him. Hartstein didn't understand for a moment. Maybe Brannick couldn't come any nearer for some reason. Hartstein went to him instead. It seemed to take forever. At last they clasped hands, Brannick pulled hard, and Hartstein lurched forward onto the Agency's recovery stage. He stood there for a while, breathing hard, shaking, looking at Brannick. The sergeant studied him gravely until Hartstein had control of himself again.

"Decided to take the long way home, didn't you, Corporal?"

"I guess so, Sergeant. But you don't know what I saw—"

"Stow it, son. I know. I've been in that place, too. I've been there more often than I want to think about. I've seen those things and I know. What you got to do is get over it as fast as you can. You're going to be dreaming about it for a while and every now and then you're going to start remembering and you're going to get the shakes. But it doesn't really exist, Hartstein. That place doesn't exist. Those . . . *things* don't exist neither. There's nothing to be afraid of."

It sounded as if Brannick were playing at mommy, going "There, there" and making it all better. Hartstein shuddered. "You're sure of that? How do you know they're not real?"

"For one thing, if they were real, we wouldn't be here now. The world wouldn't be here. They'd've eaten it by now. They'd've eaten all of time. How are you feeling?"

Hartstein looked around the familiar hall, and he felt giddy with relief. "I'll be all right," he said.

"Sure you will."

Hartstein watched as Brannick prepared a hypodermic syringe. "What's that for, Sarge?" he asked.

Brannick only smiled as he reached for Hartstein's arm. "You're going to be debriefed, soldier. Just relax. This won't hurt a bit." The last thing Hartstein thought before losing consciousness was that if his quasi-past had died and faded around him, then the same thing must have happened to Melissa Spence. Only there was no one to pull poor Melissa out of that evil place . . .

Hartstein awoke in his own bunk. He felt much better. He knew that the Agency had done something to him, had somehow removed the last traces of his fear, and he was grateful for that. He wondered what else they had done.

There was an envelope sitting on a chair beside his bunk. He reached for it and took out a sheet of paper. It said:

Enclosed please find one set of sergeant's chevrons. You came back with the goods. Brannick.

"I came back with the goods?" Hartstein mused. "How about that."

There was a knock on the door. "All right to come in?" called Sergeant Brannick.

"Sure, Sarge." Hartstein was curious if it was just coincidence that Brannick showed up as soon as he awoke. It could be just his usual trick of knowing what everybody had done and was going to do.

"You can call me Brannick to my face now, but remember I'm still top kick. They're giving out these stripes like they was only worth a nickel on a bar of soap. It's not like the old days." Brannick sat down with a grunt in the chair.

"What does this mean?"

"What? That note? Figure it out. It means while you were dreaming away, safe and sound and all tucked in nice, you had another review and they upped you another rating. A few days ago I was saving your ass, and today they think you're a sergeant." He shook his head mournfully.

Hartstein frowned. "A few days ago?"

"Uh huh. You still don't listen so good. The docs put you out for your own good, otherwise you might have had permanent hangovers from that time you spent you-know-where. When I was a recruit, they didn't think that was necessary. A lot of my pals are sitting around hospitals to this very day going *mrmee-mrmee-mrmee*. You guys sure got it soft now. Especially you, Hartstein. You keep lucking out. Since you came back, a lot of things have been going on. You missed a battle, a big one. We jumped on the Underground somewhere in prehistory. I don't even know when it was, we didn't see anything but prairie. It was one of their main assembly points. We must've knocked off a quarter of the rebel soldiers. Even captured one of their ships. Nothing too impressive; their ship, I mean. Couldn't have done it without that crazy stuff you brought back, the partial numbers business. That's what got you the promotion. *Not* the going AWOL."

"Does this mean I have to lead a platoon of my own men? I don't think I'm cut out for that."

"I don't think so, either. But you're a Special Agent, Hartstein. Just like me. I picked you and I trained you. You're kind of like my successor, son. That's why I risked scrambling my own brains to get you out of that fix you got yourself into."

Hartstein just blinked.

"Thank me or something," said Brannick.

"Thanks, Sarge. I didn't think I understood that number idea well enough for you to dig it out of my head."

"You didn't. But our weapons development people don't need much to go on. You brought back enough. That's what we sent you for, and you came through."

"Ah. So that's what you sent me for."

Brannick gave him a disappointed look. "What do you *think* we sent you for? Pineapples and coconuts beside the hula-hula ocean?"

Hartstein remembered what had happened on Easter Island. He remembered Pā-Eh-Ah-Me-Ah and Tipchak and the slaughtered natives and Melissa Spence. He knew better than to ask if it had all been worth it. "Anyway," he said, "it was fish and yams. Tell me what happened to the Underground forces on Easter Island after I left there."

Brannick shrugged. "We used their own trick on them. We pinched them off. They're stranded now, stuck between one millisecond and the next. It may take a billion years for that millisecond to pass."

"So they're in a kind of suspended animation? For a billion years?"

"I guess so; I've never experienced it myself. So that takes care of that runt, Tipchak. *And* the Commander. He's given us a lot of trouble in the past, but now he's socked in tight for a long time."

Hartstein thought of Melissa again. "There's no way to find her?"

"You mean the rebel woman?" Brannick just shook his head.

"Somehow you knew about her idea, and you sent me back to get it away from her. And you're just going to leave her in that awful place?"

"Listen, son, there's nothing we can do. Besides, she *wanted* to go there."

"Huh?"

"Didn't she tell you that she picked it out herself? That it was her fantasy past?"

Hartstein was confused. "You mean she's back in Africa? I thought—"

Brannick laughed, one brief, sharp sound. "You thought she was lost forever screaming in the dark in Cleveland."

"What do you mean, Cleveland?"

"Cleveland's what we call it, Hartstein, we veterans who've been there and seen the fog and seen those monsters munching away on time itself.

Because it's the deadest, emptiest place in the universe. There's a special little insignia you'll be getting, just for walking around in the place, like when you sail across the equator. You see, you basically blunder through and you come back and get promoted and ribbons and everything. I don't get a damn thing for bringing you back. Not that I'm complaining. But about that Spence woman. She did get herself to where she wanted. Her theory seems to work. But she wasn't able to do the same for you. When you jumped out of her past—which was a real past, but one she had created with her partial numbers—you jumped back into the flow of quasi-time. So you went back to a quasi-Alexandria."

Hartstein sat back, relieved. "Then she's happy," he said.

"I hope so," said Brannick. "And she's bottled up in her own private past. No one can get to her from here."

"That's good," said Hartstein.

When Hartstein awoke, he was in his own bed. Not in the Agency barracks, but at home, in his parents' house. He sat up and threw off the heavy feather comforter. It was chilly in the room. For a moment he couldn't remember why he was back in his parents' house. He thought about it a little longer; he still couldn't remember. He was dressed in flannel pajamas with cowboys on them. Some strong-smelling mentholated gunk had been smeared on his chest, like when he was a kid and had a cold. He hated the way the pajama top stuck to the stuff. He swung his feet out of the bed. The floor was cold. There was a pair of bunny slippers, and he put them on. Then he went to the bedroom window, high up under the eaves of the old house. He pulled aside the curtains.

The moon on the breast of the new-fallen snow gave a luster of midday to objects below. He could see the garage. The snowdrifts piled high against the door, glittering and sparkling and promising exhaustion if he was the one who was going to have to shovel that driveway clear. There were the tracks of a small animal across the snow in the backyard. The tree that had supported his old basketball hoop had been cut down the year before he graduated from high school, but it was standing now, just the way he remembered it. It was black and barren in the frozen winter night. He saw Lucky's doghouse. Poor old Lucky . . .

Hartstein didn't know what to make of all this. He put on his bathrobe and went downstairs.

His mother was waiting for him. "Look who finally woke up!" she said, laughing. She shook like a bowlful of jelly.

"Merry Christmas, son," said Hartstein's father gravely. He handed Hartstein a small package.

"Merry Christmas, Dad. What am I doing here?"

Mr. Hartstein led his son into the living room. There was a big Christmas tree near the picture window, full on the bottom, skinny on the top, just the way Hartstein's father liked it. He always said that he liked his women and his Christmas trees shaped like pears; everybody always got a laugh out of that. The tinsel had been put on carefully, branch by branch, and the little colored lights blinked a warm, happy welcome. But best of all, asleep on the living room carpet beside the couch in his old place, was Lucky.

"Lucky!" cried Hartstein. The old spaniel rolled over in his sleep.

"Sure, son," said Mrs. Hartstein. "What would Christmas be without Lucky? Or without the three of us together?"

Hartstein unwrapped his package. Inside, there was an envelope. He took out a sheet of paper. It said:

Sgt. Hartstein: This is not a quasi-past, although in some ways it may look like one. This past has been created for your benefit, but it is in every other way independent of the present. You could stay here forever, but we're not going to let you. You have work to do. You came back from Easter Island with serious doubts about the purposes of the Agency. It's not just for your peace of mind that those doubts must be answered—the fate of the world may ride on it. We are preparing another mission for you as soon as you return, which will be in twenty-four hours.

CAPT. D'AMATO

P.S.: Your folks sure are darn nice people.

"Who is Captain D'Amato?" asked Hartstein. He sat down on the plastic-covered couch while his father began to dig through the pile of presents.

"He came and he left that for you, dear," said Mrs. Hartstein. "He sure was a darn nice young man."

"This is for you, Ma," said Mr. Hartstein, handing her a big square Christmas package. "It's from Dick and Jane."

"How nice of them," she said.

Hartstein felt very uncomfortable. This scene seemed to be made up from memories he had of holiday seasons from his childhood. He could understand why the Agency would send him back here to rest and recuperate. But how did they expect him to find his answers? There was nothing here to sway him in either direction.

"Son," said Mr. Hartstein, "I'm glad you're awake now. I wanted to talk to you about the Agency."

"Uh huh, Dad," said Hartstein.

"You know, the Agency is doing its level best to make things good for everybody, not just here and now, but all around the world and in the past and in the future. They're a swell bunch of folks, and I really think you could do a lot worse than helping them out as much as you can."

"Your dad's right, son," said Hartstein's ma. "Do you remember that time your grandmother slipped on the ice and hurt her hip? Who do you think took her to the hospital? The Agency ambulance, that's who. And do you remember when your Uncle Ned didn't have the money to open his own hardware store, who loaned him the money? The Agency did."

"How are Grandma and Uncle Ned?" asked Hartstein.

His father looked at him curiously. "They're both dead, son. You know that."

"Oh. I just thought—"

His father cut him off by raising a hand. He looked just like the Commander doing that. "I know we haven't always seen eye to eye, my boy. And I know that sometimes I'm a gruff old man who seems to have lost touch with what you kids are up to these days. But believe me, son, I've never had anything but your best interests at heart. If you love your mother and me, you'll promise us that you'll do anything the Agency tells you to do."

Something was just a little fishy here, too. "Dad, I—"

The doorbell rang.

"Land sakes!" said Mrs. Hartstein. "It's five o'clock in the morning. Who could that be?" She got up and answered the door.

"Excuse me, ma'am, but I saw your lights on. I know it's awful early and Christmas morning and all, but I've had an accident. I was hoping—"

"Sergeant Brannick!" cried Hartstein. "What are you doing here?"

The burly Agent came into the living room, shaking snow off his handsome uniform. "Private Brannick, young man," he said, "but I hope to become a sergeant someday." His voice was serious but kindly.

"Sit down, Mr. Brannick," said Hartstein's father. "Maybe we have a Christmas present here for you too."

"So," said Brannick with a smile, "your son likes the look of the Agency uniform, eh?"

"I'll say he does," said Mrs. Hartstein. "All the young men of our community do. And I'll bet it's a hit with the young ladies, too."

"Ha ha," said Brannick, "I guess I can attest to that. Son, how do you feel about the Agency?"

Hartstein paused. This was just too much. "I love it," he said. "I love everything about it. I think it's the greatest thing in the whole wide world."

"Good boy," said his father.

"You have a sharp son there, sir," said Brannick.

"Don't we know it," said Mrs. Hartstein.

"Well, I guess I have to be going," said Brannick. "Merry Christmas to all, and to all a good night." He went back into the darkness from which he came.

"Is this real?" asked Hartstein.

"Of course it is, darling," said his mother.

They opened a few more packages and Mrs. Hartstein began making hot chocolate. The sky began to lighten a little above the Sikulowiczes' house across the street.

There was a knock on the front door. "My goodness," said Mr. Hartstein. He answered the summons. "Hello?" he said.

"Mr. Hartstein?" said a man's voice. "I was wondering if I could have a few words with your son."

"Certainly. Come into the living room. That's my boy right there, in the cowboy pajamas and the bunny slippers."

The gentleman who entered the room was very tall and lean. He had a handsome face that seemed to radiate intelligence. His eyes were dark and quick and magnetic. He wore an elegant camel's hair coat and he was smoking an expensive French cigarette. If the man hadn't evidently been so full of Christmas good-fellowship, his eyes and his pointed beard might have made him look absolutely satanic.

"Dr. Waters?" asked Hartstein, wonder in his voice.

"My boy," said the inventor of time travel, "I just want to tell you that if you had any doubts about what to do with your life, about where your talents would be put to the best use, about how you might guarantee your happiness and that of your loved ones, well, I'm here to tell you that the Agency is your best bet."

Hartstein gulped. He knew that few people had ever had the privilege of meeting Dr. Bertram Waters in person. "Dr. Waters, don't you remember me? You made a recording that I saw in the Mihalik Building. In the Time Museum."

Waters and Mr. Hartstein exchanged glances and chuckled. "Mihalik Building?" said the scientist. "Time Museum? I've never heard of them. And why would they want me to make a recording?"

Hartstein understood: this was a young Dr. Waters. "I must have been dreaming, sir," he said.

Dr. Waters nodded pleasantly. "Well, you're young enough to have your dreams in peace, son. But sooner or later you'll have to take up the responsibilities of adulthood. You'll have to do your duty so that other people, folks just like your wonderful mom and dad, can continue to dream in peace. And that's just what the Agency is all about."

"I know. God bless the Agency."

"By the way," said Waters in an offhand way, "this was buried in the snow outside your door. It's addressed to you." He gave Hartstein a soggy Christmas card. On the front was a sketch of a mouse in a nightcap, all settled in for a long winter's nap. Inside there was a message from the Time Marshals themselves. It said:

Sgt. Hartstein: You have done excellent work in the past. We hope you will continue to fight so diligently for the cause of truth and justice. You can aid us most by locating the headquarters of the Underground and getting as much information from them as possible. They seem to like you. We'll take care of the military end, but you must do the sensitive reconnaissance. Hope you and yours have a pleasant holiday season.

The Highest Echelon

"They want me to infiltrate the Underground again," said Hartstein with some disappointment.

"The Underground?" asked Dr. Water. "The Temporary Underground?"

"Yes, sir. But the only time I've ever encountered them has been in a quasi-past. I wouldn't even know how to begin looking for their headquarters in the present."

"Oh," said Dr. Waters, "I have their number right here." He gave Hartstein an embossed business card. "They have a toll-free listing, too, but that's just a recording. Well, got to run now. Merry Christmas, everybody." He let himself out.

Hartstein's mother came in with the hot chocolate. "Did that nice young scientist leave? Well, I guess that about wraps things up. Son, you ought to go back upstairs and get some more rest. You've got a busy day ahead of you."

CHAPTER SEVEN

THE DIFFERENTIATION OF SERGEANT HARTSTEIN

When Hartstein awoke, he was back in his bunk in the Agency barracks. "Refreshed?" asked Sergeant Brannick.

Hartstein rubbed his eyes. "Why, I've just had the strangest dream. And . . . and *you* were there, too."

"How curious. But it was only a dream, son. You were here all the time. Well, we've got a full day's work ahead of us."

"Yes, so my mother told me. You know, I didn't really trust that dream, Brannick. It felt too real. And too unreal at the same time. How do I know that I'm not still sleeping? How do I know that this isn't just a dream, too? How do I know that I'm not still in that foggy dark hell, what you called Cleveland? I could still be there. Maybe you never got me out of that place. How do I know I'm—"

Brannick looked stern. "We don't have time for that. You're supposed to be over all that by now, Hartstein. You're just going to have to take our word for it. You were just asleep, right here in your bunk. You didn't go nowhere."

Hartstein was skeptical. "If I didn't go anywhere," he said slowly, "why do I still have this?" He held up the embossed business card. Under the legend TEMPORARY UNDERGROUND and the phone number, it said *Operators Are Standing By to Take Your Call.* "I'll just bet they are," said Hartstein.

"I put that card into your hand," said Brannick.

"Dr. Waters gave me this card himself."

"Dr. Waters? Ha ha, that's a good one. *The* Dr. Bertram Waters? What would Dr. Waters want with a brainless ape like you? No, I put that card into your hand while you were asleep."

"Why?"

Brannick shrugged. "I was on my way out. I got tired of waiting for you, so I put it in your hand so you'd find it when you did wake up."

"I dreamed about this card. How could I do that?"

"Just a coincidence; happens all the time. Now, come on. There's a big mission on for today. You want to be briefed or not? If you'd rather lounge around all morning, we can send you into danger completely unprepared. It's your choice. You can end up holding your breath through all eternity just like that weasel, Tipchak."

"I'm coming, Brannick," said Hartstein grumpily. He dressed quickly and put the Underground's card in a pocket. "So what kind of mission is it?"

"You'll love it," said Brannick.

They walked down the hall to the Special Agents' briefing room, where the complex and carefully orchestrated operations of the Agency took shape. The room was already half filled with the regular officers and Special Agents who would carry out this fierce attack on the Temporary Underground. Brannick nodded to a man in a major's uniform. "He's all right now," said the sergeant, indicating Hartstein. The two sergeants took seats near the rear of the assembly, and the major went to the podium.

"Gentlemen," the major said, "today we will strike a crushing blow against the enemy. If fortune is with us, if we all do our jobs with precision, this may be the beginning of the end for the Underground. Captain D'Amato will give you the details of the combined operation."

Captain D'Amato was a handsome man in his early forties. He was tall and athletically built, with short, wavy blond hair and clear blue eyes. He wore a carefully trimmed blond moustache that gave him the devil-may-care appearance of a World War I fighter pilot. He carried a riding crop as a kind of personal signature. "Thanks to the invaluable work of Sergeants Brannick and Hartstein," said D'Amato, "we now have in our possession a weapon of terrible power. It is a mathematical concept that permits us to alter the reality of the past or future as we will. It also enables us to have certain limited control over how that past or future may influence our present." A murmur passed through the ranks of blue-and-silver-tunic-clad Agents. "Yes," said the captain, "we can now restructure certain aspects of reality by mathematical means. The exact process involved is most secret, so let us move on to how this weapon will affect what you will be asked to do today."

He pointed to a large map of the world. His pointer struck it in the middle of the Atlantic Ocean. "Here, gentlemen, is today's battlefield. Yes, I know it looks to you like an immense expanse of white-capped salt water, rising and falling in restless swells that mirror the infinite imagination of that Spirit which created and inhabits us all. That was the case yesterday, but it is not so today. This morning at approximately eleven hundred hours, the Temporary Underground will be attacked upon the beaches, upon the landing grounds, in the fields and in the streets, in the hills of the continent of Atlantis. I know what you're going to say: 'Captain D'Amato, there *is* no continent of Atlantis.' And how wrong you'd be. Today, there is a continent of Atlantis. It is occupied by the Temporary Underground, and we are going to go there and take it right away from them."

There was a pause while everyone tried to understand what the captain was talking about. Then, when only limited understanding came, a great and enthusiastic cheer went up instead.

D'Amato waited for the shouts to die away. "Atlantis was created in the following manner: There is a quasi-Atlantis which is often visited by tourists and is well-known to some of you. But it exists only in a vague and short-lived quasi-past, only because a sufficient number of our contemporary citizens have a kind of belief in Atlantis. If that belief were strengthened and made more definite, Atlantis would take on an even more elaborate existence in this quasi-past. As it is, the place fades away and dissolves into between-time in roughly sixty minutes.

"Using the new concept of partial numbers, we have been able to lift Atlantis out of its quasi-past and bring it to our present. We can maintain it here as long as we wish. We can throw it back into the past at any moment, or we can continue to support its existence here. It is the ideal place for a showdown with the Underground, endangering no civilians and subject to no accidental interference from them."

None of this seemed relevant to Hartstein, because he already knew what his assignment would be: to infiltrate the main body of the Underground at their objective-time headquarters. It didn't occur to him that they might have their headquarters elsewhere, in a quasi-past or future, moving from one to another as conditions required, or that they might have used Spence's partial numbers to establish a command post in a tailored pocket-universe to which the Agency would never have access.

"I think," said Captain D'Amato, "that since all the unit leaders have received their mission indoctrination files, that the best thing now would be to break up into your groups. Your unit leaders will give each of you your individual assignment and answer all your particular questions. Should there be any difficulties, please direct your inquiries to Major Li or myself. You'll have about two and a half hours to complete your planning sessions and to relay the orders to your platoons. Be sure to leave plenty of time for your logistical needs. There will be no ESB prep for this operation, because in moving Atlantis to the present we shifted all language and cultural factors of this novel setting to match our common present-day social environment. So you need not be concerned about the nature of the people of Atlantis, unless the Temporary Underground has been able to wrest those factors out of our control. In that case, no ESB prep would be effective in any event."

Sergeant Brannick indicated that Hartstein should follow him. "Our orders differ from theirs a little," he said.

"We have to dig our way into the Underground," said Hartstein. "At least, I have to. I don't understand why you're including yourself in; the Underground knows you too well. You won't be able to get by their security people."

Brannick nodded. "They know you, too, Hartstein. But that doesn't make any difference. They know we're coming, and they're waiting for us. Believe me, they want to talk to you. And they hope they'll be able to pry some secrets out of me. They won't. But their headquarters are on Atlantis, you know."

"Atlantis? But what about this card? With the phone number on it?"

Brannick dismissed the card without a glance. "That phone number is a dead end. All you get is their answering service. Their real headquarters are on Atlantis. It used to be in the quasi-past, phasing in and out of existence every sixty minutes to avoid falling into between-time, maintaining an objective continuity in a subjective time frame. They did it with Spence's partial numbers."

"So they're using that weapon too. I was afraid of that."

Brannick indicated that he, at least, wasn't terribly concerned. "The Underground and the Agency are able now to make massive adjustments in the rate of flow of time in any direction, and to the proper relationships in space as well. This war must end soon, or all the normal circumstances that human beings think of as sane and rational will disappear, and the world—the entire universe of observable phenomena—will dissociate into random, unpredictable events. All because of Melissa Spence."

"The Agency wouldn't allow that to happen," said Hartstein. "That sounds very much like the Underground's principal goal. Allowing a mathematical weapon to have that effect would be a tacit victory for the rebels."

"Exactly," said Brannick. "We have to use their tactics and their weapons for a little while, as much as we abhor them."

"At Easter Island, the Underground created more order than the universe required. And in Atlantis, the Agency is undermining order. The two sides have made a complete turnaround, a one-for-one reversal of roles and swapping of ideologies."

"So?" said Brannick. "We use whatever weapon comes to hand. We use the enemy's own program against it. And they do the same to us. Ironic, I suppose. But nevertheless, the end justifies the means, or else the Agency wouldn't even consider adopting the Underground's methods even for a minute. You can trust me on that, son."

They entered their ready room, where they could study their unique assignments as part of Operation Surf City. They sat at a long table and Brannick opened their envelope of orders. "Brannick?" said Hartstein. "I just thought of something."

Brannick said nothing; he gazed at the young man tiredly.

"If the past is subjective," said Hartstein, "and so is the future, that means to a large extent the present is subjective, too. There's no such thing as the present. Our world—I mean, the *real* world exists out there just as a matter of consensus. There's nothing to make the present any more solid than any random quasi-past we visit."

Brannick chewed his lip. "Son," he said, "every single person you've met since you first walked in the Agency's front door has been trying to tell you that. I've told you that at least three times. The people in the past and in the future told you. Melissa Spence told you. Your friend the weasel told you. Even the Commander himself—damn his eyes—tried to tell you. But you've been too bubblebrained to understand. You've clung to the ancient idea that the earth is something special, and that there's something holy and inviolate about the present moment. It's the only thing that's hindered you as an Agent. Until you made that realization, you were doomed to spend the rest of your life as a mudface sergeant, taking orders and charging blindly into the claws of the enemy. But I sure am glad to hear you say what you just did. You should be fine from here on."

"Thanks, Brannick, I guess. But you didn't catch what I meant. How can the Agency rationalize fiddling around with the present? Introducing a whole new continent full of cities and people and culture that we'll have to deal with. Fighting like that in a quasi-past is fine and good, but tampering with the present seems an unforgivable act of desperation."

Brannick put down the papers he was looking at. "Hartstein, you're not seeing the big picture. The Underground is right, as far as a few points are concerned: the universe is tied together by a single very simple set of laws. Those laws can be expressed easily in equation form, although some of the equations themselves require complex and sophisticated mathematics. Your friend Spence was right about all that, but she was wrong when she thought the Agency's beliefs contradicted hers. We have to believe the same thing; otherwise, why would we be so concerned about what the

Underground wants to do? The rebels are trying their best to disrupt these equations. On one hand you have the Underground threatening not merely to harm the world, but to eliminate it entirely. From that point of view, all the Agency is trying to do is maintain the status quo. And yes, we are desperate. Desperate to stay alive. Do you have any moral objection to that?"

"No," said a chastised Hartstein. "But I wonder why the Agency has chosen to be so shifty. So out-and-out fraudulent. I can see right through its ploys sometimes. For instance, why is everyone so nice to me? I mean, when I visited my folks in that 'past,' my father was acting like kindly old Dad. He never acted like that in real life. You were kindly old Private Brannick. Kindly old Dr. Waters. And the Underground is the same way —kindly old Commander. Do you people think I'm buying that act? I'm not as stupid as I look. I'm going along with everything until somebody slips up. I wouldn't be at all surprised to find out that the Agency and the Underground are the same people. And every one of you is old and kindly."

"Uh huh, Hartstein. Are you finished? Because we have other things to worry about. Atlantis, for one."

Atlantis was a nice place. It looked a little like the Greek islands. There were low, round hills of bald rock with small goats climbing around looking for something to nibble on. There were short, broad trees bearing strange-looking fruit and scrubby bushes with exotic flowers. There was the fragrance of roses and the faint sound of reed pipes everywhere. Fluted columns as creamy white as magnolia blossoms lay in ruins on the hillsides, and in the distance there were the baroque towers and battlements of the capital of this unreal land.

The main attack was centered on the southeast side of the island continent. Brannick and Hartstein were delivered farther to the north, about four miles from the battle. They had another mission.

If the number 2 means the same thing to everyone in the world, if it can be counted on to stay the same thing forever, then human minds can proceed to learn, to build, to provide for themselves necessities and luxuries, life and culture. Civilization is based on a few essential definitions, many of them unspoken because there has never been a need to enunciate these things: that life is better than death, that right is better than wrong, that civilization is worth something after all. But the Temporary Underground had done the thing no one had ever had the mad courage to do; they declared these things and then rejected them, one by one and in combination.

How would the world look today if man had not been able to trust the universe to stay constant in some regards? Perhaps there would be no people at all. Perhaps without a means of exploiting his natural intellectual superiority, man might have been eliminated by stupider and stronger natural foes. If, for instance, the number 2 was made equal to 1.999996, there would have been no basis for human minds to build the towering edifice of civilization upon. The number 4 would still be the same by definition, but it would not equal 2 times 2, which now equaled 3.999984000016. From the discrepancy between the two, a powerful force was released which could destroy forever the progress of millennia. It was possible now to do just that, to assign new values to old constants, to make the rock-solid science of mathematics a quicksand which would swallow up first physics and chemistry and then cosmology and ultimately all life itself. But it was the Agency's weapon, and the Agency had no intention of destroying the universe, only that little bit of it that represented its enemies. It was a weapon that could only be used with the greatest caution.

"Take a look at that," said Sergeant Brannick. He passed the field glasses to Hartstein. They were crouching behind a low wall of bright yellow ceramic tiles that bordered a wood of aromatic evergreens. A broad road paved with some tough green material led through the trees; at the far end of the road there was a large estate of some kind, a palace or villa, with a collection of smaller buildings nearby, all roofed with strange squat domes and towers of brilliant polished metal.

Hartstein looked through the glasses. The glare from the bright roofs hurt his eyes. There was a banner hanging from a balcony of the main building: BRANNICK AND HARTSTEIN YOU ARE FOOLS AND YOU WILL DIE LIKE FOOLS. "Oh hell," murmured Hartstein.

Brannick laughed. "You got to learn to expect that, son. It's just a psychological trick of theirs. Don't let them have the satisfaction of upsetting you."

"But how did they know we were coming?"

"They knew, that's all. And we knew they knew. So we're coming anyway, because they won't expect us to."

"Did they peek ahead? Is that how they knew?"

"Right," said Brannick.

"Then when they peeked, they saw that we knew they knew, and that we were coming anyway. So they won't be surprised."

"Well, when we peeked, we saw that they knew we knew, and we gave up and went away. So we won't."

"So what good is all this peeking if it doesn't necessarily mean anything?"

Brannick shook his head. "You have to have some kind of military intelligence to go on. You just can't waltz into a battle unprepared." To Hartstein, Brannick's reason sounded about as effective as the native warriors on Easter Island jumping and whooping around a bonfire before a fight and waiting for a mystical sign from the Sun God.

"What do we do?" asked Hartstein.

There was silence while Brannick stared through the glasses for another few seconds. "We do what we're ordered to do. We reconnoiter around the Underground's headquarters. We make a decision concerning the possibility of attacking and capturing the building and its contents, and we return with that information to Marshal Farias. This is how we're going to do it. You go all the way around through the woods and approach the building from the rear. Stay out of sight as long as you can. Estimate the number of Underground troops guarding the place, inside and out, and the number and type of weapons they're using. See what they have in the way of defenses, gun emplacements, armored vehicles, and so forth. I'm going to go straight down the road and try the same thing from the front. I don't expect to get very far, but it will take the heat off you."

Hartstein frowned. "What are you going to do if you get captured?"

Brannick gave him a little smile. "I've got my temporal tap. I'll just hop back or ahead a little."

"That's no good, Brannick. If you stay in the future for ten years, when you come back to now you'll still be a prisoner."

"Maybe I just won't come back. If they have me lined up against a wall and I'm staring down the barrels of their rifles, I'll go and I won't come back."

"But—"

"Shut up, Hartstein," said Brannick softly. "Just go do your job."

The two men went in opposite directions. Hartstein looked over his shoulder; Brannick was not looking back. He was marching slowly down the long road toward the headquarters of the rebel army. Hartstein thought that the sergeant had the best posture of anyone he had ever seen.

The sky was as clear as if God had washed it and left it out in the fiery sunshine to dry. A light breeze whipped the upper boughs of the evergreen forest. Birds sang and called to each other; Hartstein wondered what kind of birds they were. He angled through the trees away from the building until he covered what he guessed to be about half the length of the road. Then he cut back toward the Underground's headquarters. After about a quarter hour he came upon the back of the spacious clearing in which the villa stood. He lay down among the slender saplings on the edge of the clearing and studied the rear of the stone building. There didn't seem to be anyone about. He saw no defenses of any kind; that bothered him a great deal. There was nothing to stop him from rushing from his place of concealment and reaching either of the two large bronze doors that led into the villa. That bothered him, too.

About now Sergeant Brannick should be reaching the front of the building, encountering whatever sort of defenders the Underground had stationed there. Hartstein heard nothing but the twitter and chirp of birds high above him. Then, suddenly, there was something more. There was a low hum and a rumble, so far away that he felt the sound more than he heard it. The vibrations increased in strength and the pitch of the noise rose until it became almost painful. The ground shook and the trees flailed the air as if caught in an invisible storm. A small pane of glass shattered in one of the villa's windows.

And then a familiar craft screamed down to a shuddering landing on the grass, not fifty yards from Hartstein. The outline of the thing was unmistakable. If it wasn't the Commander's craft from the quasi-future, then it was a sister ship. Hartstein thought for a moment, undecided whether he should continue with the reconnaissance and risk being spotted by the crew of the Underground destroyer, or return to the Agency invasion headquarters to report the ship. The weapons that craft carried could devastate the Agency positions.

An amplified voice boomed from the destroyer. "SERGEANT HARTSTEIN! WE SEE YOU IN THE BUSHES. THERE IS NO REASON TO BE AFRAID. PLEASE, COME ABOARD. WE ARE MOST ANXIOUS TO SPEAK WITH YOU."

"I'll just bet you are, anarchist swine," Hartstein growled.

"THERE ARE FACTS CONCERNING THE AGENCY THAT ARE KEPT HIDDEN FROM YOU. WE FEEL THAT IF YOU KNOW THESE THINGS, YOU MAY BE PERSUADED TO WORK WITH US WHOLEHEARTEDLY. YOU ARE UNDER NO OBLIGATION OTHER THAN TO LISTEN TO OUR ARGUMENTS WITH AN OPEN MIND. OTHERWISE YOU WILL BE BLASTED INTO YOUR CONSTITUENT ATOMS IN TEN SECONDS. NINE. EIGHT. SEVEN. SIX—"

Hartstein jumped to his feet and sprinted across the carefully trimmed lawn to the Underground ship. He pounded on the place where he thought the sliding hatch should be. "Let me in!" he cried. "I'll listen, I'll listen!"

The hatch slid. "VERY GOOD, SERGEANT. PLEASE, COME IN."

Hartstein stepped into the craft; the hatch closed behind him, and in the blackness he felt as if he had been swallowed by a giant fish. That was him, all right, Old Jonah. Or Pinocchio, at least.

Pinpoints of colored light flickered around him. There was a low-pitched hum and a rattling racket that sounded like an ice machine. Once again Hartstein wondered where all the crew members were. He wondered how he was going to find his way about the ship. This one seemed identical to the Commander's, which was still locked into the Easter Island quasi-past. Even if it were identical, Hartstein wouldn't know his way around. The only part of that craft he remembered clearly was the pantry where he had had such an interesting conversation with Melissa Spence, but he knew he couldn't hope to find even that familiar place in the maze of gangways.

"So, Hartstein, we meet again."

"Yipe," said the young Agent, startled. He turned around, but he saw no one in the darkness. "Who's there?"

"Me," said the voice, "Tipchak."

"Tipchak! But you're—"

"Dead? Not me, pal. Not old Tipchak. I'm too tough to kill. It'll be a long time before the Agency finds a way to get rid of Terrible Tipchak, Time Rogue."

"Then this *is* the Commander's ship. But it's supposed to be stuck back on Easter Island. The Agency played the Underground trick of distorting the temporal coordinates. You're all supposed to be trapped forever in some kind of stasis."

Hartstein heard Tipchak's disgusting snicker. "But we're not. The Commander gave orders to follow you and that Spence person after the two of you disappeared. Our monitoring equipment registered your escape, but it gave us ambiguous data about your destination. The Commander was not at all pleased about losing Sister Spence and her partial-number theory, although it was all recorded in our ship's computer. But he was afraid that she'd given it to you, and that you'd take it to the Agency. Which is, after all, precisely what happened. But he's willing to let bygones be bygones. He's a very forgiving man, Hartstein."

"So you left that quasi-past before the Agency sealed your particular Easter Island off. I can't say that I'm thrilled to see you again, Tipchak. I thought you were something I never had to worry about again." His eyes had grown accustomed to the darkness, and he saw the little weasel standing nearby.

"Let's go. The Commander is waiting." Tipchak turned and headed down the corridor. Hartstein followed, lost in urgent thought.

After a while they stood before the metal bulkhead that was the entrance to the Commander's wardroom. The bulkhead vanished, just as it had on Hartstein's previous visit, and the Commander was just as he had been then, seated at the table, drinking quasi-sherry from a cut-glass decanter. The Commander smiled broadly at Hartstein. "Come in, Sergeant," he said. "Join me. You've made quite a name for yourself since last we spoke. Tipchak, go find something to do. Leave us alone."

There was a resentful grunt from Tipchak, and the small man went off to do something despicable in another part of the ship. Hartstein took a seat across from the Commander. The kindly old Commander, he reminded himself. This leader of the Underground was not as trustworthy as he wanted Hartstein to believe.

"Some sherry?" said the Commander.

"Sherry? Real sherry this time?"

"Yes, real sherry. I stocked up when we returned to our base. Atlantis is —or was, I should say—a major producer of sherry in ancient times. Or it is now, after I made a few adjustments in their reality. Just a matter of altering a few numbers here and there. But it's actually quite acceptable as sherry, don't you think?"

"Very nice. You want to talk me into betraying the Agency, isn't that it?"

The Commander laughed, a pleasant, innocent sound. "You seem very defensive today, son," he said. "The last time you were here, you enjoyed yourself more. A shame Sister Spence is no longer with us, but if you look around, perhaps you'll discover that such friends are easy to find in the Underground."

"You can stop throwing your women at me, Commander. I'm not going to sell out the Agency and allow you to destroy the universe for the sake of a few moments of pleasure."

"I didn't mean anything of the kind," said the Commander. He looked a little hurt. "Sometimes young people forget who their real friends are. But enough of that. Let me make a few points about the Agency. Then I want you to think over what I tell you, ask me any questions you may have, and be certain that I'm not trying to con you into anything you don't want to do. That's all I ask, that you listen to the truth, and that you evaluate it fairly."

"Fine," said Hartstein. "Where's Sergeant Brannick?"

"Brannick? Did he come with you?"

Hartstein bit his lip and said nothing.

The Commander decided that the best thing was to change the subject. "Have you ever wondered whose Agency it is?" he asked.

"What do you mean, 'whose'? It's everyone's Agency. It's a service to everyone."

The Commander allowed himself a brief smile. "How naïve you are. I don't believe I've ever met so naïve a sergeant before. Do you know what they call you behind your back? They call you 'The Candide of Time.' Hartstein, the Agency controls a vast, almost unimaginable amount of power, not to say material wealth. Are you so certain that this gathering of power is for the benefit of all mankind?"

"You can't deny that the Agency has provided material comforts to every single person on earth. There is no poverty anywhere. Great steps have been taken to eradicate many diseases. The—"

"I know. I do grant the Agency its due in these areas. But these things were unavoidable, don't you see? Even the most evil governments in history provided some benefits to their populations. And next you'll tell me that the Agency is not a government, but I disagree. It has all the privileges of a government without the blessing of legitimacy. The Agency has been consolidating power for many years, and those who control the Agency therefore control the world—the world as we know it, the world as we'd like to know it, the world as we will wake up tomorrow and find it. However that may be."

"No one controls the Agency," said Hartstein.

"You're wrong," said the Commander softly. *"One person* controls the Agency. The supreme power and wealth that the Agency has accumulated is all in the hands of a single demented man. Would you care to take a shot at guessing who it is?"

"I don't have the slightest idea. Sergeant Brannick, maybe."

"You fell into an elementary trap, son, although in this case it happens that I was telling the truth. When I asked you to guess, you said that you couldn't, which implies that you have accepted the premise that someone is, in fact, in control of the Agency. Which is true, as I said, but you still shouldn't let people bully you with polemical gimmicks. No, it isn't Sergeant Brannick. It's Dr. Bertram Waters."

"Dr. Waters! That's crazy. Dr. Waters died more than fifty years ago."

The Commander drummed his fingers on the table impatiently. "The fact that Dr. Waters died in any given year does not rule out the possibility that he may have lived the majority of his life in a time decades later than that year. We have time travel now, son."

"I know that. But when you go into the past or the future, it isn't real. I've spent months having that drilled into my head. So if Dr. Waters lived many years ago and invented time travel, and used it to go into the future to live, he arrived in a quasi-future, not what we call the real present. He couldn't be here to control the Agency."

"There! That was fine reasoning." The Commander beamed at his ace student. "But you neglected one thing. What if Dr. Waters had help from the real future, from a time when legitimate time travel has been perfected, when people can travel back to the true past or ahead to the true future?"

"That couldn't be," said Hartstein. "There's never been the slightest sign of any such visitation from the true future."

"None that you know of," said the Commander. "Maybe the Agency or a part of the Agency is guarding that knowledge jealously, for its own nefarious reasons. Maybe Dr. Waters is alive at this moment, manipulating you and the rest of the Agents who are out there giving their lives, and manipulating the Underground too and the poor citizens of the world. Can you grant that possibility?"

It took a little thought. When no one was speaking, the Underground destroyer made gentle background noises like a kitchen full of appliances at midnight. "Commander," said Hartstein at last, "if I grant that possibility, *you* must grant the next logical step."

"Which is?"

"That from this war the Agency must emerge the victor, in order that the world survives into that future from which Dr. Waters has received the help in the first place."

"My, somewhere in the last few weeks you've really learned to think. But no, what you're saying isn't necessarily true."

Hartstein felt it happening to him again; a thundering wave of words and fallacious arguments and convoluted reasoning towered above him, ready to crash down and drown him. "How can it mean anything else?" he cried.

The Commander took a deep breath and let it out slowly. "Although there is a 'true' future, son, it is only true in the sense that it exists as a result of our actions in the present. What we mean by 'true future' is in reality a finite though immense set of alternate futures each of which could develop with equal probability from the world as we know it at this instant. With every passing second the set of possible futures changes; some futures are eliminated as impossible under the new circumstances, while others are created by the same situation. Dr. Waters received help from people in one or another of these potentially true futures. But there are futures equally likely in which the Underground wins this conflict, and you know what that entails."

"Hopelessness," said Hartstein.

"We prefer to think of it as an absence of the degradation of the nature of the universe."

"Whatever."

"Did you know that the Agency has begun a program of educating people through their ESB sessions that not only is the Agency all-powerful, but that it has *always* been all-powerful?"

That point bewildered Hartstein. "What good does that do?" he asked.

"It reinforces the Agency's grip on the present. Soon people all over the world will believe that the Agency has been in existence since the dawn of time; then, when anyone visits a quasi-past in any period or place at all, the Agency will be there. As the ruling force. At that point, the Agency will have won the last shreds of power remaining in the hands of the free individual. There will be a tyranny such as the world has never known, and it will last forever because no one on earth will think it possible to exist without the Agency."

The notion chilled Hartstein. He knew it was very plausible; the Agency certainly had the means, and they had been giving tourists and students and adult citizens ESB training for many reasons for years. It would not take long for the Agency to accomplish what the Commander suggested. "That's the most horrible thing I've ever heard," said Hartstein.

"Good! Then you'll—"

"But eliminating the universe altogether isn't a rational solution, either."

The Commander wasn't upset by Hartstein's ambivalence. "We never expected you to become our fanatic supporter, lad. We don't count on your working tirelessly toward our ultimate goal, although we'd love to have you. We ask but one thing from you, and that's this: help us to keep the Agency from winning *its* ultimate goal of absolute and eternal domination. Your conscience will be clear; you can do that without necessarily aiding us. Do you see?"

Hartstein nodded slowly. Perhaps there was a way of blocking the Agency without clearing the way for the Underground. And vice versa. It required some thought . . .

"Will you work with us?" asked the Commander.

"Yes," said Hartstein, "up to a point."

"Fine. We will not ask you to compromise your principles or endanger yourself or your friends."

Hartstein had yet to see how that was possible. "What do you want me to do first?" he asked.

"We want you to prevent the Agency from destroying the Underground command center here in Atlantis. If we can win this battle today, we will move our headquarters elsewhere, and Atlantis can be returned to its proper quasi-past."

"A stalemate," said Hartstein. "I suppose you have just the right way for me to go about it, too."

"Of course." The Commander smiled and poured him some more Atlantean sherry.

Captain D'Amato looked worried. This operation wasn't going so smoothly as headquarters had hoped. Agency men were dying by the hundreds on the beachhead. The Underground seemed to anticipate their every move. And the Underground had some grotesque weapons that the Agency knew nothing about. Of course, the Agency had a few tricks left up its silver and blue sleeve.

The captain stroked his blond moustache and waited. He could do nothing more until he received reports from the forward positions. Marshal Farias himself would arrive in a few minutes, and then the headquarters staff would begin to revise the strategic timetable. It was obvious now that some revision was necessary.

The Agency had taken over a farmhouse just south of the landing areas for use as a makeshift field command post. Captain D'Amato looked out a window toward the ocean. Bright violet beams of energy split the air above the Agency positions. There was the eerie, intermittent noise of a battlefield, the booming of guns and the cries of dying men reduced to mild and gentle sounds by the distance. A young lieutenant knocked briefly on the door and entered the room. "Captain," he said, "Sergeant Hartstein is back."

"Just Hartstein? Brannick's not with him?"

"No, sir." That was more bad news.

D'Amato rubbed his temples and waited for the news to get worse.

"Captain D'Amato, sir," said Hartstein. "I've just come back from the Underground headquarters in Sector Six. I've had an interview with the Commander."

"The Commander! But he's supposed to be out of this war. Or did he come here from a point before we trapped him in the Easter Island quasi-past?"

"No, sir," said Hartstein. "He and that destroyer from the future managed to escape. But he believes that I'm willing to cooperate with the Underground, and he thinks he has reason to trust me. I have the entire rebel battle plan."

D'Amato just stared for a moment. This was news better than any he could have hoped for. The difficult situation in Atlantis could yet be turned around. "First," he said, "before we discuss that, what of Sergeant Brannick?"

"Captured, sir. He's somewhere in that main building, I'm sure. I was too closely observed to do anything about him. I felt my primary duty was to get back here with their strategy."

"Exactly right, Sergeant; but don't worry about Brannick, he'll take care of himself. They won't get anything out of him. And we'll get him out of there if we have to take this whole unreal continent apart stone by stone. Now, let's see what you have."

Hartstein took a seat by the captain's table and began telling him the falsehoods invented by the Commander. Hartstein knew this would cost the lives of thousands more unlucky Agents; he felt like a filthy traitor.

In response to the deceptive Underground plans, Captain D'Amato ordered a company of men to charge the enemy's left flank. The left flank was supposed to be vulnerable; it was not. The company was decimated, and as twilight fell on Atlantis the news of the disaster came to the darkened farmhouse. Marshal Farias brought it himself, muttering orders into his wrist-communicator. The noise of the weapons never ceased, nor did it grow quieter as it should have, had the Agency forces been able to leave the beach and storm inland toward the Underground stronghold.

"Did you send Company B into the Underground's left flank?" asked Marshal Farias. He seemed almost exhausted by the long and terrible battle.

"Yes, sir," said Captain D'Amato. He and Hartstein stood at attention.

"And you did so without consulting Major Li or myself?"

D'Amato winced. "I thought it necessary to take advantage of a momentary weakness in the enemy's position, sir," he said.

"A weakness that did not, in fact, exist."

"Yes, sir."

Marshal Farias gazed around the bare room. "Where did you acquire this information?" he asked.

"From Sergeant Hartstein, sir, who had just returned from the Underground's headquarters."

Farias turned his cold black eyes on Hartstein. "Why—"

Hartstein touched his temporal tap and was gone.

The Commander had promised him two things in return for Hartstein's aid: that Hartstein would be able to escape into the real future, with the assistance of the Underground and its manipulation of partial integers; and that when Hartstein wanted to return to the present, he could do so at whatever place he wished. Hartstein had chosen to return to the Underground's Atlantean villa, figuring that if the Underground was going to hold off the Agency in this battle, then it would be foolish to return behind Agency lines, to try to explain to Marshal Farias and Captain D'Amato what had gone wrong. And if the Agency did win the battle after all, then he could be there for the moment of victory.

"So this is the real future, at last," murmured Hartstein. He looked around; he wasn't in Atlantis any longer, but rather back in the Agency Building. It was familiar and comforting. When he looked through the windows, he saw no towering needle-thin skyscrapers or monorails or fourteen-lane highways or any of the things he had seen in the subterranean quasi-future he had visited. Hartstein reminded himself that this wasn't, in fact, *the* real future but *a* real future. He walked down the hall toward the Agents' briefing room. He stopped by a door that in the present opened into an administrative office suite. Now there was a peculiar legend on the door: DR. BERTRAM WATERS, CHAIRMAN, PLASMONICS DEPT. Hartstein paused with his hand on the knob, then shrugged and opened the door.

Inside, there were two people in white lab coats standing beside an immense wall of complicated electronic equipment; it was all bizarre futuristic stuff, and Hartstein recognized none of it. He did, however, recognize the two people. One man, tall and dark with magnetic eyes, was the elder Dr. Waters he had seen so often in historical documentaries. His chief assistant was himself, the Hartstein of this future.

It was a little startling to see himself standing there smiling, looking no older, no more the worse for wear. "Hello," said Hartstein$_1$.

"Hello," said Hartstein$_2$. "We've been expecting you. I suppose you've come from the Battle of Atlantis. Operation Surf City, right?"

"Yeah. Do you remember that?"

"Sure," said the Hartstein of the future. "Do you want me to tell you how it all comes out?"

"What good would that do me? I can't trust anything I learn in a quasi-future."

Hartstein$_2$ laughed.

Dr. Waters nodded sagely. "This isn't a quasi-future, son," said the inventor of time travel. "Do we look like insubstantial spooks to you?"

"You look like all the other nonexistent people I've ever met. How do I know this isn't a quasi-future?"

"Because the Commander explained that he was sending you into a real future, didn't he?" asked Hartstein$_2$.

"Can I trust the Commander?"

Dr. Waters went to a desk and unlocked a drawer. He took out a file folder and handed it to $Hartstein_1$. "This is for you," he said.

"What is it?"

"It's a complete summary of everything you need to know to function without your usual handicap of ignorance," said $Hartstein_2$. "Everyone has been telling you the truth, but only in part. Of course, everyone has been lying to you some of the time, too. Those pages will clear up everything for you and give you some ideas about how to handle the next few important developments. Consider it a gift from an infinitely benevolent universe."

"Thanks," said $Hartstein_1$. He glanced at the folder; there were twenty-five pages of notes, covering both the Agency and the Underground, along with suggestions for improving his relationship with his father, good grooming hints, and a recipe for a radical variety of futuristic doughnut. Of course, this was merely one of a set of possible real futures; if the Underground won the war, this future would never come into being, and these notes would be totally fraudulent and meaningless. But Hartstein felt he had to put his faith somewhere . . .

"Now you have one more important step to take," said Dr. Waters, seemingly looking into $Hartstein_1$'s very soul with his uncanny eyes.

"I have to take all this material back to the present and explain myself to my superior officers."

"Well," said $Hartstein_2$, "that, too, but first you have to go farther into the future. You must talk to ourself one year from now to find out what the results of our giving you that information will be."

"I see," said $Hartstein_1$.

"Taking that information from us alters the nature of your present, which is our past. Consequently, this possible future of yours may not exist after you take the folder back. So you must go ahead before you go back, to be certain that we've done the right thing."

$Hartstein_1$ nodded. He didn't want to inspect their reasoning closely; what they were telling him opened a can of worms that only the Bird of Time itself could love. He thanked both himself and kindly old Dr. Waters, said goodbye to them both, and touched his temporal tap.

Nothing much changed. He remained in the room. Some magazines and journals on the desk were replaced by others, but otherwise everything was the same. Dr. Waters and himself stood waiting for him. "Right on time," said Dr. Waters.

"You're here for the data," said $Hartstein_3$.

"Uh huh," said $Hartstein_1$. "A year ago you were concerned about my taking this information back to the present. My present, I mean."

"A good thing you came here," said Hartstein$_3$. "We have another folder of supplementary material for you. Without it, the first batch would have been ambiguous, and could have gotten you and the Agency into a lot of trouble." He gave Hartstein$_1$ a second folder. There were an additional twenty pages.

"Thanks a lot," said Hartstein$_1$. "Well, I have to report back to Captain D'Amato now. This will give me a good excuse for why I ducked out of Marshal Farias's interrogation."

"You can't go yet, son," said Dr. Waters. "You must do the same thing as before: jump ahead a year to see what the effects of this second folder will be. Then you can return to your present. Better safe than sorry, you know."

"An ounce of prevention," said Hartstein$_3$.

"Of course," said Hartstein$_1$. "Well, thanks again." He touched his temporal tap and leaped ahead another year.

"Welcome to the World of Tomorrow," said Hartstein$_4$.

"Never mind that," said Hartstein$_1$. "Just give me what you have to give me and let me get going."

Dr. Waters laughed tolerantly. "Ah, the impetuosity of the young. I wish I could have that kind of energy again. What I'd accomplish in my old age, with youthful vigor coupled with the experience of a lifetime!"

"Don't you have something for me?" asked Hartstein$_1$ impatiently.

"Ha ha," said Dr. Waters, holding out yet another folder.

"Thanks," said Hartstein$_1$. There were sixteen pages of new information. That meant another jump. He jumped.

Hartstein$_5$ gave him twelve and four-fifths pages.

Hartstein$_6$ gave him ten and a quarter pages.

Hartstein$_7$ gave him eight and one-fifth pages.

Hartstein$_8$ gave him six and two-thirds pages.

Hartstein$_9$ gave him five and a quarter pages.

Hartstein$_{10}$ gave him four and one-fifth pages.

Hartstein$_{11}$ gave him three and two-fifths pages.

Hartstein$_{12}$ gave him two and two-thirds pages.

At that point, Hartstein$_1$ got fed up. "This can go on forever," he screamed.

Dr. Waters raised a placating hand. "Almost forever," he said.

Hartstein$_{12}$ shrugged. "I know how you feel. I remember it as if it were only yesterday, instead of more than a decade ago."

"What did you do about it?" asked Hartstein$_1$.

"I asked Dr. Waters here, just as you're going to do."

"What should I do, Dr. Waters?" asked Hartstein$_1$ furiously.

Dr. Waters began to pace up and down the room, ignoring the blinking signals and whispering voices coming from the elaborate electronic equipment. He lit one of his rare French cigarettes. "It seems to me that every time you jump a year into the future, the next Hartstein gives you new information, but fewer pages each time. Am I correct?"

"Yes," said both Hartsteins.

"Well, it's a simple matter of finding out what the sum of the series is. You can say that the information you're obtaining is the function of the particular Hartstein who gave it to you. Eventually you're going to reach a point where the Hartsteins are giving you very small bits of new material, which will be negligible enough so that they won't have much effect on your present if you choose to ignore them. What you must do is find out the operative limit of the valuable material, and then integrate the corresponding number of Hartsteins."

"Ah," said $Hartstein_1$. "How do I do that?"

"He doesn't yet know as much mathematics as I do, sir," said $Hartstein_{12}$.

Dr. Waters took out a pen and wrote something on the folder $Hartstein_{12}$ had given to $Hartstein_1$. "This is what you need to solve:

$$f(x) = y \qquad \therefore \qquad \lim f(x) = \sum_{i=2}^{\infty} f(Hartstein_i)$$

$$x = Hartstein_i \qquad (Hartstein_i)^{-1} \to 0$$
$$y = \text{new information}$$

That is, the sum of all the pages all the various Hartsteins will give you from now until the end of time. Although this is an infinite series, it has a finite solution. We'll just ask our impressive and generally quite dependable machinery here to see if there's a common pattern to the number of pages each Hartstein has given you in your first eleven stops. Then we will simply integrate the equation, adding up all the separate areas under the Hartstein curve, as it were." Dr. Waters laughed as if it were some kind of clever joke. $Hartstein_1$ was just plain ticked off.

A moment later, the electronic equipment delivered its verdict: there was a ratio between the number of pages from each Hartstein, making the whole a geometric progression amenable to solution. The formula for that sum was: $S_{infinity} = a_1/1 - q$, where q represented the ratio in question, and a_1 represented the number of pages in the first group. In this case, q equaled a fraction in the neighborhood of $4/5$ and a_1 equaled 25. Therefore, $S_{infinity}$ came to a total of 125.

"When you get a hundred twenty-five pages," said Hartstein$_{12}$, "you might as well quit and go home. Any further jumps into the future would be pointless."

"I could say that about the last several jumps as it is," muttered Hartstein$_1$ grumpily.

"Now, now," said kindly old Dr. Waters. He was an inveterate peacemaker. "According to the formula, you'll have a hundred and twenty pages after you meet Hartstein$_{16}$. From then on you'll just be receiving fractional pages from us. So just make four more jumps and then you'll have plenty to show Marshal Farias."

"He'll be real happy about it," said Hartstein$_{12}$. "I remember the look on his face. He was relieved and grateful and frankly admiring of our ingenuity."

"Uh huh," said Hartstein$_1$. He wondered who was going to try to make sense of the 120 pages while thousands of Agency men were being blasted into drifting vapor on the beaches of Atlantis. He hoped that the Chronic Marshal would suggest that the data was better off under the scrutiny of more agile minds than Hartstein's. "Thanks for everything," he said, then touched his temporal tap. He was in no mood to put up with any such nonsense from Hartstein$_{13}$.

After he had made the additional four jumps, Hartstein returned to the present. "I'm back!" he shouted. The Underground's headquarters was noisy with celebration. Champagne corks were popping like bottle rockets; the tiled corridors were slick with dropped cake and ice cream. Paper napkins and plastic cups littered the grounds just as if the rebels had gone into the franchised fried-chicken business. No one paid very much attention to Hartstein and his bundle of papers. All the Underground soldiers and technicians were singing drunkenly in the villa's dark rooms. Vague shadows of rebel men and women coupling on the vast lawn gave the place an air of harmless abandon. Hartstein was happy to see that the Underground was able to let its hair down now and then, yet he dreaded witnessing the reason for their party.

The Commander joined him as he wandered about looking for Brannick. "What's this?" asked the Commander, indicating the pages Hartstein had received from his selves.

"Oh, nothing. I'm looking for Brannick. I can't go back without him. I owe him my life, you know."

"Ah yes. Well. I was hoping we'd get to keep him, but if you're claiming him then I suppose we'll let him go. He and I have a kind of rivalry, you know. Goes back a long time. But this round is mine. He'll know that when he wakes up. You'll have to help him back to your lines. He's not in great shape, I'm afraid."

Hartstein's stomach began to hurt. "You didn't torture him, did you?" he asked.

The Commander laughed. "No, of course not. We're not animals. We just drained his mind a little. He'll have to lean on you all the way to the beach. That's five miles or so. And your folks are trying to get the hell out of here, so it's good that you came back when you did. You wouldn't want to be stuck here when this place goes back into the quasi-past. We're probably going to seal it off there, you know. No more Atlantis for anybody."

The Commander led Hartstein to the cell where Brannick was lying unconscious. It took a few minutes for them to get Brannick roused enough to stagger along with Hartstein's support. The two Agency sergeants began the long walk down the green-paved road, beneath a full orange moon and a sky of bright stars like the dust of broken glass. The Commander stood on the lawn in front of the villa and waved goodbye, a good suburban host after a long night of fun and games. It had been pleasant, but now it was time to go to sleep. Everyone had to get up early in the morning. Tomorrow was another day.

CHAPTER EIGHT

THE SOUND OF n HANDS CLAPPING

Hartstein accepted the praise graciously and walked proudly from the assembly. Sergeant Brannick followed him, no expression at all on his rugged face. Hartstein reached out to push the polished brass doors, but they were pulled open by Agency corporals in dress uniforms. They saluted Hartstein. He would have to learn to get used to it.

Brannick called to him, and Hartstein stopped and turned around. "I'm happy for you, Lieutenant," said Brannick. "I'd like to shake your hand. You never stop making me proud of you. And besides that, I owe you something. You know that I've never been very good at—"

"Sergeant," said Hartstein, "I never want you to think that you owe me something. You've saved my neck more times than I want to remember, so it made me glad that I could return the favor this once. But I'm still a few rescues behind. Just because they made an officer out of me, it doesn't mean that our relationship has changed any. You're still my teacher and my friend. And I'd rather you didn't call me 'sir.' At least not in private."

Brannick relaxed and gave the youth an easy smile. "Good to hear that," he said. "I didn't think you'd get all inflated on me, but sometimes the bars on the collar warps a kid's mind. And this war ain't over yet; you're still going to need your tail saved now and then. I hope it's me that's there to do it. You're the best I ever trained."

"That's enough of that, Brannick. Let's forget all about it and concentrate on what we've got to do next."

Brannick agreed. "Whatever you say. But I'm not forgetting that you could have left me with them. With the Commander. I'm not forgetting that you got me out of there under fire, at risk to yourself."

"So tell me, did they promote me for that, Sarge, or for bringing back the hundred and twenty pages they're so excited about?"

"Ha," Brannick snorted, "I'd like to think my wrinkled old hide was what they were worried about; but I know better. Those pages are a superweapon, Hartstein, maybe just what we need to end this war. They're drawing up plans for the final battle right this minute. We'll hear about it before morning."

Hartstein understood well enough. The Agency didn't have the precious time to waste, not after the calamitous defeat in Atlantis. The thing to do was to strike back quickly with every weapon at the Agency's disposal. They had to recoup their losses.

"When you were promoted," Hartstein asked, "were you reviewed personally by the Overlords themselves?"

"Of course not. They have better things to do."

"Then why do they give me their personal attention?"

"I don't want to tell you."

"Why the hell not? Do I have to order you to tell me?"

Brannick's shoulders slumped a little, but then he recovered. "Every time I tell you, you get mad. The Overlords are interested because they know you're someone particularly important in this war. They know that somehow the outcome of the conflict involves you. They know because they looked ahead and saw it."

"You're right, Brannick, I don't want to hear about it. Melissa Spence thought I was someone special, too. That's why she approached me with her idea."

"Not quite. You're important, but you're not special, son. You may be the hinge that the future turns on, but you're expendable and easily replaced. You are not the active will of the universe, but the physical machine through which it will work. You are not the engine, but the transmission. You're just Lieutenant Hartstein, the Fulcrum of Fate."

It didn't make things any better. "Can I resign that job?" he asked.

"You might not have to. You might get killed tomorrow. Maybe that's how you're supposed to make your contribution."

"Great. Wonderful. Just make sure they spell my name right on the victory monument."

What Sergeant Brannick hopefully called the final battle was a concentrated effort that would attack every known Underground cell in the present, the quasi-pasts and futures, and the limited real past and future. It would be the largest combined military operation in the history of the world.

It was also the greatest gamble anyone had ever taken. The five Overlords felt the immense pressure, but they were chosen to lead because they were able to think and reason clearly in such grave situations. There wasn't a single Agent who doubted his leaders, and each one was prepared to go into battle wherever and whenever he was sent, in defense of his continuum. If the Agency failed, very soon there would be nothing left in the universe to recall the existence of either faction.

The preparations for this final struggle were huge and time-consuming, but they could be made in the past and returned to the present when they were completed. Thus, the attack itself could be launched with as little as twenty-four hours' notice. Hartstein felt a slight nervousness because whatever he was assigned, it would be the most important mission of his career. He was a lieutenant now but he was still a Special Agent, working alone on the lonely battlefields of time. He paced his narrow quarters and thought of the weight of responsibility on his shoulders. He thought of his father; since Hartstein had joined the Agency, he had seen his parents only in the unreal Christmas visit. What would Mr. Hartstein think of his son now? Had Hartstein at last earned his father's respect? The answer to that was in the future somewhere, a future that would not be at all unless Hartstein and his fellows succeeded in their objectives.

Hours later, after dinner, Captain D'Amato called Hartstein into a conference room. Hartstein was surprised to see that the captain was alone. "Sit down, Lieutenant," said D'Amato. He moved restlessly in his plush armchair; he was holding a sheaf of papers, and his hand trembled.

Hartstein said nothing; he sat in the other chair and waited.

"Your assignment, Lieutenant Hartstein," said the captain, holding the papers up. "It's a difficult one."

"I don't expect any of them are particularly easy, sir," said Hartstein solemnly.

"Exactly so. But this is a vital mission. Your success could undermine much of the Underground's theoretical basis, and therefore render them virtually helpless. Much of their math weaponry would cease to have validity, and we would then be in a position to eliminate them quickly and without danger to our own forces."

Hartstein raised an eyebrow. "I'm honored to be given such a job, sir," he said.

"Glad to hear it. Briefly, son, you are going back into the real past, to ancient Greece. You are going to impersonate an Athenian philosopher, and you are going to introduce ideas contrary to those of the Underground. Now that we're able to make the present responsive to changes in the past, these philosophical notions will have the force of Euclid, Plato, and Aristotle. They will alter the perception of the universe just slightly, but just enough to make the existence of the Underground impossible."

"Philosophy, sir?" asked Hartstein. "I thought that we were fighting this war with pure mathematics. How does ancient Greek philosophy have any effect?"

"Sometimes there is a fine line between science and mathematics on the one hand, and philosophy on the other, particularly when you're dealing with the very large or the very small, the infinitely new or the infinitely old. Even though those philosophers lived twenty-five centuries ago, and few people today read their works or even know their names, their ideas have colored the thinking of every generation that came after them. Their theories and attitudes have been passed down through all the years as a heritage, that which we call civilization. Change the ancient foundation of scientific thinking, and you change the way we look at our world today. That is what you must do—but carefully. If you operate too broadly, the result may be disastrous."

"I don't know if I'm quite the right person to carry this out, Captain."

"You are the right one, Hartstein, we are all certain of it. But you needn't worry too much. We have a detailed outline of just what you're supposed to say and to whom you're supposed to say it. Take it and study it tonight, and in the morning report to ESB for your preparation."

"Yes, sir."

"Good luck, Lieutenant," said D'Amato.

"Good luck to you, sir, and to the rest of the Agency. I hope when I finish in Greece and return, it will be to a world without the Underground."

"If we fail, son," said the captain somberly, "you won't have a world to return to."

That night, Hartstein read the briefing thoroughly; but he had had very little previous education in philosophy, and some of the arguments he read made no sense at all. An introductory note said that he shouldn't worry about that, because the ESB treatment would give him insight into the Greek philosophers he needed to understand. Finally, after the second time through the difficult material, Hartstein gave up, trusting to the Agency to endow him with whatever he lacked. He dropped the pages to the floor, turned his face to the wall, and fell into a deep and dreamless sleep.

In the morning he decided that there was one thing more he had to do. Sometime in the night the realization formed that it wasn't only philosophy he needed to learn, but more math as well. If he hoped to protect himself and do his job, he required a more fundamental grasp of the major weapon of this war. He was curious why the Agency hadn't seen fit to instill that knowledge earlier. It was as if they had sent him out with a slim dagger to fight unknown enemies in the dark.

Fortunately, it would be easy to remedy that situation. He dressed quickly and decided to skip breakfast. He went first to the ESB department reserved for the use of the Agents. This was a more elaborate facility than that used by tourists to prepare for their brief holidays in the quasi-past. Virtually anything an Agent had to know in order to carry out orders was available to authorized personnel. It was a quick and efficient way to learn languages, history, and the basic ideas of any science or art. What the Agent did with this knowledge, of course, depended on that individual's own talents and inclinations.

A young woman, an Agency corporal, sat at a desk processing a large pile of forms. It was early in the day, but she was already harried and unhappy. "Excuse me," said Hartstein.

She looked up, not pleased by the interruption. When she saw that he was a lieutenant, she gave him her attention but not her enthusiasm. "Yes, sir. What can I do for you?"

"I would like to take a course or two in intermediate mathematics. From algebra through plane geometry, trig, calculus, and so on. Enough so that I'll be able to handle myself where I'm going. It seems like all the Underground agents I run into have a much better education than I do."

The corporal nodded. "I see. But I'm afraid, sir, that information is classified."

"Classified? But it's basic high school and college math. How could it be classified?"

"Since the disaster in Atlantis, all potential weapons sources have been declared top secret, and mathematical training is now given only on a need-to-know basis."

"But I need to know." Hartstein felt the familiar frustration of dealing with low-level personnel, the men and women who sat at desks and stood behind counters and decided his fate. How rarely they understood that circumstances vary from person to person, and how less likely they were to venture beyond the safe limits of their specific orders.

"We'll see what you're cleared for, sir," said the young woman. She took Hartstein's identification and typed it into her terminal. A moment later the data appeared on her screen, out of Hartstein's sight. She turned to him. "I'm very sorry, sir," she said. "It says here that you're cleared for any amount of math you wish to take. Take this card and follow the blue line. The technicians will give you whatever you need."

Hartstein took the card she offered and followed the blue line. It led to the ESB treatment booths. A tech sergeant took his card, saluted, and led Hartstein into one of the booths. The couch was comfortable and the lighting dim. "Which course do you want, sir?" asked the sergeant.

"General mathematics," said Hartstein. "From algebra through calculus."

"Yes, sir. Just relax. We have an excellent new course in vector analysis and another in game theory. Would you like those as well?"

"No, I don't think I'll need all that. I just want to be a little ahead of the ancient Greeks. None of them will know calculus, so it ought to give me an advantage. And then I'll be on an even footing if I run up against any rebels from here on in."

The treatment lasted only an hour, and Hartstein emerged from it feeling no different, with no obvious flood of mathematical appreciation coloring his thoughts. Just as he had not consciously been aware of the insertion of the Egyptian language and customs prior to his first tour of Alexandria, so now his new knowledge of elementary and advanced math slept in his mind, waiting for him to call it forth.

While he was in the ESB section, Hartstein also took the prep he needed for his mission to ancient Greece. Hellenic philosophy, culture, the language, and hints as to the strategy he should follow in debating with the great analytical minds of antiquity filled his unconscious. It was almost time for him to report to the transmission screen. He had only one more stop to make.

"Well, well, well," said the young man in the costume and props department. He looked at Hartstein critically, one hand on his hip, the other languidly stroking his downy cheek as he thought. "A *lieutenant* now, I see. And the absolute darling of the Agency. You know, you're quite a celebrity to us poor clerks. I like to think that in some small way I've contributed to your marvelous, cometlike ascendancy."

"I'm an officer now," said Hartstein, "and I expect to be treated like one."

"Oh," said the corporal, feigning chagrin, "*please* forgive me. You want me to salute, don't you? Is that it? Please say it is. I've been simply *praying* that you'd make me salute." There was an intrinsic precision and snap missing from the young man's salute.

Hartstein returned it anyway. "I need to be fixed up for Greece," he said.

"I'll say you do."

"I'm going back to ancient Greece, about 460 B.C. I want to look like a respectable philosopher."

"Just leave yourself in my capable hands."

Hartstein didn't intend to reply to that suggestion. He waited for the corporal to go into the storeroom and return with an appropriate costume. It did not take long.

"Here you are, Lieutenant, sir." He put a plastic bag on the counter. The costume inside was more voluminous than anything Hartstein had worn except, perhaps, the Palestinian outfit. Still, it was only a white togalike mantle and a pair of sandals.

"I'm glad to see those," said Hartstein. "I'm tired of going back into periods where I have to run around risking my neck with nothing on my feet but bruises."

"Barefoot boy with cheeks of tan. My, my, how I'd love to see you in your element. It must be thrilling, sir."

Hartstein didn't know if the props corporal was mocking him or not. He let it pass. "No jewelry or anything else?"

"Just this." The young man handed over a long, slender staff. "That's your badge of office, you know. You can't be a good peripatetic educator without your staff. If one of the boys gets out of line—you know, spitballs and paper wads—you go whoops! with the old stick. Spare the rod and spoil the child. That's how the West was won, *n'est-ce pas?*"

There was a moment of silence while Hartstein tried to gauge the corporal's attitude; it was impossible. For an instant Hartstein wanted to inaugurate his staff across the young man's skull. He took the costume into a dressing room and changed. One of the makeup artists supplied him with an appropriate beard and hairstyle. When Hartstein appeared again, the props corporal was astonished. "Oh my heavenly days!" he cried, clapping his hands together. "Why, look who it is! It must be Socrates himself, or Zeus, or Sir Laurence Olivier or *somebody!* I wish I had my autograph book with me today. How grateful I am that I'm not just some poor scullery maid in the cafeteria. I wouldn't miss this for the world."

Cold air had no problem finding a way up under Hartstein's toga. "If the Greeks were so civilized," he muttered, "why isn't there decent underwear?"

The corporal pretended to blush and avert his eyes. "I just can't stand it anymore," he said. "What are you up to in that outfit?"

"I'm going back to change the Greeks' ideas of mathematics and the universe."

"Oh, how rugged and sly we are. But do you know enough to take them on? I mean no disrespect, my lord, but they have people like Pythagoras playing on their team."

"I took an hour's worth of ESB math training this morning."

The young man looked honestly impressed. "Say something in equations for me."

Hartstein shook his head. "I can't. You know how it is. It won't come until I need it."

The corporal was enthusiastic. "I'll coach you. 'If a point is that which has no part . . .' "

"What's that?" asked Hartstein.

"That's Euclid's very first definition, you ninny. I mean, sir."

"Uh huh. 'A point is that which has no part.' " A look of amazement crossed his face. "Why, then it follows that straight lines parallel to the same straight line are also parallel to each other! And, of course, that if an equilateral pentagon be inscribed in a circle, the square on the side of the pentagon is equal to the squares on the side of the hexagon and on that of the decagon inscribed in the same circle! And then . . . and then . . ."

"Ah," murmured the young corporal, "only Euclid and Hartstein have looked on beauty bare."

Hartstein could not reply as he stared off toward infinity, visions of the endless minuet of numbers moving stately through his head. His mouth hung open and he began to teeter just a little.

"Hello?" said the props clerk. He prodded Hartstein a bit with a forefinger. The lieutenant started a slow, magnificent topple. The corporal caught him by one arm.

"Thanks," said Hartstein dreamily.

"Are you all right?"

"It was beautiful," Hartstein murmured. "All . . . white and hard and clean."

"Well, at the risk of depressing you utterly, I ought to remind you that you have an important mission, and that we're not just doing this to get you ready for the masked ball of the Krewe of Proteus."

"Yes, of course." Hartstein returned the young man's salute and stumbled away toward the purple glow of the transmission screen.

A few minutes later Hartstein was wandering the hills beyond Athens, sometime during the Golden Age of Pericles. The chilly air of early spring refreshed him and cleared his still-dazzled mind. Goats and sheep tore at the sparse grass around him. Bald discolored stone, the bones of the earth, gaped through the black soil. Not far away was a grove of trees, empty and barren but promising a future of fruit. In the damp wind, with patches of snow still clinging to the ground in protected places, that future seemed impossibly far away. On a hilltop in the distance, Hartstein saw the Parthenon as Euripides and Sophocles had seen it, unbroken and proud. Grasping his long staff, Hartstein began to walk toward the city.

After a quarter mile, a young man, evidently an aristocrat, joined him on the road. They greeted each other, and the Athenian youth asked respectfully, "Are you then a teacher?"

"Yes," said Hartstein. "I have come to set the others right. For all their greatness, your philosophers have ignored a simple truth and entertained themselves with inventing various false semblances of truth. Only they are wise enough in the ways of argument to see their deceptions, but I will open the eyes of the unschooled. Thereafter these wicked teachers of Athens will no longer lead young minds astray."

His words excited the Athenian. "My name is Brosias, son of Diogoras. I am a student of Gorgias of Leontini and his followers."

"Ah yes. The Sophists. It is they whom I have come to challenge."

"May I walk with you, sir? I'd like to hear your arguments."

"As you wish. Was it not Gorgias himself who said 'Nothing exists; but even if it did, we could not know it'? Your teachers pride themselves on being able to confuse and bewilder, rather than to make clear. They value rhetorical athletics over genuine knowledge and wisdom."

Brosias shrugged. "That is nothing new, sir. That's the same thing Socrates is telling everybody. Nobody listens to him, though."

Hartstein laughed indulgently. "They will, soon enough. That ugly old hound has an idea or two worth considering."

They skirted the Acropolis proper and came into the Agora, the broad area at the foot of the north slope. This part of the city has often been described as the marketplace, but that gives only a little of its flavor: yes, there were tradesmen and craftsmen here, a bazaar of Greek and imported commodities for sale; but one found new ideas here as well, and the excitement of discovery. New machines, new theories were unveiled, demonstrated by geniuses or charlatans to fascinated audiences. Ethics in business and private life developed in the Agora in an attempt to govern relations with domestic neighbors and foreign nations. Taking these accomplishments one step further into the abstract, philosophers questioned their fellow citizens about matters no one had ever bothered to think about before. Perhaps to the average Athenian such subjective problems had little practical value, but then they could not know that nearly three thousand years later the fate of the world depended on them.

"Look, sir," said the honest Brosias, "there is Protagoras, the finest lawyer in the city. He is a Sophist, and he is able to win any case at all through the force of his logic."

"Not his logic," chided Hartstein, "but his manipulation of mere words. He tangles the listener up in trivial considerations of various words and their meanings. Meanwhile the sense and spirit of the vital question itself dies ignored at his feet. He cares not for the truth of his argument, but only for its success. Can you not see where that leads?"

Brosias frowned, deep in thought. After a moment he gave up. "No, I can't," he said.

"It leads to the assumption that all arguments are equally valid. And then it follows from that, that *no* arguments are essentially valid, and therefore such things as philosophical inspection and the pursuit of justice are based on worthless notions, and are completely without objective merit."

"I have no difficulty accepting that," said Brosias.

That gave Hartstein some trouble. He was prepared to speak with people who still felt that truth and morality were constant and desirable. But if the Sophists had persuaded some of these youngsters that such abstract concepts are purely relative, then his assignment would be more difficult than he had imagined.

"Lo, my teacher himself is speaking to those artisans," said Brosias as they approached a part of the Agora given over to potters, leatherworkers, and other craftsmen.

"I can see by his staff that he is a philosopher."

"I shall introduce you, sir. I'm afraid you didn't tell me your name."

"I am Epimander of Miletus." Epimander was the name of one of the authors Hartstein discovered in his first visit to the Library of Alexandria, the perpetrator of *Self-Realization Through Hubris*. There was no record of any actual classical philosopher by that name, and it sounded good to Hartstein.

"Miletus, the home of obsolete thinkers," said Brosias with an impudent grin. "That's what Protagoras calls it."

They stood beside the Sophist and listened to him debating with the Athenian citizens. Hartstein was not impressed either by Protagoras's philosophy or his skill with words. Perhaps the man had earned a great reputation here, in the early morning of civilization; but where Hartstein came from, the Greek would have a tough time holding his own with a high school senior.

"Sir," said Brosias, "I wish to introduce Epimander of Miletus, who has come to question you about your methods."

Protagoras turned around and smiled. He held out a hand in a very unclassical gesture. "Hartstein, isn't it? I've been waiting for you."

Hartstein's spirit sank. Here, too, the Underground was ahead of him. It was not going to be just a matter of adjusting the attitudes of these ancient Greeks: it was going to be a deadly contest for the hearts and minds of the audience, using rhetorical skill as a weapon. He shook the man's hand. "How are we going to work this?" he asked.

The rebel looked around at his listeners. "Why don't you go ahead and attack my way of thinking. Then I'll try to enumerate your errors. When one of us looks like a big enough fool, it'll be over."

Hartstein was frightened. He was sure that someone else should have been sent in his place. This Underground impostor was certainly well trained and confident. Hartstein himself had only the benefit of his brief ESB treatment that morning. He prayed that it would be enough. "I understand that you teach your students to argue either side of a legal case," he said.

"Yes, that is true," said Protagoras. "First, it enables them to plead on behalf of all clients, even when my students have no personal interest in the matter. Second, it stretches their imagination and forces them to think in new and creative ways."

"That sounds good at first hearing," said Hartstein, "but I would like to show how destructive such a technique will prove to be in the long run." He turned to one of the attentive potters. "You, sir, do you feel that if called upon to sit on a jury, that you would be able to render a good and true verdict in the best interests of justice and the state?"

"Why, of course," said the potter.

"And are you of the same opinion?" Hartstein asked another man.

"All Athenian citizens would be," said the second man.

"And what is it that makes you so confident?" asked Hartstein.

The first man thought for a moment before replying. "One man may be mistaken or misled or of dishonest inclinations," said the potter. "But a jury must have an inner sense of justice. As a group of sincere and disinterested citizens, a jury is able to find the truth in any legal dispute. That is the basis of our system, and one of the foundations of our great state."

"I agree," said Hartstein. "Yet this man Protagoras is teaching his students to argue even the unjust side of a question, to mislead a jury in deliberate fashion for the profit of a guilty client. He is able to persuade men through the art and craft of his words, which may sound more truthful than they are in fact."

"Aristophanes made the same complaint in his new play," said a silversmith who had joined the crowd. "He portrays a contest between Just and Unjust Argument, and it is Unjust Argument who wins every time."

Hartstein paused to consider his next step. "But such a thing goes against all reason. There *must* be a general knowledge of what is right and what is wrong, even though all the philosophers in the world play with their meanings. Each man knows inside when an action is right, and when it is wrong."

"Do you mean to say that there are such things as absolute universal laws?" asked Protagoras, still smiling placidly.

Even without his ESB preparation, Hartstein would have recognized this as the first stage of a rhetorical trap. "I say that a man may invent justifications for wrongdoing, yet still know that it is wrong."

"Yes, that is true," said the Underground agent. "Right is right, and wrong is wrong. All things that are, are; and things that are not, are not. And it is the man himself who knows these things: that 'right' and 'wrong,' 'being' and 'not-being' exist. Will you accept that?"

"Yes," said Hartstein hesitantly.

"Then what is it about a man which enables him to know these things?"

"Only his mind, sir," said Brosias.

"Good lad. His mind, of course. Man is the measure of all things. Or more precisely, in the words of Anaxagoras, 'Mind orders all.' "

"That is a primary tenet of our beliefs," said one of the leatherworkers. "The mind of man is the source of all blessings which do not come directly from the gods or nature. We take the growing things and cultivate them for food. We take stone and build houses. We shape our environment as we will."

"Very good," said Protagoras. "Therefore, it follows that justice also does not exist except in relation to the mind of man. Truth exists only in relation to the jury selected to find it. By this I mean that the truth and justice of a matter before our court may not be the same as that before a court of, for example, the northern barbarians, if indeed they have one. Our ideas of justice do not always reflect the ideas of the Egyptians or the Scythians or the Persians."

"But, sir," said a second potter, "what you are saying cuts us off from any great and everlasting notion of truth. Surely you are not denying the existence of the gods and their institutions?"

"No, no, of course not. But what we as mere mortals perceive as truth and justice and honor are ideas that have developed because of man, not gods. They exist because men live together in communities and so must formulate abstract concepts in order to keep peace with each other. There is no truth or justice beyond the mind of man."

"Your predecessor, Gorgias, said that nothing exists," said Hartstein. "Is this an example of how the mind of man orders all things?"

Protagoras laughed. "Gorgias was merely demonstrating that as the knowledge of the world is not constant but relative to the observer, then it is impossible for one man to convey his precise knowledge to another, for each man has his own view of the world."

It was clear that Protagoras was well on his way toward persuading these Athenians of the Temporary Underground's view of the universe. Hartstein had to do something to counteract the rebel's success. "Tell me once and for all, sir, if you believe in any set of fundamental laws of human behavior, independent of whatever cultural influences may be used to modify them."

Protagoras shrugged. "Will you accept the statement that only that which is, exists; and that which is not, does not exist? As you granted earlier?"

"Certainly," said Hartstein.

"And if anything exists, my friend, it must be either finite or infinite. Do you not agree?"

"I suppose there is no third alternative."

"Yet through simple logical means, with which no one has found fault, Parmenides arrived at the conclusion that what exists is pure being, and is necessarily infinite."

"That is a well-known hypothesis we have all studied," said Brosias.

"And another philosopher uses precisely the same method to prove that pure being must necessarily be *finite* in nature. Only a false proposition, my friends, can lead to such a contradiction. Therefore, I submit that nothing exists, but only the *illusion* of existence exists; and that the universe is content to have nothing exist, and that the universe and the mind of God would be blessed to have the illusion of existence removed forever."

Hartstein opened his mouth but found nothing to say. All the others in the audience turned to him, waiting for a devastating refutation of Protagoras's reasoning. It was clear to Hartstein that such a confrontation was pointless. He had another plan: he touched his temporal tap and was gone. He conceded the first round to the Underground.

Jumping ahead to twenty years after the death of Protagoras, Hartstein went to visit Democritus, the man who organized the atomic theories of earlier philosophers such as Leucippus. "Let the Underground have Protagoras," thought Hartstein. "I'll provide a firm foundation for the materialist side. A tendency to accept the idea of atoms here will result in a clear advantage for the Agency in centuries to come."

Democritus came to Athens as a young man, drawn by the excitement generated by the circle of thinkers assembled by Pericles. At first, Democritus had felt rejected and just a little resentful. Hartstein wondered if the Underground had warned the Athenians not to speak with the young Democritus, that his theory of atoms was dangerous and impious.

Hartstein found Democritus in the middle of the Agora, trying to interest passersby in his little hard bits of matter. He was shouting and waving his staff, but no one was listening.

"You know," said Hartstein, "that sounds very interesting."

"I'm glad you think so," said Democritus. "It's almost impossible to get these Athenians to pay attention. Those Sophists screwed everything up for a long time. Listen to this, I heard it from a young woman, one of their students. A woman, yet! She said, 'Either things exist or they don't. If they don't exist, then there can't be atoms. If matter does exist, it is either finite or infinite. If it is infinite, there cannot be atoms, because there must be a quantity of not-being between each atom, which would necessitate an infinity of not-being for the entire universe, and an infinity of not-being would not permit the existence of any matter. If matter is finite, then once again there cannot be atoms, because in this case as well there must be not-being as a separater of atoms, and I cannot accept the being of not-being, or an argument that claims both the existence and the non-existence of something at the same time.' *That*, my friend, is Sophistry, even more absurd than that of the damned Protagoras himself. It is all just verbal tap-dancing."

"Tap-dancing? I didn't know there was tap-dancing in ancient Greece."

Democritus blushed. "What do you mean, 'ancient'?"

But Hartstein wouldn't be so easily bluffed. "You aren't from this century, are you? You're another agent of the Underground."

"Well," said the false Democritus, "you found me out. What can I say? Be careful, Hartstein. We'll meet again." The rebel touched his temporal tap and disappeared. Hartstein did the same.

The appearance of the Agora hadn't changed very much. It was now several decades earlier, during the height of Periclean Athens. Hartstein needed to speak with Anaxagoras and change that great thinker's mind about a few things; in that way, Hartstein could destroy the arguments of Protagoras in advance and prepare the Greeks to accept the atomic theory of the true Democritus. He decided not to waste a moment; he stopped a wealthy merchant walking through the marketplace with his wife and three children. "Excuse me, sir, I am looking for Anaxagoras, the scientist and philosopher. I am new in this wonderful city, and I was hoping you could point him out to me."

"I hope you enjoy your stay," said the merchant. "That's my little shop, right over there. If you need anything in the way of rugs or fabrics or dyes, come see me. Nothing I like better than doing business with newcomers to our city. A good way to expand my export business, you see, if you tell all your friends at home about my line."

"*This* is my home," said Hartstein curtly.

"Yes, of course. You're looking for the scientist. That's him, right over there, hitting that poor slave over the head with his staff."

"Thank you. Good day to you and to your lovely family, sir." Hartstein crossed the way and waited for Anaxagoras to stop punishing the slave.

"Are you waiting to address me?" asked the philosopher.

"Yes," said Hartstein, "when you're finished. I understand that you believe mind orders all things."

Anaxagoras looked astonished. "I have considered that idea, yes, but I haven't told anyone as yet. How could you know about it?"

"I have a way of knowing all that is of importance to me. You are quite certain of your conclusion?"

A wary expression crossed the Greek's face. "Of course I am. What else would order all things?"

"Perhaps there is a divine will that defines everything so that the human mind may comprehend them."

Anaxagoras looked afraid. "Divine, you say? You are not . . . divine yourself, by any chance? Apollo, perhaps, or one of those?"

Hartstein laughed. He wanted it to be deep and booming, but it wasn't. He sounded more like a pet cockatoo than one of the Olympians. "You're still superstitious, I see. But I wonder, do you mean that each individual has a separate and equally true world, or that the total consciousness of human minds creates the world by cooperative effort? For if the former is true, how can we co-exist in different worlds? And if the latter is true, then the world must change from day to day, as the consciousness of it changes."

"Interesting, very interesting questions. I see that you are more than a mere educated Athenian. I will tell you. In the beginning all things were mixed together, except Mind. Mind set the mixture in motion, and the heavy particles drifted to the center, while the lighter particles were forced to the outside. Thus the sun, moon, and stars are hot stones thrown out of this vortex into the sky. They are not, as our ancestors believed, gods."

"And do you have equally mechanical explanations for other phenomena, as well? For rain, for instance, and lightning?"

Anaxagoras looked unhappy. "These Athenians are not going to be pleased to hear my ideas. My new philosophy requires a complete change in beliefs. It will not be a simple matter to persuade them all."

Hartstein nodded sympathetically. "Perhaps I could suggest a way to make it easier for you. You must make a slight change in your conception of the nature of matter. Nothing that would change your creative framework, just a greater emphasis on atoms and less on the generative power of the mind."

"But—"

Hartstein would not be interrupted. "Your idea of religion is that there is a Mind that remains pure and unmixed in all things. That's a sound idea in some ways, but you're right—these people won't buy it. They'll think it's atheism. They picture their gods sleeping on clouds and plucking lyres. Forget about mind for now; just rely on the Athenians' willingness to believe in the existence of tiny particles. Everyone understands tiny particles."

Anaxagoras shook his head. "I'm sorry, sir, but my sponsor would not approve."

"Your sponsor?"

The philosopher pointed. "Yes. Over there. It is Pericles himself."

Hartstein looked. Smiling at him across the marketplace was the same rebel agent who had impersonated Protagoras. Once again, the Underground had anticipated Hartstein's plan.

As Hartstein saw it, the Underground had taken the first skirmish as Protagoras; there had been a draw with Democritus; and the rebels controlled Anaxagoras. Hartstein felt that a solid victory with Zeno of Elea would even the score, for much of the logic used by the later philosophers derived from Zeno. So the Agent jumped a few years back and many miles to Elea in Italy.

Zeno is most famous for his four paradoxes of motion. Of these, the most familiar is his "Achilles and the tortoise." According to Zeno, if Achilles gives the tortoise a head start of any amount in a race of any length, the poor man can never catch up to the animal. This is because before Achilles can pass the tortoise, he must run to point A where the tortoise started the race. But the tortoise has moved on to point B, so Achilles must run to that point, but the tortoise has moved on to point C, and so on until the torpid creature crosses the finish line. Meanwhile Achilles, swift of foot, has been reduced to tippy-toeing in microscopic fractions of inches after it. Zeno's other three paradoxes are also entertaining and treacherous; Hartstein wanted to get this master puzzler on the side of the Agency.

When Hartstein popped into the Eleatic academy, Zeno was going over the tortoise paradox for the benefit of the young men in his class. It did not take long for Hartstein to recognize that "Zeno" was the same Underground agent who had posed as Protagoras. "There can be no such thing as atoms," said Zeno loudly, for Hartstein's benefit as well as the class. "Parmenides has proved the nonsense involved with postulating a 'void' or a 'not-being' that separates points of time or space. The same is true of matter. If something is not, then it has no properties, and thus cannot hold atoms apart. We must conclude that there are no atoms, and therefore there is no matter. There is only Mind, or something like that. But as to matter, space, and time, they are the imposition of human limitations upon the perfect order of the universe."

Hartstein interrupted. "It seems I'm following you backward through time, listening to you palm off that anti-atom line in one form after another. You're doing the philosophical equivalent of taking out a cigarette lighter and astonishing the natives."

Zeno smiled unperturbably. "You know that and I know it, my friend, but these children will never learn it. And do you know, I am not so far from the truth. With the development of partial numbers, these old paradoxes have gained new meaning. If we assign a partially negative quantity to Achilles' velocity, not only does he never overtake the tortoise, he *loses* ground with every stride! But that is too much for these young minds to comprehend. You must look elsewhere if you hope to destroy all our work, Hartstein. I have won this engagement as well."

Hartstein was very hungry, but he didn't have a penny or an obolus or whatever the ancients used for cash. He hadn't planned to take so long to accomplish his mission. He thought he'd visit ancient Athens and have a little talk with Socrates or somebody, and that would be that. He didn't figure on running into the Underground on the same errand—and once again nobody had bothered to warn him of the possibility. Now he needed, besides lunch, a complete reevaluation of his strategy. Next before Zeno, chronologically and ideologically, was Parmenides. If Hartstein failed there, too, he would try Heraclitus. Before Heraclitus there was Pythagoras, a big shot in the pantheon of both the Agency and the Underground. If Hartstein could claim Pythagoras, it didn't matter how many later philosophers the rebels cornered. But if the Underground co-opted Pythagoras first, then the only thing to do was travel further back and try for the philosophers from Miletus: Anaximenes, Anaximander, and, finally, the world's first philosopher, Thales.

Things went worse for Hartstein the more he delved into the past. The Underground had set up a little intellectual boundary around each philosopher that prevented him from disrupting what the rebels had accomplished. The Underground had mixed, distorted, misquoted, and perverted the rational thought of centuries in order to support their own position. If left undisturbed, mankind would develop through the ages with a firm, unspoken, unconscious conviction that the world does not truly exist, that there is no such thing as matter, and that what we view as reality is only an uncomfortable illusion that annoys the universe. In the present, it would be the Underground that had the support and backing of the people, not the Agency.

In the time of Parmenides, the Underground taught that only being exists, and that being is unchanging.

Before Parmenides, Heraclitus paved the way by saying that the universe may seem like eternal flow and change, but behind that evident strife is a cosmic order—the *logos*. That's as far as Heraclitus took the idea; but when the Underground finished with it, they made everyone believe that the *logos* wasn't really crazy about the flow and change and strife and would really appreciate it if we'd all go away. Parmenides was the same rebel agent who had been Democritus, and the part of Heraclitus was played by the gently smiling man who had previously impersonated Protagoras and Zeno.

The scene shifted to Crotona, a city in southern Italy. Here Pythagoras made his home. Combining the roles of religious leader and philosopher and scientist, he was one of the most influential men in that part of the world. The Pythagorean philosophy favored neither the Agency nor the Underground, but balanced between them. It stated that numbers were things, which the Agency found useful; but it also said that things were numbers, which the Underground could definitely use in order to rid the universe of both things *and* numbers. Before Pythagoras, the Milesian philosophers said "To be is to be material." That was a fine notion for the Agency to encourage and defend. Unfortunately, Pythagoras took his second thesis and ran very far with it, into the realm of abstract and mystical applications. That was the kind of stuff the Agency wanted people to forget about.

Hartstein was expecting to find an academy of young men sitting around Pythagoras chanting "Things are numbers" and "Numbers are things." He was very wrong. He was very surprised, too. When he arrived, he did find an academy of young men sitting around Pythagoras (he was the immoderately serene rebel again). But they were chanting a syllable that sounded like "Ōm." Hartstein hadn't been prepared for that at all.

"What's all this?" he cried. "What have you done?"

Pythagoras gazed at him blissfully. "May this unworthy one humbly offer your honorable self a cup of tea from this miserable pot?" he asked.

"Are you kidding? What's this oriental stuff going on here?"

"Zen," said Pythagoras. "Listen to the words of Lao-tze: *The Tao never does, yet through it everything is done; If princes and dukes can keep the Tao, the world will of its own accord be reformed. When reformed and rising to action, let it be restrained by the Nameless pristine simplicity. The Nameless pristine simplicity is stripped of desire. By stripping of desire quiescence is achieved, and the world arrives at peace of its own accord.*"

Peace. Meditation. Oneness. Nothingness.

"Nothingness!" shrieked Hartstein. "Oh my God!" He saw immediately what a disaster that could mean for the Agency in the present. The Underground had sidetracked pre-Socratic philosophy from a consideration of the material nature of the universe to a preoccupation with nothingness. There could be no worse catastrophe. Hartstein decided to skip both Anaximenes and Anaximander, and leap all the way back to the beginning, to Thales of Miletus. He adjusted his temporal tap and jumped.

When he arrived, the first thing he saw was the Commander's destroyer. "Well, well, if it isn't Captain Future," said Tipchak. "We meet again, Hartstein."

CHAPTER NINE

NO TIME LIKE THE PRESENT

This was the third time Hartstein had been aboard the Commander's destroyer, but it was the first time he had gone anywhere in it. There was no sensation of motion—an advantage of technology from whatever future the craft came from. They left the Ionian past and traveled back to the present, to the great rallying of forces that would culminate in the final battle between the Underground and the Agency. Or, rather, the battle which was already raging around the world and all along the tortuous avenue of time.

Everyone on board was very friendly. The Underground men and women knew Hartstein and were aware of the service he had rendered to the rebel cause. They weren't aware that some of that service had been entirely unintentional. The Commander, for instance, was under the impression that Hartstein's poor showing in pre-Socratic Greece had been a conscious effort to blunt the Agency's attack. "We owe you one, my boy," said the Commander in a fond way. "We can appreciate a man who lives by his principles. I don't suppose you're yet entirely sympathetic to our cause, but it makes me glad to know that you're no mindless tool of the Agency, either."

"You say that you owe me one," said Hartstein coldly. "If you win this battle and have your way with the world, how will you repay me?"

The Commander laughed. "Oh, I guess we won't need to worry about that anymore," he said. Hartstein didn't share his amusement.

He was wearing a tunic borrowed from one of the Commander's aides, and a pair of patched trousers donated by another rebel soldier. He was still wearing the Greek sandals and the false beard. It itched so much he wanted to tear it off.

Rebel soldiers made sure that he was comfortable, brought him food and free drinks and magazines to read. There was stereo music for him to listen to, with a choice of eight different programs. There would be a holofilm after lunch, and then they would arrive in the present. There was a rare feeling of expectation aboard the ship, one which Hartstein shared in a sickened way. It was the end toward which they all had worked, one way or another. It was the final battle, and it felt like graduation day.

As if Hartstein's appetite hadn't already been thoroughly spoiled, it was ruined completely by a visit from Tipchak. The weasel felt like gloating, and he couldn't get anyone else to listen to him. "Say, Hartstein," he said, smirking. "I never thought when I first ran into you that you would end up to be a hero. And an Agency hero and an Underground hero, too. How about that?"

"Yeah, right, how about that." Hartstein was listening to a recording of an Armenian goatherd singing to her animals. He couldn't understand a word of it, and the girl's voice creaked like a five-hundred-year-old windmill, but all in all it was preferable to Tipchak's notion of conversation.

"You getting butterflies in your stomach?" asked the small man.

"Butterflies? What for?"

Tipchak raised his eyebrows in surprise. "I'd've thought you'd be getting butterflies. The end of the world and all that; some people would be upset about it. Not me, of course, because I'm a loyal Underground soldier and I have my convictions to comfort me. But you don't have that, or, at least, not so's you'd notice. So what's it like, knowing you're going to snuff out like the flame of a candle in the next couple of hours?"

"You tell me, scumsucker. Convictions, my ass! If you have any convictions at all, they're for high crimes and misdemeanors. Just leave me alone."

Tipchak shook his head pityingly. "Butterflies. You've got buzzards flapping in your gut." He turned and left the narrow room where Hartstein had been billeted.

Tipchak's departure immediately improved the environment, but it was still far from pleasant. Hartstein had enough of the shrill goatherd and threw the earphones across the room. He wondered how the Agency was doing against the rebels in the present. It wouldn't be long before he found out, but the trouble was that he wasn't going to like the situation regardless of who was winning.

It had all come down to this: the final battle, with but two degrees of disaster to choose from as the ultimate result. Take your pick—absolute and eternal slavery, or peaceful nonexistence.

There was a knock on the door and the Commander looked in. "Mind if I come in and chat?" he asked.

Hartstein didn't answer.

The Commander sat in a chair beside Hartstein's bunk. "Having second thoughts?" he said.

It occurred to Hartstein that if the Commander wasn't sitting in that chair playing friendly neighborhood psychiatrist, it was Brannick. It was time to put a stop to it once and for all; there wouldn't be much opportunity to speak his mind later. "Do you mean, am I having second thoughts about helping the Underground? Yes, I am. I'm having second thoughts about helping the Agency. I wish there had been a way to blow the whistle on both gangs of lunatics; but I thought there would be a way out of this without anybody getting hurt, and without the poor, average man-in-the-street ever finding out how close he came to having the farm bought for him."

"You sound bitter, son."

Hartstein's anger flared. "You don't have to patronize me anymore, you son of a bitch. There isn't anything left to get out of me. I'm just a passenger and a spectator from here on in."

The Commander smiled. "I can appreciate how you feel. You think you've been used, don't you? You think you've been manipulated and lied to and cheated. Well, all of that is true. But you've never been able to see this whole thing in perspective. Sometimes it's necessary to cheat and lie in order to perform an ultimate good. The end justifies—"

"*Nothing* justifies what you're doing. Or what the Agency's doing."

The Commander paused. "Then there's nothing more I can tell you, son." He stood up. "We'll arrive in the present in about thirty minutes. We'll be touching down in the Seychelles, a pretty string of islands. The weather's beautiful this time of year. Why don't you go down to the Ops Center and ask for Sister Ojani? She's been waiting to show you our new superweapon, the one we're going to use to rid the world of the Agency's filth forever."

"A superweapon?" asked Hartstein. "More powerful than partial numbers?"

The Commander seemed amused by the idea. "Partial numbers are not an offensive weapon, lad. They are like the Trojan Horse, in a way. They are the ultimate dirty trick, like giving a Z-Ray projector to the most conscienceless murderer in history. When I stumbled upon partial numbers, I knew immediately that their misuse by the Agency would do them more damage than correct use by the Underground ever could."

"When *you* discovered them?"

"Oh yes. Who do you think gave Melissa Spence the idea in the first place? It was all an elaborate and clever plan to get the concept into the Agency's hands. Why, *of course* I lied to you and dear Sister Spence, but it was all for the greatest good. I wasn't foolish enough to think you'd believe that, so I arranged the little charade for your benefit."

Hartstein's belly felt as if it had been filled with foul chunks of dirty ice. "Did she know about all that?"

The Commander's expression was kindly. "No, son, of course not. I'm not so evil as that."

Hartstein had something to say to that, but he didn't. There was no point. "And you have something up your sleeve that makes those partial numbers look like nothing, I guess?"

"Just something I've forgotten to tell you about before. Come with me." The Commander led Hartstein to the Ops Center. They said nothing to each other in the corridor. Just inside the Ops room, the rebel leader pointed to an old woman. "That's Sister Ojani," he said. "She'll answer your questions. I must go now. We only have a little time left." He turned and went back into the passageway.

Sister Ojani was an elderly woman with wispy white hair and deep black eyes. Her face was as wrinkled as a dried plum, but her expression was as cheerful as a clear conscience could make it. She seemed to be anticipating some great and transcendent joy. "Lieutenant Hartstein?" she said in her thin voice. "Sit down beside me."

Hartstein did as he was asked, feeling like a timid young boy in an ancient fairy tale. Sister Ojani was either a wicked witch who would roast him for lunch, or an enchanted beautiful princess who would let him wake from this nightmare safe and sound.

"I'm only going to say this once," she said. "The whole is greater than the part."

"I know that," said Hartstein.

"The whole is greater than the part. That is one of the basic definitions on which Euclid's geometry is based. In fact, almost all of mathematics comes from simple, commonsense ideas like that."

"I know that."

"*Everybody* knows that. But what few people realize is that the whole is also greater than the sum of its parts." She covered his hand with her ancient fingers. Her dry skin felt like old paper.

Hartstein blinked. "That's a truism, ma'am. That's a kind of folky proverb that sounds good but isn't real in any kind of mathematical way. A triangle with three sixty-degree angles still totals a hundred and eighty degrees. The quantity $a + b$ doesn't equal anything more than $b + a$. Even if one or both of those unknowns are partial numbers, the commutative and distributive laws still hold."

Sister Ojani laughed. It was a dry, shrill, cackling sound. Hartstein gave up on the beautiful-princess theory. "Wrong again, little one," she said. "Do you not see? The process of addition has a value of its own. Two quantities sitting in different seats in a theater have no relationship to each other at all, yet when we add them together, a mystical bond is created that moments before was unthinkable. It is the *act* of addition that brings that bond into being. The act of addition is responsible for a new unity in the world. The process has a value of its own, independent of the values of the quantities. Man has always ignored that specific value, because he wished the mathematical operations to have a classical simplicity and logic. We have clung to that ancient idea, blinding ourselves to the truth and inventing all sorts of constants and other factors to make our equations work out correctly. We must say, 'Oh, this formula comes close to predicting what happens in real life, but we have to figure in K one way or another to get true accuracy.' What is the use of a formula that contains some made-up constant K that we can never put our finger on? And all the time the trouble has been caused by our refusal to abandon outdated ideas of arithmetic, ideas that predate the earliest written mathematical texts."

"What are you saying?" asked Hartstein. "That two plus two equals something more than four?"

"That's right, that's absolutely right. Assuming both twos in that equation are purely positive, the sum is on the order of four plus $1/10^n$, where n equals the objective operations value."

"The objective operations value," said Hartstein. "I suppose there is such a value for all operations: subtraction, multiplication, and so on." Sister Ojani nodded agreement. "And the precise value of n—"

"Must be determined by the context," she said. "It is a difficult and time-consuming procedure, even for our computers."

"But that would mean that everything we know about the universe, everything from the circumference of the earth to equations like force equals mass times acceleration, all those things are slightly incorrect."

"You got it, son. And, naturally enough, the act of adding the $1/10^n$ requires the addition of an even smaller but discrete value, and adding *that* . . ."

The potential for disruption in the world at large was immense. It was an even greater threat to mankind than the theory of partial numbers. It was something the Agency must know about as soon as possible.

Sister Ojani cackled again. "You are thinking about telling the Agency," she said.

The wicked-witch thesis seemed ever more likely. "Yes," he admitted.

"How do you know it isn't a second dirty trick?"

"I don't know that," said Hartstein.

"And they probably figured it all out for themselves by now. They buy their computers from the same people we get ours from."

"Then—"

"Then it will be pure hell when we arrive in the present. With both sides attacking each other with partial numbers and objective operations values, the concept of reality will mean very little. I'm not looking forward to seeing what's left of it."

"I'm a little afraid, too," said Hartstein. "I just hope—"

An alarm rang through the ship, warning them that timefall and land-fall were imminent. That was as much of the Underground's ultimate secret as Hartstein was permitted to learn.

"Do you know what I see, Lieutenant Hartstein?" asked the old woman.

There was a loud scraping noise, and then the scream of the braking jets drowned out all conversation for several moments. When the sound died away at last, the ship had come to rest somewhere in the present. No one was in a hurry to run outside and find out what was going on.

"What do you see?" asked Hartstein.

"I see you, dear, hurrying to the Agency lines with this new informa-tion, hoping to spare your friends and save your own life, hoping that they will round us up like obsolete outlaws. You would be a hero, the Sergeant York of Time. That is what you want. It will not happen."

Hartstein turned away. "You know that for certain?" he asked.

"No, of course not. The whole world's turned upside down."

Hartstein smiled. "That's what the band played when General Corn-wallis surrendered."

"Who?"

"Nobody," said Hartstein. He was planning his escape.

"It's all a game," mused Sister Ojani.

The alarm for General Quarters sounded, and suddenly the ship was all movement, noise, and purpose. Men and women ran to their battle sta-tions, fetching sidearms and helmets and other equipment. Sister Ojani did not stir from her chair. "It's all a game," she murmured.

Something about her sentiment annoyed Hartstein. "I'm glad you can see it like that," he said. "A game! A goddamn game of cosmic chicken is what it is." He stood up and left the Ops Center. He wandered into the corridor with no clear idea of where he was going. He walked toward the bow of the ship, flattening against bulkheads to let grim-faced rebels pass in the narrow gangways. He still had no idea where the Agency forces were, or what his next few moves might be.

The Commander came up to him and put a friendly hand on his shoulder. "Don't be frightened," he said.

Hartstein was astonished. "Aren't you supposed to be, you know, commanding or something? Why are you just out walking around like I am?"

The Commander smiled. "These people have been drilled so well that they really don't need me to tell them what to do. As a matter of fact, my job is almost over. It's all in the hands of the soldiers and the math artillery people. I guess I'll just oversee everything and make suggestions to my officers if things don't work out as planned. But other than that, I'm probably going to be just as much a spectator as you say you are. Why don't we go into the solarium and see what's happening outside?"

Hartstein wanted to be alone, to find a way out of the ship and on his way to the Agency lines with his new knowledge. The last thing he wanted was to be in the personal retinue of the enemy leader.

"Were you planning on getting out of here?" asked the Commander. "You can just forget about that. I'm not letting you go until this battle is over. You'll have to consider yourself my guest while—"

The bulkhead behind the Commander glowed a lovely lavender shade, the color of wisteria in April. There was a low hum that increased in volume as the bulkhead began to melt away. There was no heat, although the futuristic alloy dripped and sloughed and vaporized until there was a gaping hole large enough to admit an adult bison. And there were a lot of adult bison just on the other side of the breach. The bone-jarring hum disappeared suddenly, but rang in Hartstein's ears for some time. He looked at the Commander, who was evidently displeased by this damage to his ship. "What's that?" asked Hartstein.

"A hole," said the Commander. "I'm going to have to report this to damage control, but there's not a lot they can do about it now."

Hartstein looked outside. He couldn't imagine what had caused the damage. There was nothing out there but bison and prairie and low mountains in the distance. "Where are we?" he asked. It was supposed to be an island in the Seychelles, which are not famed for their prairies and bison population.

"How the hell should I know?" said the Commander in a surly tone. He turned and hurried away. Hartstein was all alone in the passageway. He put his hand on the outer bulkhead, cautiously testing the edge of the hole. It was not hot; he took advantage of the situation, wriggling through the hole and dropping to the ground.

He immediately felt he had made a bad mistake. He landed heavily in the coarse grass, and when he looked up the Commander's ship was gone. It had vanished silently, without leaving the least sign that it had ever rested on the prairie. But then, when Hartstein stood up and brushed himself off, he saw that the prairie, the bison, and the mountains had vanished as well. It occurred to him that perhaps *he* had done the vanishing, but he didn't want to get his points of reference confused. For the sake of continuity, he preferred to think that the world had vanished or changed, and that he had stayed in the same place. It didn't really make any difference.

A man in fifteenth-century plate armor, mounted on an armored horse, rode up to Hartstein. "Lieutenant," he said, "you must make the final disposition of the knights."

It was no difficult matter. Hartstein had fought in many battles, and so had these hand-picked men. The only problem was the weather; it was cold and wet, and the army had traveled a great distance in the last few days. The battle would take place in the morning, but until then the knights had to solve the problem of passing the night without caking their armor in mud and rendering it useless for the conflict. Removing it and sleeping on the ground was out of the question.

"Perhaps this rain will stop soon," said Hartstein. The constant beating of the raindrops on his helmet was driving him crazy.

"We cannot count on that, Lieutenant," said his aide.

"Then we will have to spend the night in the saddle. There's no other way."

"Yes, sir. The damned English have been living on just nuts and bad meat, and we must nap fitfully on our chargers in the cold, wet air. It will not be a pretty engagement on the morrow. Both armies will be ragged and miserable. If the English don't kill us, we will die of sickness from these conditions. Twenty-five thousand French knights assembled at Agincourt, and the king will be lucky to see the return of twenty-five hundred."

"Enough, Godchaux, that sounds like treason. Pass the word among the knights: they are to keep their equipment in fighting condition, whatever little sleep they get tonight. After the battle, they will be able to sleep as long as they like."

"Those who haven't been put to eternal rest already," murmured Godchaux as he kicked up his mount.

Hartstein turned to consider the disposition of the army. At dawn, the English would try to break through the French position between the two woods. At least, that was what he expected them to do. After all, the English had invaded France, so it was up to them to test the defenses. Hartstein could keep his knights reined up in the gap between the woods forever. Let the English try to get through!

Of course, he thought, his army outnumbered the English four to one.

Perhaps a massed charge could obliterate the enemy threat once and for all. Hartstein knew that he would spend all night long arguing strategy with himself. He felt cold and lonely and very weary, but he was not afraid.

At dawn the rain stopped. Hartstein awoke, realizing that he had fallen asleep sometime during the long hours after midnight. His muscles were stiff and sore, and as he stretched he saw that he was in the midst of a dense forest, a jungle, to be exact. Tall ferns towered above him, shutting out some of the light but none of the heat of a tropical sun. Dragonflies the size of owls flitted through the steamy air. Strange, frightening cries broke the stillness. There was a rank, fetid odor in the air that brought Hartstein close to nausea with every breath. He turned around and saw a bubbling black pond not far away. There was a huge dark shape in the middle of the pond, struggling to free itself from the viscous stuff. The creature filled the air with its savage, hopeless screams. Hartstein turned away. A man approached him through the gigantic ferns.

"Hartstein," said the man. It was Tipchak. He ran toward the young Agent.

"What is this?" asked Hartstein.

There was the crash of a fern not far away. A tall gray-blue thing slunk among the boles. Smaller animals skittered through the underbrush. Something leaped from branch to branch over their heads. The helpless beast in the tar pit voiced its dying rage.

"I don't know," said Tipchak, his eyes wide with terror. "About a quarter-mile through there, I was captured by these seven-foot-tall African natives. They dragged me to their village and put me in a big iron pot. They were going to cook me, Hartstein! It wasn't real. It couldn't have been real. It was like a bad joke."

The two men stared at the prehistoric scene around them, wondering which way to go, in which direction were sanity and stability and safety.

"Back the way I came," said Hartstein. "Staying here is no answer. The Agency and the Underground have let all hell loose. We've got to find some secure place in our own time. The Agency must have a headquarters near here where they're maintaining the present. It's our only chance."

"You're not taking me into no Agency headquarters, Hartstein," said Tipchak in a wild voice. "They'll kill me. I'd never get away alive. We've got to find the Commander."

"Forget the Commander. We're going this way." It began to rain, a slashing, hot, heavy rain that stung his skin. Thunder rumbled and lightning struck around him with sharp, deadly cracks. He felt Tipchak's hand on his arm, pulling and tugging in the opposite direction.

"*This* way, Hartstein. I saved your neck once, and it looks like I have to again."

Hartstein slapped the little man's hands away. "I don't ever want you touching me again, Tipchak, remember that. We're going my way. If you don't like it, find your own way through this jungle." He turned his back. A moment later a towering creature, an allosaurus, broke through the ferns and stared down at them with small red eyes. Saliva drooled from its huge, dagger-toothed jaws.

"Christ, Hartstein," muttered Tipchak.

"Don't move." From somewhere, Hartstein thought he heard the powerful strains of Stravinsky's *Rite of Spring.* A bolt of lightning illuminated the carnivore's immense head, followed instantly by a detonation of thunder. Hartstein looked up at the dinosaur and held perfectly still. He was sure that he couldn't outrun the beast; maybe it couldn't see well enough to identify the two men as prey if they stood absolutely motionless. Tipchak broke first; he turned and ran, and the allosaurus almost grinned in pleasure. Its tremendous thighs lumbered forward for a few steps, and then it lurched into a thundering, ground-eating lope. Tipchak looked over his shoulder and gave a single inhuman shriek. The allosaurus had almost overtaken him before Tipchak tumbled head over heels down a low bank and into the tar pit. He cried for help, but Hartstein could do nothing for him. The allosaurus stood at the edge of the pit, waiting for Tipchak to extricate himself; but the weasel would never be able to do that. Hartstein was sickened. He backed away from the terrible scene, up against the trunk of a giant fern. When he turned around, he was somewhere else.

He was in the middle of a vast parkland. On the horizon, in a full circle around him miles away, were tall hemispherical structures. He had never seen anything like them before. There were paths radiating from the very point where he stood, as if he were at the center of the world. The paths were paved with a perfectly smooth cream-colored material, straight and wide. He began walking along one of the paths, toward a hemisphere that was tinted the green of new spring leaves.

He walked for many minutes, and the hemisphere soon loomed above him, a vast city in a green glass bottle. He could see that inside, near the top of the dome, a bright ball of yellow floated like a miniature sun. He saw houses and carriages and steeples and children playing innocent games on the sidewalks. He saw gardens and theaters and civic buildings with stern, fluted columns.

"How do I get inside?" he asked himself. There was a frail-looking steel ladder on the outside that allowed him to climb up toward the north pole of the hemisphere. He started up the hanging ladder. Men and women on the inside of the bottle gathered and pointed at him in wonder. He climbed up and up and up. He grew dizzy and tired. The sun beat down on him and his head swam, but still he climbed. He climbed above the level of the rooftops on the inside. He did not dare look down at the ground. His hands holding the metal sides of the ladder perspired, and the rungs themselves dug painfully into the soles of his feet.

There was a narrow landing built into the dome near the top, an inlet of perhaps four feet square, with a heavy green metal door leading inside. Hartstein tried the door; it was locked fast. He pounded on the door, sure that someone in the city must have climbed up to meet him and now stood waiting to unlock the door at his knock. Was this a city of the future? Had he somehow stepped across some new wartime threshold of the eons, from the Jurassic to a distant time yet-to-be? He panted with exhaustion; he tried again, but the door still would not open. He turned away, determined to climb higher, but the ladder had disappeared. He stood now not hundreds of feet in the air, but upon a broad marble stairway in a great castle or palace.

Shadows thrown by gaslamps flickered on the damp stone walls. Many graceful statues, miniature copies of classical figures, stood in niches up and down the staircase. Hartstein started down the steps hesitantly, unsure where he was now. A man in a dark cloak appeared below. "Rupert of Hentzau," Hartstein muttered.

The other young man looked up and noticed Hartstein. "My king has returned to Zenda," he said brightly. He drew his sword.

Hartstein did not descend further; let Hentzau come to meet him, while Hartstein enjoyed the superior position. He, too, drew his sword. "I have desired this meeting," he said.

"As have I," said Rupert. He tossed his handsome head and waited, the point of his sword down as if in no concern at all for his life. He loosed his cloak and let it fall to the floor. Every movement had such an unstudied grace and carelessness that it was impossible not to admire Rupert, for all his ambitious and self-serving ways. "If you intend to wait there upon me," he called to Hartstein, "then this will be a very long night indeed, for I shall not give you such an advantage."

Hartstein understood. "Then will you permit me to join you down there?"

"Why, of course, sire." The sarcasm in his tone was heavy though without rancor. This final duel was inevitable, but it was not motivated by hatred. It was merely a matter of leaving to Fate the decision of who was to be master of a woman's affections.

Hartstein went down the venerable stairs. Both men took their positions calmly and silently. They saluted each other; Rupert added an elaborate flourish that only underscored the irony in his attitude. They touched blades, and then Rupert leaped to the attack.

Hartstein parried and riposted; Rupert danced backward. Hartstein followed, then fell back before a feint and a lunge that touched him on the shoulder. It was not a serious wound. They cut and leaped at each other in grim silence, back and forth in the cold hall. Far away, a larger and more deadly battle was taking place for the future of the kingdom, but it was not fought with more determination and skill than this wordless duel for the hand of the beautiful Flavia.

At last Rupert maneuvered Hartstein into a position where the Agent could retreat no farther. Backed against a wall, Hartstein fought on with renewed strength, yet he was unable to make Hentzau give up an inch. With a devilish twist of his blade, Rupert disarmed him; Hartstein's sword clattered across the stone flags with a terrible racket. "My prayers are with you," said Hentzau with a sardonic smile. "I shall tell her that you died as you lived, but she will not understand precisely what I mean." He thrust home, but Hartstein flung himself to the side, only to receive a stunning blow with the flat of Rupert's blade. Hartstein fell to his knees, dazed, one hand to his throbbing temple. He awaited momentarily the final thrust.

When it did not come, he raised his eyes. He was sitting in a narrow enclosure, the cockpit of some flying machine. He was far above the black storm clouds, flying into the sun with three other fork-tailed aircraft beside him. "Pull up, Hartstein, pull back on your stick, you're drifting down," came the voice of Captain D'Amato in the receiver in his helmet. Hartstein pulled back on the stick and the P-38 climbed to its proper position. They flew onward in formation, toward some dreadful destination. All was peace and serenity high above the war-torn ground. The perfect blue of the heavens blessed Hartstein with a feeling of warmth and quiet.

It was not to last. A voice—it was Major Li's—cried, "Six bandits at ten o'clock low, climbing fast!"

Hartstein tipped his right wing up a little and looked down. He saw the enemy fighters approaching in a tight V formation. As he watched they spread out, making a more difficult target. They were single-engine fighters, no match for the P-38s in speed and high-altitude performance, but much more maneuverable. They roared through the Agency formation, firing their guns and screaming on into the sky.

Hartstein chose one and followed it up. The Underground pilot wasn't aware that Hartstein was on his tail, and slid over into a shallow, lazy dive, searching the air for something to attack. Hartstein announced his presence with a long burst from his .50-caliber machine guns. "Stay on him, Hartstein," called D'Amato. "Wax his tail, boy."

The enemy pilot, suddenly aware of the trouble he was in, turned over hard right and dropped out of sight. Hartstein followed him down, shrieking through the wind. The rebel plane was highlighted against the dark clouds, flashing in the sunlight, helpless.

"They suckered you, Hartstein! Now you've got one in your deep six! Shake him!"

Hartstein turned hard right and dived until he had accelerated beyond 350 miles per hour. He leveled out in another turn and slipped to the left. The enemy plane hadn't anticipated the maneuver and was now silhouetted against the clouds. Hartstein climbed to the level of the others in his formation, ignoring the bandit that had been on his tail because he saw that two of the enemy were diving on Marshal Hsien's plane.

"Two coming down on you from your three o'clock high," he called to the Overlord. "I'll be there in a second." He turned into the path of the rebel planes and, choosing one, flew directly at it, machine guns stuttering a deadly greeting. Hartstein saw a series of hits stitch the rebel, then he was by it and turning in a swift, tight circle. Marshal Hsien had skidded out of the Underground's way to momentary safety. Now the Overlord and Hartstein looped back, on the tails of the enemy fighters.

"Thanks, Hartstein," said Marshal Hsien. "I never saw them. You saved my life."

"Later, sir," said Hartstein. He hit his firing button again and his tracers drew a fiery white line across the fuselage of the first Underground plane. It fell into the storm clouds, trailing a ribbon of black smoke. The second enemy made another pass at the Overlord's plane. It began to fire short bursts, but Hartstein did a quick wingover and looped down and around to the left and then climbed into the bandit. The rebel sat in his sights like a duck on a frozen lake, and with his first burst Hartstein saw it explode into a blinding yellow fireball.

"I owe you my life again, Hartstein," said Marshal Hsien. "*Captain* Hartstein."

"A battlefield promotion!" said D'Amato. "Congratulations, son."

"Thank you, sir. How about the rest of these rebel monkeys?"

The other enemy fighters broke off contact and were running into the sun. "Let them go," said Hsien. "We have more important work to do."

"Right," said Hartstein. He was still glowing from the excitement of the battle, and the thrill of the sudden promotion.

"Hartstein, wake up!"

He had been daydreaming. He focused his attention on what Marshal Hsien was telling him.

"We cannot escape, Captain," said the Overlord. "Not with that gang of rebels guarding the road. If our army is to survive, someone must clear the way. I want you and that ragged company of yours to do the job. I've told you many times that your men are not soldiers in the sacred tradition, but you also know that I count on their skill and courage. That is why I give you all the most important missions."

"Yes, sir," said Hartstein. "The men are all ready to show you that your trust is well placed."

"Good. Do your best and good luck to you. All our lives depend on your success."

Hartstein saluted and returned to his men. As Marshal Hsien described them, they were a motley crew of veterans. There was Weng, the grizzled old dogface, scarred and blind in one eye and humorless, but a veritable killing machine; Chu Jen, the kid, the handsome young dandy whose youthful appearance belied his deadly skill with the bow; How San, the fastidious swordsman whose reputation as a ladies' man he always denied; Bo Bo, the comical old worrier and complainer; and, of course, Sergeant Brannick and Mademoiselle Zaza, the beautiful French volunteer whose darkest secret no man would ever learn.

"Well, is there some action, Captain?" asked Weng hopefully, as Hartstein ducked into the rickety hut they had taken over.

"Enough for all of us, pal," said Hartstein. "Get all the others and bring them here. We're going to clear the road for the Overlord."

"Okay!" Weng ran to a small wooden shack where the rest of the Jade Cloud Jokers were gambling away their future pay. Hartstein smiled proudly. The regular army called them "jokers," but that was just envy. The Imperial Chinese Army had no other platoon like Jade Cloud; their shining record of victories was what permitted them a degree of autonomy, almost a perverse individuality. The Overlords themselves beamed benignly on the men of Jade Cloud, amused by their appearance, pleased by their fighting strength.

They came running, with old Bo Bo bringing up the rear as usual. "Sit down, men," said Hartstein. "And ladies," he added, nodding to Mademoiselle Zaza. "We've got a tough nut to crack today. I wanted to tell you about it myself, knowing how much you all like impossible assignments. Well, you apes, we haven't faced anything like this since we took on the Mongols and their ten-foot giants."

"Yeah," said Chu Jen, grinning, "but we cut them down to size, didn't we, Captain?" Weng clapped the kid on the shoulder in comradely good spirits.

"Yes, we did. But now we have the whole Underground advance party camped on the road between here and the Agency lines. They've got us all sewn up here, and that includes Marshal Hsien. So the regular army passed the ball to us and told us to kick those rebels the hell off our doorstep. Then the Overlord and his boys can go on with the business of winning this war."

"That suits me," said How San.

"But there is only six of us," complained Bo Bo, "and there are at least a hundred of them."

"Zair are seven of us, *mon ami,*" murmured Mademoiselle Zaza in her languorous voice.

"Oh," said Bo Bo, sighing, "in that case, it's different."

Everyone laughed at Bo Bo's anxiousness.

While the entire army could not move surreptitiously around the Underground position, the Jokers could. They cut through the woods and found themselves some two hundred yards behind the rebels. "Captain," said How San, "let me take Weng, and we'll account for at least twenty of the bastards. We'll take care of that unit on the left side of the road."

"All right, pal. But first I want Chu Jen to take his bow and pepper their rear. That'll soften them up for you."

"*Mon capitain,*" whispered Mademoiselle Zaza, "I too can make ze attack on ze rotten rebels. I weel keel *une douzaine* of zem, as zey keeled my seestair. I weel make ze diversion for ze rest of you."

"Very good, Zaza," said Hartstein. "Bo Bo, Chu Jen?"

The fat old man and the handsome youth looked at him. Their quirks of personality were gone now; this was a matter of life-and-death. They waited to hear their orders. "Yes, Captain?" said Bo Bo in a level voice.

"After Chu Jen punctures a few of those rebels, I want you and him to charge the main body on the right side of the road. Weng and How San will join you when they've finished off the other gang. Meanwhile, Sergeant Brannick and myself will cut back to hit them from the other side. We'll catch the suckers in a three-way squeeze."

"Very good, Captain," said Bo Bo. The Jokers moved out silently, each intent on his own part in the plan.

"Let's go, Captain," said Sergeant Brannick.

Hartstein tested the edge of his sword. It was perfect. He nodded to Brannick, who was armed with a sword slung across his back and a bow. "One moment, Sergeant," said Hartstein. "I want you to know how much

I've appreciated the help you've given me. I couldn't have bullied those lugheaded gorillas halfway across China without you."

Brannick grinned. "Don't thank me, sir. It's you they look up to. Now let's go get them Underground sons of bitches!"

They charged out of the cabin, but there was nothing there. "There's nothing here!" cried Brannick.

"I can see that, Sergeant." Hartstein felt fear choking his throat. His breathing came rapidly. The road, the shack, the trees had all vanished. There was nothing to see in the dim light but the gentle fog, curling in wisps around their feet.

"It's . . . it's between-time, Hartstein!"

"I know. I don't know what it means."

"But this isn't a quasi-past! It's the *real* world! The real world can't fade into between-time. How can this be happening? Maybe it's those things, the time-eaters. Maybe they've finally destroyed us all. *This can't be happening!*"

"Tell it to the Marines, Sergeant," growled Captain Hartstein. Then he screamed and screamed and screamed.

CHAPTER TEN

BETTER LATE THAN NEVER

Hartstein ran through the fog, as he had done once before. This time he felt anger rather than fear, because he was certain that the meddling of the Agency and the Temporary Underground in the nature of the universe had caused this. They had adjusted and altered and reshaped reality to fit their needs, and perhaps they had tinkered once too often, had made one too many little changes. A pleat here and a tuck there could be assimilated by the universe, but the wholesale renovation caused by this struggle for power might have weakened the entire structure of reality. Hartstein despaired of learning what had finally brought the real world down around his ears and, to tell the truth, he didn't really care who was at fault. It was too late for that. It was too late for blame, or for victory or defeat.

Here he was in Cleveland, in the endless world between the worlds, but this time there was no one to save him. The whole universe had decayed into this dead zone of faint light and shimmering fog. If there was anything to be grateful for, it was the absence of the obscene things Hartstein had witnessed before—the devourers of the feast of time. It might have been that Brannick was right, that they didn't really exist. The monsters might have been a function of the quasi-past, and as this between-time world derived from the actual world, the creatures themselves had no existence here.

Still, it was very little comfort. The "ground" was as hard and featureless as ever. Hartstein knelt and ran his fingers over the surface: it was neither warm nor cold; it was dead, without vibration; he felt no crevices or ridges or places where edges might have been joined. The fog swirled around his chest. It could not be described other than to say that it was fog; it had no color or smell, it was neither damp nor dry. If thirst or hunger did not kill Hartstein, it would be the boredom. He stood up and walked on through the emptiness.

It had only taken a few seconds for him to lose Sergeant Brannick. Somehow in this horrible unworld distances changed with capricious frequency. The two men had stood inches apart; seconds later, without moving, they were out of sight of one another. When Hartstein walked, each pace might have been miles long, or microns. There was no use in trying to find anyone else here, or screaming for help, or sitting still and waiting for rescue. All Hartstein could do was wander alone and hope.

Time passed with the same disregard for consistent order. It was pointless to wonder how long he had searched: hours might have passed, or centuries. At last, however, a thought came to him, a notion that had been implanted with his new mathematical knowledge by the Agency's ESB treatment. He remembered a curious topological idea. If you took a map of the world or a grid of numbers, or anything broken up into recognizable areas, and placed over it a second and identical map, each point on the second would lie directly above its mate on the first. Now, if you crumpled the top map in any way or shape or form, or stretched it or compressed it or folded it, and dropped it on the bottom map, there must be at least one point on each map that still retained their original contiguity. This was called the "fixed point theorem." And Hartstein knew immediately that here was the key to his freedom. Even if this between-time world of Cleveland extended to positive and negative infinity, there would be one point where it touched the real world, where he could cross from one to the other. That was how Brannick had rescued him before, through that single point. The difficulty now, though, was *finding* that point. Of course, Hartstein reasoned, he had all of eternity to look . . .

There was something standing in the fog, a sign on a post, shadowless in the gloom. Hartstein ran to it; he had never seen a sign here before, he had never seen any object in this dead world.

Go Back! Danger! Go Back!

* * *

I heard a fly buzz when I died.
No, I didn't. I just lied.

* * *

Death, Hartstein, Destruction,
Personality Dissociation, Madness!

* * *

Go Back! Danger! Go Back!

"Go back where?" Hartstein wondered. He walked on. He came to another sign.

NEVER PUT OFF UNTIL TOMORROW
WHAT YOU CAN PUT OFF UNTIL
YESTERDAY

A third sign:

> Dear, dear,
> Bread and beer,
> If you was smart
> You wouldn't be here.

And a fourth sign:

> War is hell.
> This is war.
> This is hell.
> Turn the lights off
> when you leave.
> Drive carefully and
> arrive home safely.

Hartstein didn't realize it at the time, but the signs were the sound of the universe clearing its throat. It wanted to speak to him.

Dr. Waters approached him through the fog. "Hello, son," he said in a kindly voice.

"Hello, Dr. Waters. I understand that you're behind the Agency, that you control it and are using it to consolidate unimaginable wealth and power."

Dr. Waters chuckled. His piercing eyes glittered. "That's right, my boy, I'm as bad as the Queen of Spades. It's been weighing heavily on my conscience, particularly now since I've learned how my schemes have spoiled the world for everybody." He made a broad gesture taking in all of Cleveland. "I'd like to make it up to you somehow, but all I've ever had was my scientific genius. Perhaps I can show you a few more clever tricks that neither the Agency nor the Temporary Underground know about."

"That would be great, sir," said Hartstein.

"Look here. Partial numbers and objective operations values are all well and good, but they only indicate where the true treasure is buried. People are afraid of mathematics—"

"With good reason," said Hartstein, looking around fearfully.

"Perhaps. But mathematics can do things for us that our so-called scientific knowledge tells us is impossible. How would you like me to give you the secret of practically instantaneous interstellar travel?"

"Goddamn, Dr. Waters, that would be swell."

Dr. Waters smiled. "Then look at this diagram." He held up a complex geometric figure.*

"I have given you the universe, dear boy," said Dr. Waters after he explained his discovery. "See that you do right by it."

Dr. Waters faded away like the ghost of Hamlet's father. Hartstein glanced down at the paper the old scientist had given him, but when he opened his fingers he held only a handful of fog.

A table was prepared for him in the midst of the drifting nothingness. A silver salver had been placed on the table. Upon the salver was a single fortune cookie.

"This fortune cookie has been put here for a purpose," Hartstein reasoned. "It must contain an important clue about why I am here, and how I may be saved."

He took the cookie with trembling fingers and broke it open. There was a small strip of paper inside. He read it. It said INSPECTED BY NUMBER *12*. Hartstein dropped the paper and the cookie and pressed on through the mist.

He saw two men standing beside a box. "Hey!" he cried, running to them. They did not seem to hear him; they were looking at the box. Hartstein saw that it was a coffin. He saw that it was himself laid out inside it. He thought he looked very natural, as if he were only sleeping. One of the two men was Hartstein's father. The other was a small owl-eyed man whom Hartstein didn't recognize.

"Blessed are the dead that the rain falls on," murmured Hartstein's father.

"Amen to that," said the owl-eyed man. Hartstein recognized the scene from *The Great Gatsby.*

"But I'm not dead!" shouted Hartstein. "Can't you see me? Can't you hear me?"

The other two turned away from the casket and walked through the barren landscape. "I couldn't get to the house," said the owl-eyed man, as if explaining something.

"Neither could anybody else," said Hartstein's father.

"Go on! Why, my God! they used to go there by the hundreds."

* To see this miraculous mathematical discovery in detail, please see page 163 in *The Nick of Time.*

"What are you talking about?" cried Hartstein. He felt like Scrooge walking in on someone else's Christmas ghosts. "Why do you think I'm dead?"

The owl-eyed man took off his glasses and cleaned them. "The poor son of a bitch," he said.

A thick, dusty book sat on a battered wooden desk. Hartstein riffled through it slowly; every page in the book was printed with the same words:

Hartstein, here is something to consider. Perhaps the reason that the Underground so well anticipated your every move was that the props and costume corporal whom you so blithely disregarded was in reality a top-notch spy for the rebels. Remember, you always told him where you were going and what you were planning to do. When they're not otherwise busy, pal, loose lips sink ships.

This is either true or it is not true. Only the names have been changed to heighten the ambiguity.

More signs, like a roadside advertisement on the soft shoulder of time: Thomas Henry Huxley says: "Science commits suicide when it adopts a creed."

Morris Cohen says: "Science is a flickering light in our darkness, it is but the only one we have and woe to him who would put it out."

Sir Osbert Sitwell (Who *are* these people? Hartstein asked himself) says: "In reality, killing time/Is only the name for another of the multifarious ways/By which Time kills us."

Raymond Chandler says: "When in doubt, have two guys come through the door with guns in their fists."

And Ben Hecht says: "Time is a circus always packing up and leaving town."

And time had left town for good, as far as Hartstein could see. The whole town had left town for good, too. As far as Hartstein could see, there was nothing to see.

But then, after more walking and deepening despair, Hartstein saw a monstrous shape in the pale light. It was tall and black and unmoving, a monolith, like a fallen angel chained in place, frozen in a lake of ice. Only its huge narrow head glowered up above the curling tentacles of fog. It was the Guardian moai, the great Easter Island head that waited stoically for the end of the world. Now that its moment had come, it spoke to Hartstein.

"Welcome, Captain," it said.

"Thank you," said Hartstein. "Glad to be here."

"You are nothing, Captain Hartstein. You are a zero. Do you know what a zero is?"

"I have a passing acquaintance."

"A zero is a doughnut, Hartstein. A zero is a nothing with the illusion of a boundary around it. You are such a zero. Perhaps you are the only consciousness that exists here, Hartstein, but that means nothing to the void. Let x equal the void, the zero, the cold nothingness that desires nothing more than to exist without you. You are a quantity, a unit, a wholeness that is like a grain of sand to an oyster. You are $(x + 1)$, an imbalance, an anomaly. Let us represent x, the void, by the integral

$$\int \frac{dx}{x} \; .$$

If we integrate by parts,

$$
\begin{aligned}
x &= \int 1 \cdot (1/x)\, dx \\
  &= x\,(1/x) - \int x\,(-1/x^2)\, dx \\
  &= 1 + \int \frac{dx}{x} = 1 + x
\end{aligned}
$$

And, therefore, $x = 0 = $ Hartstein. You are zero. You are nothing."

"I understand," said Hartstein. "I'll try not to let it get in my way."

Dean Rusk says: "The pace of events is moving so fast that unless we can find some way to keep our sights on tomorrow, we cannot expect to be in touch with today."

In the murky desert of between-time, Dean Rusk's words failed to cheer Hartstein. He staggered on to the next sign.

Bette Davis (in *Dark Victory*) says: "Nothing can hurt us now. What we have can't be destroyed. That's our victory—our victory over the dark. It is a victory because we're not afraid."

That was easy for *her* to say; she had George Brent with her and the theater gave away free dishes once a week.

Out of the fog, out of the night, like mysterious travelers came Frank Mihalik, the Odysseus of Time, and Cheryl, his girlfriend. They smiled at Hartstein and waved.

"This is amazing," said Hartstein. "First I make friends with Dr. Bertram Waters himself, and then I get to meet the Odysseus of Time."

"I'm pleased to meet you, too," said Mihalik. He was a young, strong, handsome man. Cheryl, the Penelope of Time, was attractive and intelligent. They were a great team, and they had inscribed their names in the annals of courage with their exploits in the arena of time.

"Do you have any idea how we can get out of this?" asked Hartstein.

"No," said Cheryl pleasantly, "but we have a couple more incredible superweapons that you can give to the Agency. We're sure that these will be just the things to stop the Underground's merciless and inhuman master plan."

"First," said Mihalik, "you know that there are certain kinds of vectors that have no magnitude, merely direction. Well, we've perfected a kind of calculus that deals with the other kind: vectors that have magnitude but no direction."

"What good is that?" asked Hartstein.

Cheryl smiled prettily. "They help you describe certain things in the real world for which vectors and tensors aren't quite sufficient. And once you learn to manipulate pure magnitude, you can apply it in powerful ways, with undreamed-of results. Pure magnitude is a weapon the likes of which even Dr. Waters has never imagined."

"Pure magnitude without direction? Give me an example."

Mihalik thought for a moment. "Hubert Humphrey," he said at last.

"Ah," said Hartstein. He didn't bother to make notes.

"And then we have a way of factoring out the operations signs in an equation, canceling them out or otherwise removing them, thus leaving only numbers and no processes," said the Odysseus of Time. "That would be a good defense against the Underground's objective operations values. They would just neutralize each other."

"Too late now," said Hartstein.

"I suppose so," said Cheryl. "Well, Captain Hartstein, we wish you the best of luck, and may God bless."

Mihalik and Cheryl smiled and waved. They took a single step into the fog and disappeared. Hartstein was alone again. He was beginning to prefer it that way.

He walked along for a while, humming tunelessly, wondering what the universe had prepared next in the way of entertainment. He tripped over something large and heavy, hidden in the slowly creeping fog. He bent down. He was startled to find a body, the corpse of a young woman. She was pretty despite even the grotesque deformity of death; Hartstein held her, overwhelmed by his emotions. All the sadness and grief he felt for himself and for the whole world, for his family, for those he loved and people he didn't even know, all this anguish he focused on this woman who lived no longer.

There was a note pinned to the front of her shirt. It said:

Her name is Alohilani. You and she were very much in love. You must take her back to the house. Keep walking east until you get to the river. Follow the river downstream to the house. East is the direction of the rising sun. They will help you when you get there.

"East?" murmured Hartstein, afraid. "What house? What rising sun?" He set the young woman down gently. He had never known her; he had never loved her. The note was meant for someone else, but he hated to leave her here, lost forever. Yet . . .

The decision was made for him. He searched through the fog for the body, but he could not find it again. He felt over every inch within a radius of ten feet, but the corpse was gone. The nature of reality had frayed so badly that only long habit held it together any further.

PREPARE, HARTSTEIN. THIS IS IT, THE BIG FINALE. AFTER THIS THERE'S NOTHING LEFT TO DO BUT STRIKE THE SET AND RING DOWN THE CURTAIN ON ANOTHER SEASON.

Had he read that on a sign? Had he heard it? Had he thought it himself? Hartstein couldn't say.

"God wouldn't permit the existence of evil. God is infinitely benevolent."

"Who are we to disagree with the Commander? The Commander has all the information. We don't. He's in a better position to make decisions than we are."

"People know what's best for them. They'd never allow an organization like the Agency to take so much power we'd all have to worry."

Hartstein chewed his lip. He was afraid. What new kind of attack was this? He saw no one; he heard no one. There were no voices, not really, just *words*. Truisms.

"Once this war is over, we'll all benefit from the discoveries both sides have made in mathematics, science, and philosophy."

Truisms! What a fiendish scheme! Hartstein looked around himself feverishly.

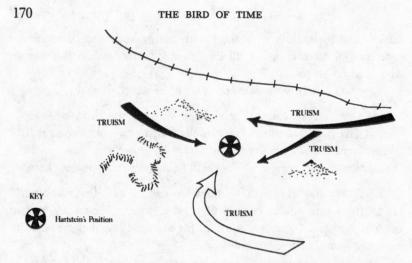

Fig. 1: TRUISMS BESIEGED HARTSTEIN

False premises gave aid and comfort to his enemies.

Outright lies eng   him.   lfed

The surface of the lies glittered like the sun on the Bay of Naples, and the words were just as insubstantial. There was nothing to grasp, nothing to fight, but Hartstein would not surrender. Trapped, he tried everything he could think of to escape. He clicked his heels together and repeated, "There's no place like home, there's no place like home." It did no good. "You don't scare me," Hartstein lied and, miraculously, he was free. Thinking he was one of *them*, *they* let him go. He ran.

"Now there's something you don't see every day, Chauncey," said a middle-aged man sitting on a park bench.

"What's that, Edgar?" asked his friend, looking up from his newspaper. "Graphics in a novel like this."

Chauncey shrugged. "Alfred Bester did it in 1956." He went back to his newspaper.

The universe lay before him in all its magnificent dullness. Vast silent spirals of light sailed through space, fleeing their ancient natal shock. Fire and ice, gases and dust aged perceptibly while Hartstein watched. Everything grew cooler. Everything spent velocity. Electrons reached a point when they just didn't feel like zipping around a nucleus anymore; the atom collapsed. Satellites crashed into their planets, and the planets into their suns. The outward rush of the galaxies came to an end at some high-water mark of the universe, and then, like an amusement park thrill ride balanced straight up in the air, everything began the long, cold slide back to the beginning. "Look at that," marveled Hartstein. The stars picked up speed as gravity drew them closer and closer together. Billions of years passed in a moment. Hartstein held his breath, hypnotized by the splendor. He saw the end and the beginning. He saw the cataclysmic collision of all the matter in the universe as it re-formed its primal egg. He watched unguessable temperatures and pressures weave a net of physics and magic until once again, with another Big Bang, the cosmos gave birth to itself. Flung outward once more, the stars flared and hissed and cooled and formed, and the cycle continued. The show was so exciting that Hartstein sat through the whole thing three more times before he paused to wonder where he was.

It seemed to be an impossibly big room. It was a hall too large to be taken in by a human mind. It was only twenty feet across and twelve feet high—Hartstein could almost jump up and touch the hanging lighting fixtures; but the hall ran to his left and right in a straight line, until all the parallel lines in the room met at vanishing points blurred with distance. The opposite walls were lined with machinery, identical banks of equipment that cluttered and whispered and clanged and clicked to itself, oblivious to Hartstein and evidently entirely self-sufficient. Hartstein shivered. For some reason, this place was more frightening than the world of between-time. Between-time was a phenomenon he could describe and talk about, if not fully understand; this place just didn't belong to his notion of the universe. After all, the universe seemed to be "down there." Hartstein stared through one of the many TV-screen-shaped ports, back toward the realm of time and space and matter—and back toward life and mind as well. The pinwheel galaxies were beginning to sort themselves out from the background waste material. The full course of the universe's existence now took about fifteen minutes, Hartstein estimated; each cycle was shorter than the one previous.

Each unit of control board consisted of a CRT terminal where he could enter in questions and commands, and banks of digital readouts and pushbuttons. The buttons controlled the values of constants that governed reality back in the universe. The first readout Hartstein looked at said *The value of π is now equal to: 4.29517248319+*. Beside that a button was labeled ERASE. Hartstein pushed it. The value disappeared. New letters spelled out ENTER NEW VALUE. Hartstein pushed 2.78365139200, just to see what happened. He looked out the port again; one giant galaxy turned spontaneously into colored confetti and drifted apart into auroralike veils; two others collided in a marvelous shower of flares and bursts, exactly like the New Year's bonfires and fireworks he remembered from his childhood.

Hartstein walked slowly down the long room, between the two lines of muttering machines. He felt as if he could walk forever, deathless and ageless, and never come to the end of it. Each button determined the value of one quantity: *The value of 1 is now equal to; the value of 2 is now equal to.* This cosmic Bureau of Standards evidently recognized partial numbers. There were places where he could enter in the products or quotients of different combinations of numbers; that, in effect, validated the idea of objective operations values. Hartstein decided that the universe was probably better off without those two notions. He realized he could eliminate them by simply assigning values to all the numbers and arithmetical results which agreed with what he had been taught in elementary school. He smiled. From now on, through all eternity, two plus two was going to equal four again. What other person had ever made such an aesthetic gift to the cosmos? Hartstein wished that his father could see him now: Captain Hartstein, Champion of Time.

Of course, that meant erasing and resetting every single readout in this infinite room. If there was one button for each number, then there would be an infinite number of buttons. If there was another button for each number plus another number, that was two infinities. Plus a button for each number divided by another number—well, it was a lot of infinities. And then there were the buttons for the speed of light and Avogadro's Number and all the others. Hartstein decided he would get to work right after lunch. The universe would look crazy for a while, when some of the numbers had been set back to "normal" while other functions involving them had not, but it couldn't be helped. The reality he was creating would be sound and simple and beautiful; in the meantime, everything was just going to have to get along the best it could.

He came to a door. Between two identical banks of apparatus, there was a tan-colored door. It was the only break he had seen in the symmetry of the room. He paused for a moment with his hand on the doorknob, picturing many grotesque and frightening things that could be on the other side; then he took a deep breath and went through.

On the other side of the door there was a sign that said No ADMITTANCE/AUTHORIZED PERSONNEL ONLY. He was in a small reception area. There was a desk with a small computer terminal beside the door. Three comfortable couches stood against the walls. A coffee table by each couch was piled high with old magazines. The lighting was soft, and muted music played from invisible speakers.

Hartstein passed through the reception area and went through another door. He was in a high-vaulted, pillared lobby, like that of a large bank. There was nothing much to see. A bank building might have had elevators and escalators, a small newsstand, a few shops. Here there was nothing but pillars and a shiny floor. The lobby seemed smaller than it actually was; when Hartstein began crossing it, searching for a way out, he realized that while he kept passing pillars he didn't seem to be going anywhere. He turned around, and the door he had come through wasn't any farther away. He shrugged; another weirdness here at the end of the universe, he thought. It didn't bother him nearly so much as it would have a few months before. It did indicate that there wasn't much point in trying to find a way out of the immense lobby. He started back to the reception area.

A voice called his name. Hartstein stopped, frightened. He also felt a little angry; he had already accepted his fate here, and he really didn't want to share it with any of his old antagonists. He turned around. "Hello, Sergeant," he said.

Brannick hurried toward him. "Where the hell are we, Captain?" he asked. He seemed shaken. Brannick had learned about fear very well in such a short time.

"I don't know what to call it, Brannick," said Hartstein, "but this is where everything starts."

"I don't know what you mean. A minute ago I was wandering around in Cleveland, and then I fell over something and into this place. Is this the world?"

"I don't think so. Come on, I'll show you. You can take a look outside." He led the Agency man through the reception area and past the tan-colored door.

"I don't believe this," murmured Brannick. "I didn't think Reality would be so simpleminded. You can't tell me that the entire cosmic order of the universe depends on these buttons and things."

"It seems that way. Look out the port, there. I'm going to change the Binomial Theorem."

Brannick stared out at the starscape. Hartstein pushed a button, erased one expression, and punched in another. "My God," said Brannick hoarsely, "Newton's clockwork universe."

"You know what I just figured out?" Hartstein indicated the vast array of machines. "If you can factor out operations signs, which is basically the inverse of the Underground's objective operations values, then you can come up with square roots of negative numbers that aren't imaginary. Think what you could do with that."

"Wow," said Brannick, dazzled.

"Come along, son," said Hartstein. "We've got work to do."

They went into the reception area. Brannick sat on a couch and glanced through an issue of *Sailing*. Hartstein sat at the desk and examined the computer console. There was a question addressed to him on the screen: *Do you wish time-flow here to be synchronous with time-flow in the universe? Type 0 = no, 1 = yes.* Hartstein thought it over. For now, the "real" universe out there didn't matter to him; it was creating and destroying itself again and again, every few minutes. He typed in *0*. When the mathematical substructure had been completely repaired, Hartstein would catch the universe just after a creation and then synchronize time-flows. But that was a long time away.

Another directive appeared on the screen: *The probability that you will be able to complete the reorganization of basic mathematics now stands at 0.004%. Edit?*

Hartstein typed in 99.9%, then erased the probability. He replaced it with 100%. "Might as well make it easy for myself," he thought. He was happy to learn that this console enabled him to do so much of the work so simply. He experimented some more. He entered *The probability that there is a telephone on this desk is 100%.* Instantly, as if by magic, the laws of chance caused a telephone to appear on the desk. Hartstein picked up the receiver and heard a dial tone. He laughed softly and hung up the phone.

There was a knock on the outer door, the one leading to the lobby. "Company," said Sergeant Brannick. He stood up.

"I wonder who. Must be somebody else finding his way out of between-time."

Brannick went to the door and opened it. The Commander burst past him and came wildly into the reception area. "I know where this is," he cried. "I know this place." He tried to go through the inner door, but Hartstein jumped up and blocked his way.

"Don't let him get in there, Captain," shouted Brannick. "He'll just erase all the values and wipe out the universe that way."

"You can't stop me," said the Commander. His voice was like a ravenous beast. His hair was disheveled and his usually calm expression was manic and fierce. Brannick slipped his arms around the Commander in a full nelson, and the two men wrestled each other to the floor. Neither spoke. Hartstein stood and watched, knowing that this was indeed the final battle, that this was the ultimate struggle between the Agency and the Temporary Underground, between totalitarianism and anarchy, between eternal torment and the illusory peace of death. If Brannick won the battle, he was at liberty to recreate the world with an everlasting tyranny of the Agency; if the Commander won, he could just wash the universe clean of itself. Hartstein could help neither man, neither cause; that was what Jesus had tried to tell him so long ago. Months earlier, Hartstein would have been paralyzed with indecision. Now he knew just what he had to do.

The probability that Sergeant Brannick and the Commander are conducting their fight in this reception area is only 0.000001%. The probability that the fight is happening in the lobby beyond the outer door is 99.999999%. The two men vanished. Hartstein went to the outer door and looked out. Brannick and the Commander stood locked together, sweating and grappling and groaning in their exertion, neither able to make the other give an inch of ground, neither willing to let the other gain even a modest advantage. Hartstein watched in fascination for many minutes. It was a mythic scene, a struggle worthy of ancient gods and heroes. It was Thor against Loki, Ormazd against Ahriman, Osiris against Set, although Hartstein couldn't have said which of the two men was good and which evil. On and on they would wrestle while the universe ticked calmly along, while the blazing ships of the galaxies careered upon the face of the Deep. Perhaps one or the other would eventually achieve victory. Perhaps through strength or guile or good fortune Brannick or the Commander would toss his opponent aside; then nothing would stand between him and the sanctity of the universe but two thin doors and Captain Hartstein.

"All right," called Hartstein in a strong voice, "I'll give you guys one last chance to learn to live together in peace and harmony." He glanced grimly at each of them in turn. They ignored him. He turned his back on them then, shut the outer door behind him, and sat down at the desk. At the computer terminal he typed, *The probability that Pamari will come through the outer door carrying two large roast beef sandwiches and two bottles of beer is 100%.* A moment later, the most interesting woman in the world came in. All Hartstein could see were her beautiful eyes and her shy smile. She joined him at the desk, and he forgot all about the sandwiches.

After a while Hartstein remembered where he was and what was happening in the lobby. He typed, *The probability that there is a fully charged static pistol on this desk is 100%.* The gun appeared; Hartstein picked it up and examined it, then put it down again. If anyone else ever came through that door, Hartstein was going to blast him to atoms. Meanwhile, Captain Hartstein, the one-man Time Patrol, and his lovely Pamari settled down comfortably to wait.

Contest Results

The response to the contest included in my last Doubleday science fiction novel, *The Nick of Time*, was very gratifying. As promised, the following people who submitted entries will receive autographed copies of *The Bird of Time*. The fallacy in the nuhps' plan for instantaneous interstellar travel is concealed in one step of their proof. Following the process of differentiation, the result is $\underline{db} = \underline{b}$. The unspoken assumption is that
$$\text{da}\qquad\text{a}$$
$\underline{db} = \Delta\underline{b}$, for which no necessary and sufficient reason is given. If that
da$$$\Delta$a
equation is false, then it follows that b does not equal a, after all, invalidating the conclusion that the distance between two points is equal to the distance between any other two points. I must apologize for an error that crept into the problem during the manufacturing process of the book. It is not stated whether the differentiation is done with respect to a or b; however, the solution remains the same in either case. Those who solved the problem or were on the right track, recognized this.

The winners are:

1. Rana Jones, Cole Camp, MO
2. Chris Ford (the pretty one, not the former player for the Boston Celtics), Naples, FL
3. Mary Richardson, Sikeston, MO
4. Mark Somerville, Austin, TX
5. Frank Mihalik, Santa Cruz, CA (is this for real?)
6. Sam Tomaino, Point Pleasant Beach, NJ
7. Robert Leathers, Saunderstown, RI
8. Janet R. Boleroff, Talledega, AL
9. Corey Boettcher, Hutchinson, MN
10. Charles Emmons, York, PA
11. Ben Cruz-Uribe, Green Bay, WI (second try)

About the Author

George Alec Effinger's first novel, *What Entropy Means to Me* (Doubleday, 1972) was nominated for the Nebula Award. Since then, he has published many more novels, including *The Wolves of Memory, Death in Florence,* and *Heroics,* while maintaining his reputation as one of the finest short story writers in the Science Fiction field. His short fiction has been collected in *Mixed Feelings, Irrational Numbers, Dirty Tricks, Idle Pleasures* and *The Nick of Time,* the previously published companion novel to *The Bird of Time.* He lives in New Orleans, Louisiana.